the mourning after

rochelle b. weinstein

Copyright © 2013 Rochelle B. Weinstein

ISBN: 1484015584
ISBN13: 978-1484015582

Library of Congress Number: 2013909635

In memory of my beloved mother,
Ruth Gratz Berger

sunday, october 14, 2007
12:07 a.m.

The road curves in front of the two boys as the car speeds along the tranquil, dimly lit streets of Miami Beach. It is dark, well past the hour when children their age should be out driving on deserted roads. The passenger is upright and pinned against the worn black leather seat; his hands are knotted, clenching the seatbelt close to his chest. The driver casually drapes one hand along the wheel while his foot presses firmly on the accelerator. The balmy Florida air pours through the sunroof and whispers through the caps of the boys' hair, sliding down the napes of their smooth necks.

As the glaring red sign comes into view, there is no time for the driver to stop. A car is heading right toward them. He turns the wheel in an impulsive, desperate attempt to thwart the imminent collision. The jerking motion is frantic and commanding, jostling the driver and his passenger. What he hasn't expected is the tree. Florida is legendary for its lofty palms, jaunty against the backdrop of blue sky, but tonight the sturdy, thick trunk is camouflaged in darkness. When it emerges in front of the young driver, it is too late; the car is traveling too fast. The impact tears into the sleek exterior and swiftly crushes the people and parts that make up the interior.

The other car speeds by, oblivious to the debris it has left in its cloud of exhaust. Silence permeates the street. The collision leaves a tangle of blood, bark, and metal. Not even the sturdy roots are capable of unraveling from the mess left on the side of the road—the weeds that will run wild and uproot an entire family.

"Are you okay?" the boy asks, tugging on the other's bloodied shirt.

The words come out as a dubious gasp, hurried and uncontrolled. "Yeah," he says, "I think I'm okay."

In the distance, a dog howls. The young boy unbuckles his seatbelt and reaches for the motionless figure by his side. He starts to say something.

"Shhh, don't move," says the other.

"I can't," he breathes.

"Mom's gonna kill us," one of them whispers into the darkness, paying careful attention to the mangled metal fragments that are hovering close by.

"We'll worry about her later."

"Bro, there's something I need to tell you."

chapter 1

"I'm sorry about your brother," they say.

Something about the sentence is contrived—obligatory—and although it aims to quell the pain and anguish ricocheting around the room, it pierces Levon where it hurts the most. The gaping hole spreads rampant through his plump body like a virus. Fiddling with the tie that his father apologetically wrapped around his neck, his hand fingers the silky fabric and loosens the knot so he can breathe.

"This must be very hard for you," another mourner adds.

Levon nods; he doesn't know how to answer. He is fifteen, and this isn't supposed to be happening.

Surveying the room, he captures the span of space and furniture and is reminded that this is his home, the place he *should* feel safe though never has. Throngs of people fill the room: his grandparents, aunts, uncles, cousins he barely knows, the rabbi, teachers and faculty from the junior and senior high schools, and a few others Levon has never seen before. The muscle-heads from David's football team are by the piano. Nearby are the cheerleaders, with Rebecca Blake holding court before her followers.

Levon notices the imaginary line drawn down the center of the room. To the left are the young, the uncompromising group pent up with shock, disbelief. To the right, perched on the sofa in close confines, are the elder realists, the disillusioned assembly of those who have witnessed the finite passing of days. They are the generation who understands what it means to bury a child, to bury hope.

Levon isn't sure where he belongs. He follows the invisible line through the phalanx of hunched over bodies and crossed feet. There he finds his parents standing alongside a table brimming with shiva essentials: an overload of bagels, cold cuts, salads, and dessert spreads. It is fitting for Levon to find his parents looming by the food. Hadn't food caused enough problems in their lives?

Levon's little sister, Chloe, approaches his mother, and Levon watches. His father turns away from them, seemingly annoyed at the interruption. His yarmulke slips from his head—exposing the thick, dark hair splashed with gray—and drops to the floor. When he leans down to pick it up, his pale, blue eyes meet Levon's. It's impossible for Levon to overlook the swell of accusation in his father's stare. When Craig resumes his full height, Levon remembers the strapping palm tree—resilient and far-reaching—and finds poetry in the distinction. Later he will write in his journal: *My father, perfect and tall like a Florida palm, is weak in the presence of Mother Oak.* Levon's eyes follow the outline of his father's back as he makes his way toward the kitchen. *Weeping willow is more like it.*

Levon turns toward Chloe. She looks tired and wan, inconsistent with her normally animated face and gleaming eyes. She tugs on their mother's skirt, and Levon notices that the innocent gesture makes this ten-year-old seem younger and smaller than usual. He watches how his mother—with her brunette version of Eva Peron's famous bun—transforms when around Chloe, pushing aside the hurt and sorrow so that she can brighten for her needy little girl. He doesn't blame his mother—Chloe *is* a spirited blessing. "Honey, what's the matter? Are you feeling all right?"

Levon notes the conversation he's heard so many times—though the one-sided, spontaneous flurry of instruction that escapes his mother's mouth can hardly be called an exchange: "Chloe, are you okay? Chloe, you can't eat that. Chloe, that's your brother's milk—the blue one is yours." The excessive worry directed solely at the sick child precludes any remnants of maternal concern for him.

Levon burrows his hands in the pockets of his shamefully tight jacket, palms fisted into knots while his heavy legs drag him toward the remains of his family. If the mirrors weren't covered by sheets, he would catch his reflection: the dark brown eyes on a trusting face, the not quite black hair, the bandage on his pale cheek.

"You okay, Levon?"

It's Rebecca. She has extracted herself from the crowd and accosts Levon with the superiority of the entitled queen bee. Rebecca is painful to look at. She is beautiful and fresh—mahogany-colored eyes and flowing chestnut hair. Her lips are dotted in red and the shine leaves him breathless, as he remembers the countless nights he would hear her voice and laughter coming from his brother's room.

Rebecca stops to greet Levon en route to his mother and sister; her arms tentatively fit around his wide body as if his blubber might be contagious.

"Does it hurt?" she whispers, referring to the line of stitches across the side of his face. She smells like coconuts and orange.

Keenly aware of how close her body is to his, Levon answers, "No," as he pulls away from the ill-fitted hug. She starts to say something and hesitates, backing away, her graceful, outstretched arms falling to her sides. She holds her head down, and still Levon can see the gentle streaks of tears, the sun-kissed complexion marred in grief. When her eyes eventually reach Levon's, they lock, and she is unable to break free. Levon wants to touch her cheek and respond to the question her pleading eyes ask.

"I know it hurts," she says.

He isn't sure if she is talking about the stitches or the unseen, unspoken pain. Whatever she's alluding to, Levon gobbles up the attention. His eyes hold onto hers longer and deeper than they should. Levon's grief for his brother is entangled with his fixation on Rebecca. Is there the slightest possibility that she understands, that she might interpret what his eyes are saying? Levon exhales, expunging himself of the emotional burden that has lodged in the cushy softness around his stomach. *Does she know?* he hears himself say out loud, though no words escape. His eyes remain fixed, unblinking. He knows if he snaps a picture—blinks and clicks the camera—the feeling will surely pass, and he wants to believe that she might understand for a few moments more. He is feeding on redemption and, unlike the meals before that have left him full and ashamed, this particular gluttony leaves him proud.

It is his mother who ultimately breaks the spell he shares with Rebecca. Chloe needs her cornstarch, and Madeline has sidled up to her middle child with the presumption that he will be the one to run to the store and get it. Rebecca has by then retreated from his side, and Levon watches as she returns to her "Betty and Veronica" hierarchy. The room respectfully splits to allow her to pass through the crowd, and Jughead turns to face his mother.

"I didn't get to the store this week," she says, wistful and likely drugged.

They are the first words Madeline Keller has spoken to her son since they left the cemetery earlier that morning. They are a question, an accusation, and an order all rolled into one.

Levon's response begins in the hollow of his stomach and rises like fire through his throat where it is stifled by a deep swallow. What she really meant to say was the same thing she screamed in the hospital so that everyone within earshot turned away: "How could you? How could you do this?" Then she broke down, sobbing uncontrollably, falling onto the floor where she lay until two nurses and a doctor carried her off to an empty room for proper sedation.

Levon had been sobbing too, though she hadn't seen that.

The police officers at the scene were as perplexed as his mother. When they approached Levon's father in the hospital, they were quick to ask if he wanted to press charges against the underage driver who killed their son. Levon's plight turned into horror when his father answered, "He's my son, officer." The men, formerly businesslike, intent on delivering justice, grew compassionate. For a split second, Levon actually wondered if his father would turn his back on him too.

If not for the track of stitches across Levon's cheek, no one would ever have believed he was also a victim. That he got out unscathed was a Pandora's Box that no one dared rifle through.

He stares at his mother, who's asking him to go to the store; he can't find her once tight, unflawed features. All of her friends used to tell her she resembled the famous author Danielle Steele. Yet, the face bearing down on him is more bloated than smooth, and it's swollen where it used to be firm. He is surprised that he only now notices the wrinkles that line her eyes. Maybe they are his fault too. He hears the indiscreet humming of whispers filling the room, the question on everyone's tongue: why did God take the handsome, golden boy?

"Levon, did you hear me?"

He wants to cut her some slack, to hug her, to apologize to her again, but he is in pain too—a quiet suffering—and some mercy on her part might heal him instead of making him want to grab a handful of chocolate rugalah and shove it into his mouth. As she fumbles through her pocketbook for some money, Levon tries to say something. His eyes are blinking at her. If she bothered to meet his in return, she would see the tears pooling over and the ache inside of him.

When she finds the right denomination of bills, she tosses them in his direction without looking at him. The wadded up money lands on the floor by his feet. Getting her to notice him has always been a practice in both humility and futility, and now, Levon's defining act is sealed: he will always be the boy who got behind the wheel of the car that killed David.

Levon closes his eyes and feels David in the air. David wasn't just a muscled, lean, good-looking teenager. He possessed a presence that extended well beyond that of his seventeen-year-old physique. Belying the stereotypical young superstar in his prime, he was kind, he was good, and he was going places.

Levon worshiped his brother. And despite their obvious differences, Levon never begrudged his brother's popularity or the plethora of talents that came to him so easily. Levon was proud to tell people he was David's younger brother, and he would have done anything for David, anything, even if it meant leaving Chloe alone in the house to help him on that fateful night.

"You know I can't," was Levon's first response, when David called from a party asking him to come pick him up.

"It's not a big deal, bro. You have a restricted license."

Levon knew everything about it was wrong, yet the desire to help David, to swoop in and save the day, chipped away at his ordinarily conservative streak.

David never had to ask Levon more than once to do anything. This time, though, there were serious consequences to consider.

David continued, "I need to get home. It's only a mile away; just get here soon."

Something in David's voice triggered a response in Levon that was both foreign and dangerous. The desperation had Levon thinking heroic thoughts—now was his chance to help David out of a tough spot, just like David, so many times, had helped him when he was having difficulties.

"Mom and Dad will never know," David went on, "don't worry."

Levon's body shuddered in response to what his mind began to wrap around: David was in trouble. He checked in on Chloe and made note of the time. She wasn't due for a feeding for three more hours; his parents weren't due back for two. He didn't allow himself to consider contingencies, like how a flat tire could render Chloe straddling the fence between life and death. Instead, the excitement and anxiety settled in his belly. The idea of embarking on a private mission for his brother negated all other dangers. He got up and reached for the jeans that were strewn across the foot of his bed. He pulled them up and around his waist and didn't remember them being as snug as when he had put them on that morning. He reached for his favorite T-shirt—the one that read Fat People Are Hard to Kidnap—pulled it over his shoulders, and grabbed his wallet and the keys to David's car.

His mother despised the shirt, however he found that self-deprecating humor and self-loathing worked well together. Somehow, they canceled each other out.

Levon drove no more than fifteen miles per hour with both hands glued to the wheel. The party was not a mile away—it was more like three. Levon could hear his mother's rumbling voice, "Most accidents occur within a five mile radius of your house," as the odometer's numbers gradually increased.

When he approached the driveway of his destination, David was already outside.

Levon was always struck by the sight of his brother. He had read about Adonis— the baby that had an unearthly beauty and how measures were taken to safeguard him. Sometimes he'd see David from his parents' perspective, and, in their eyes, he was an Adonis. "What's wrong with you?" Levon asked, as David hobbled to the car, his face showing only a vestige of its usual calm.

"I feel like shit."

"You look it. What happened?"

"I gotta get out of here."

chapter 2

Levon is huffing and puffing on his bicycle en route to the nearby Publix supermarket. It is fall in Miami—at least that's what the calendar claims—and it remains unseasonably hot. A sticky moisture packs the air and fuels the tropics with storms that have innocuous names, like Erin and Irene. Wilma had thrashed ashore two years ago in October, bringing rampant power outages, school closings, and general misery with her.

Pedaling faster, Levon thinks about how much he hates riding his bicycle. The effort tires him. Because of the accident, he's pretty sure he'll never get a driver's license in any state. Now with his restricted license revoked, the bicycle is his only means of transportation. He can already see his mother calculating the number of calories he'll burn by the end of the summer.

Madeline is a substitute teacher at their high school. Levon has had great difficulty conjuring up the image of his cool, indifferent mother in front of a classroom and being taken seriously while tackling subjects like logarithms and deciduous forests. He was blown away when he learned that Mrs. Keller was the favored substitute across all four grades. This can't be his mother they're praising, he tells himself. She's one of the most impatient, self-absorbed women he has ever known. She should *suck* as a teacher! Levon dares not speak these harsh words aloud, instead, he writes about it in his journal:

My mother is uninterested, unresponsive.

My mother is a ridiculous woman who has managed to hold her place in our community with the flimsy bobby pins that clasp her updo.

I am invisible to my mother; when she chooses to look at me, she sees everything I'm not.

Rounding the corner of Sixty-ninth and Collins, the wind whips past Levon, and the smell of the ocean streams into his nose. His eyes rest on the valuable piece of untouched beach that sleeps cozily between two of Miami's latest trendy boutique hotels. Miami Beach has become more of a concrete jungle than a land of sand and surf, as residential high-rises and tourist destinations sweep the city and its expansive views from sight.

"The Beach isn't what it used to be," his father would repeatedly say to him.

Everything changes, Levon thinks to himself, glimpsing the crisp turquoise that a week ago could at times fill him with hope.

Turning from the ocean, Levon steers into the strip mall's parking lot and pulls up alongside the rusty bicycle rack. On any other day, he would, without question, run into someone he knows in the store. They might say hello and ask about Chloe or applaud David for his most recent victory on the football field. Then, they would turn abruptly, pretending not to notice him hovering over a display case with the Chips Ahoy or Nutter Butters. But today, most everyone he knows is sitting shiva at his house. Today, he could walk the aisles and purchase whatever he wants without public humiliation.

"Hey, Levon," comes a friendly voice from behind the customer service counter. It is Sally, and Levon instinctively knows it is Tuesday. The flow of days is confusing, though he is sure it is the first day of mourning, the third day since he last spoke to his brother. And it is Tuesday because Sally always wears her platinum hair stick-straight on the day she religiously visits the beauty parlor to have it ironed.

"Hi, Sally," he waves.

"I heard about your brother," she drawls. "What an awful shame."

Levon wants to back away from the counter, but Sally is leaning forward and her hand is stroking his shoulder. She is pretty in a petite, pixie way; her veiny hands are a sharp contrast to her youthful face. They resemble aged leather, coarse from sun damage.

"Your mom called ahead. I have the box of CS ready to go."

Sally liked to call Chloe's medicine "CS." She thought cornstarch wasn't befitting—not important enough, she'd say—for the serum that kept Chloe alive.

"I rode my bike…" Levon says.

"Don't you worry, sweetie pie. Take a bag with you now; I'll drop a box off on my way home. How's your mom doing?"

Levon hands Sally the wadded up money his mother had thrown at him earlier. His mother was worse than ever, drowning in grief, but how could he tell Sally that?

"She's trying to make sense of it all."

"It's tragic," Sally says, "utterly tragic."

As if he needed Sally to remind him of that. She hands Levon the bag, and the faraway look in her eyes can mean only one thing. "I remember the day that precious little girl was born."

Levon flipped the pages back in his mind. All Madeline Keller wanted her entire life was to mother a daughter. Two sons into her marriage, and the girl finally arrived: ten beautiful toes, ten tiny fingers, and too much gone wrong.

"A China!" shrieked five-year-old Levon, backing away from the pillowy softness of his baby sister's skin.

"It's a VA-gi-na," said his big brother, accentuating the VA part, as if he were teaching a foreign language. *Gross* soon followed as did *Don't ask me to change the diaper; I'm not going near that thing.*

"Must we focus on her anatomy?" said Madeline, resting

comfortably in one of the coveted suites at Mt. Sinai Hospital, overlooking Biscayne Bay. "Look at this face. Look at those perfect features."

"She's beautiful," Craig said. Meeting his wife's glossy eyes, he smiled. The upturn of her lips resembled something close to bliss.

"She looks exactly like David as a baby," Madeline finally said.

"I looked old and shriveled like Great-grandpa Daryl?" David joked.

And they laughed, together, because it was true that most newborns resembled the elderly with their undefined features and squishy parts. Most newborns, however, were budding flowers, their insides forming and growing. But that wasn't the case with Chloe. Her insides contradicted her perfect exterior, and at three months, Chloe suffered her first seizure. It was a momentous day because it coincided with the afternoon that seven-year-old David scored the winning touchdown and brought his flag football team to victory by concluding the season at an unparalleled 10-0. It was the beginning of what would mark a series of alternating highs and lows in the Keller household.

After the seizure, Chloe, the promising flower, began to wilt. A series of tests led the Kellers to Boston Children's Hospital, home to Dr. Max Gerald, the leading expert on Glycogen Storage Disease. There it was confirmed that Chloe was among those afflicted with the much-overlooked and often-misdiagnosed illness. Dr. Gerald explained that GSD is a rare genetic disorder of the liver, though to five-year-old Levon, it was the nameless, faceless foe that shadowed the entire family.

According to Dr. Gerald, the facts and statistics were grim: 1 in 100,000 children are born with the disease, 1 in 72 Jews are carriers. His clinical summation was offered in vital, scientific terms. Dr. Gerald would never have insulted the families with a terse explanation as to why their lives were forever changed. To the contrary, he was long-winded and detailed, careful to explain every fact because he knew that while the wide-eyed, sleep-deprived parents were listening and nodding their heads, nothing was being processed.

Over a lengthy discussion in his pocket-sized office, Dr. Gerald explained that children born with this deficiency can't release stored sugar from the liver because of a missing enzyme, making it virtually impossible to maintain normal blood sugar levels between meals without constant feedings. The abridged version—the one saved for the curious ears of the uncomprehending children—was that if Chloe didn't receive some special syrup every couple of hours, she would die.

"Cornstarch," Dr. Gerald said.

"Cornstarch?" his perplexed parents repeated.

"Mixed with water or soy milk, which is free of dairy and fruit sugar. It's digested slowly and provides a steady release of glucose in between feedings."

There was much to absorb about a disease that hinged on digestion. For the early years of Chloe's life, she would have to receive a cornstarch injection every two hours. Even when she was old enough to tolerate drinking the potion on her own during the day, an overnight feeding tube implanted in her stomach allowed for the continuous delivery of glucose while she slept. This was no reprieve for parents or caregivers who would have to wake up and administer the liquid throughout the night. They learned that cornstarch can never be mixed in drinks that contain high amounts of ascorbic or citric acid. If the cornstarch drink were heated, it would be rendered ineffective. Dr. Gerald recommended Crystal Lite or another sugar-free drink as alternatives to water or milk. "It may taste better," he added.

The sinister disease that plagued Chloe and her ability to be like other children her age was incurable and lifelong. Life, for the Kellers, was now defined in seconds, minutes, and hours.

Levon thought back to the first few years of Chloe's life, and how time became a race that could end in a premature death. There was the night when the power went out and the alarm for Chloe's two a.m. feeding failed to go off. He was only five then, but he remembered. His parents were screaming and arguing with each other, their steely voices filtering through the bedroom walls. He said she was supposed to check the battery-charged radio and alarm clock; she said she did. The doctors told them if they had slept another minute, Chloe may not have survived.

And because every year was marked as a miracle and not a milestone, Chloe's birthdays were testaments and celebrations. On her third birthday, the family ventured north to Orlando for Chloe's first vacation from home and a meeting with Mr. and Mrs. Mouse. But time, that brazen nemesis, flared its wicked head and a five-car pileup closed the highway down for seven hours. Madeline had only packed enough supplies to get through the three-hour drive. They were *lucky,* the doctors said, that they arrived at the Fort Drum rest stop when they did. Lucky, because the most common occurrences—things typically taken for granted without recourse—are death sentences to parents of GSD children. Indeed, getting stuck in traffic or running out of supplies or oversleeping can cause a child to have a seizure, experience developmental delays, go into a coma, or the unspeakable.

Sally's southern twang rips him from the exhaustive stroll down memory lane. "You tell your mom if she needs anything to give me a holler," she calls out from behind the counter, immune to Levon's heightened anxiety level. The rush that accompanied the thought of being so close to death guides him away from her voice. He maneuvers through the aisles and across rows of dairy and meat until he finds himself in front of his favorite comforts: Nabisco and Keebler. By the time he reaches the checkout line, the snack bag of chocolate chip cookies is empty—the only evidence of its past occupants, a smattering of crumbs. He knows his mother will have a fit that he hasn't adhered to his diet. He knew with every bite he took, every swallow, he was filling himself with something soothing but wrong. Maybe if he is lucky, he muses, he could eat and eat and eat, and she won't notice a mushrooming belly in the wake of the burgeoning sorrow. But *she* always noticed. This is a woman who, for the last ten years, restricted two out of her three children's diets. Chloe's diet maintained her good health while Levon's diet satisfied her right to be pissed.

Sally is ambling toward the checkout. He does not want another one of her memory's to pierce him. He is raw and unable to think clearly. "You don't need to pay for the cookies," she says with a sympathetic wink. The bag of Chloe's cornstarch is clutched in his hands. Today, although he finished off a batch of cookies, he has something valuable to bring home, and it gives him a sense of satisfaction. "Thanks, Sally."

Levon takes a shortcut home, careful to avoid an altercation with his mother for being away too long. *How much time does it take to eat a bag of Chips Ahoy!?* he asks himself. She knew. She always knew.

When he reaches his tree-lined street, the cleaning crew is pulling out of the driveway next door. They had been there all morning, but Levon was too distracted to notice. Finally, the jerk who had lived next door since Levon was a toddler had moved out. If not for his brother's horrendous death, Levon would have been rejoicing in his much-anticipated departure. He parked his bike on the side of his house, nearby the wooden planks that fenced their home and kept nuisances like Bruce out. He peered into the window of the now vacant house. Bruce was a creep by all definitions of the word. Three years out of high school and he was still living at home with his parents, making everyone's life miserable, while ostensibly deciding what to do with his own wasteful life. If it were up to Levon, he'd suggest an incurable and inoperative injury to his larynx that would prohibit him from talking. Much that came out of his mouth was either rooted in insult or was so derogatory in nature that Levon avoided him at all costs. You never wanted to be the overweight kid on the receiving end of the master bully.

He knows it is not the most appropriate time to indulge in negative thinking, but when he toys with the idea of Bruce switching places with David, it gives him a gratifying sense of pleasure. If only David's absence meant that he had moved out of the house and on to college, something less permanent, less forever. And Bruce, who will probably never decide the direction and course of his lopsided life, instead, will infiltrate a new neighborhood while the rest of us are left in his wake, scratching our heads in disbelief that the world can be so unfair.

"You're back," his mother says, when he opens the door to the house. She cannot prevent herself from glancing at her watch. The door closes behind them; she grabs the bag of cornstarch, and before she asks, he answers, "Sally's dropping off the rest later. I couldn't carry the box on my bike."

It is hard for Levon to watch his mother wince. He hears the chatter coming through the door, the gathering of lingering mourners and realizes he has to go to the bathroom. Racing through the house, he misses the moving trucks and the black Volvo station wagon that reach his block. As he lifts the toilet seat, his gaze turns upward toward the window. He can hear the trucks as they halt in front of the house, their screeching brakes sounding more like whistling steam engines. Zipping his pants and washing his hands, he takes the few steps to the window and stands on his tiptoes to see his new neighbors. At the same time, bellowing voices emerge from the hallway outside the bathroom. The muffled sounds beckon him to turn toward the door and listen.

He recognizes the delicate timbre of his father's tone against the loud, hurling accusations of his mother. He can't make out what they are saying, nor does he try. If he had his journal with him, he would be able to cite similar exchanges, even dictate the exchange himself. Lowering himself to the floor, he turns and positions himself backside against the door. An interruption from their offensive, culpable son would not bode well. Levon stares at his watch instead.

It wasn't always this way.

Levon remembered when it was just the two of them, David and him. To his four-year-old mind, his family seemed really happy.

Then Chloe came along, and life was divided into before and after. It was impossible to blame Chloe; he loved her madly, though her appearance diffused the balance of a family's once ordinary veneer. Levon's earlier memories were correlated with the bottle of Shalimar that rested on his mother's vanity. Whenever his parents would go out for dinner, his mom splashed herself with Shalimar. It was a scent that Levon first equated with being watched by his favored babysitter Roxy, and later the smell was connected to what they had lost when his sister materialized.

His mom always looked stunning those evenings with her hair falling on her shoulders, softening her face and eyes. The *pre-bun era*, Levon thought to himself, was a magical period in all of their lives. Levon tried hard to remember the precise instant when things went from carefree and wild to contained and suffocating.

Upon her return in the evenings, Levon would stir, jarred awake by the full-bodied smells of his mother's familiar scent. And though his eyes were closed, feigning deep sleep, he knew she was smiling, her cheeks ripened with laughter. At fifteen, Levon distinguished the scents: perfume, wine, a hint of garlic. At a younger age, the smells were the defining scent of his youth, bottled up in once forgotten familial happiness. It would be the scintillating mixture of Saturday nights that had come to mean love and trust.

Nestled under the covers, Levon felt her body leaning over his, while strands of her hair tickled his back. She would whisper things that he hadn't heard in years: "I love you, Sailor Boy." "How's my monkey? I missed you tonight." "Sweet dreams." Levon used to think he was silly for remembering those interludes and phrases reserved for him and him only. He had scribed the words on paper so many times the pen could write them without the will of his hand. He foolishly believed that if he wrote them down, they would be real, and the permanence would prove Levon's worth, verify that he was lovable.

She once found him cute enough to tag him with the name Monkey that combined charm and chunky cheeks. Back then, his room was hand-painted in the deep hues of the jungle, and the monkeys with their animated poses and childlike smiles often transformed Levon into a world of fantasy. Then Levon, in what stung like a swift slap of the wrist, had to switch rooms with Chloe so that her room was closer to their parents. As hastily as his mom had named him Monkey was the rapidity with which the strokes of French pink brushed over his jungle walls. They never got around to repainting what was *supposed* to have been Chloe's room, and now was Levon's. Yellow was neutral, they claimed, a term they used loosely at the time, and which would later become the cornerstone from which contempt was bred. After that, whenever Levon would see a monkey at the zoo, he would scream and cry until they stopped going to the zoo altogether.

And Levon had long since given up sailing. After capsizing three boats, you realize you were never meant to rest your curved bottom on a meager piece of fiberglass and expect it to stay upright. *Bon voyage, Sailor Boy.*

Once Chloe emerged, Madeline and Craig ceased going out for dinner, and Madeline gave up wearing Shalimar. Levon smelled it sometimes when he would accompany her to Burdines on Lincoln Road. They would walk through the cosmetics and perfume counters to get to the escalator that would bring them up to the children's department, and Levon would purposely slow his gait. She would reach for his hand and tug on him with a fervor that signaled to Levon they weren't stopping for a new bottle. They were going to ignore what was once normal. The wish that Levon so often dreamed about remained bottled up, and the only scent that would seep into their house was the kind that didn't come from a bottle. Without the elements of color, taste, or touch, it had the capacity to invade all the senses. It is what becomes of a Shalimar-less existence. It was unhappiness.

The fights were always the same. Drenched in sleep deprivation and the genuine prospect of death, accusations turned venomous and hostility burned from the ashes of exhaustion and tears.

"The next feeding's yours," Craig would grumble, crawling into bed and taking his position defensively next to his wife.

"I did the last two," she'd counter.

"I'm meeting a contractor in the morning."

"This is all your fault," she stabs at him.

"What the hell does *that* mean?" he asks and adds, "You're crazy," as he heads toward Chloe's room where he will spend another evening on her pink carpeted floor while Levon listens next door. His father ran a multimillion dollar real estate development company yet he couldn't tame his size-two, reed-thin wife who could very easily fall over if one sneezed in her direction. He was sure his great-great-grandfather, having built this house a million years ago, had no idea that the structure made it possible to eavesdrop simply by sitting up in bed. The air vent near the ceiling above his head spilled out all their secrets, telling him of their suffering. He once tried closing the silver flaps and woke up that night with beads of sweat trickling down his back, and he stood up on his bed and reopened the vents.

His mom followed his dad into Chloe's room that same night. Levon knew this because her voice trailed behind his through the duct.

"Are you kidding me?" she balked. "What if the boys wake up and find you here?

"Then they'll find me here. I think they already see the fault lines in our marriage."

"And what's *that* supposed to mean?" she asked.

"We're breaking in two."

This was when his mother became hysterical. His metaphors always preceded one of her eruptions. Once, she would brag to her friends about the intellectual genius she married. Now, his verbiage unnerved her, stripping her of solid footing. Levon imagined her bobby pins flying across the room and springing off the wall.

"I'm tired," she started, "I'm so tired." The words slipped through the creases of breaths and whimpers. "Why did this happen to us?" Her words hung in the air, the thoughts too frightening to say out loud. Finishing her thought would give credence to the next sentence, the harbinger of what was to come. "I want it to go away, Craig. Please make it all go away." She was sobbing now, and Levon wasn't sure what she meant. Did she want them to disappear? He thinks his father might have interjected something, but he wasn't sure—his voice was typically softer and harder to hear. And then she began again, her cries rising and falling in measure with her despair. "I can't take it anymore…I just can't do this."

"Yes, you can," his father said, raising his tone as if he intentionally wanted Levon to hear.

"I'm sick of your certainty," she screamed.

"We have no choice."

By then, Chloe was screaming a deafening wail, and Levon covered his ears with his pillow, drowning the sounds of everything that had gone so wrong.

From his position on the bathroom floor, Levon reaches for a hanging towel and lowers his face into the fresh scent of Bounce. He is tired of their arguments. He is tired of missing David. He is tired of holding everything inside. He longs to be free. He whispers the words to his favorite Everclear song:

I close my eyes when I get too sad
I think thoughts that I know are bad
Close my eyes and I count to ten
Hope it's over when I open them
And then he screams.

At first, it is into the soft white towel, and then he lifts his head and a high-pitched howl escapes into the air. Raising himself off the floor, he finds his face in the mirror and continues screaming. He doesn't care how ridiculous he looks. He doesn't care that his face is turning crimson. He doesn't care if his stitches pop and blood splatters across the mirror or that the words frozen in his brain leak onto her immaculate floors.

Hope my mom and I hope my dad

Will figure out why they get so mad
Hear them scream, I hear them fight
They say bad words that make me wanna cry

They start to bang on the door.

His mother speaks first. "Levon, is that you?"

Levon keeps screaming. The tightness in his throat gives way to a rising squeal. He sounds like a pig; he looks like a pig.

They are intent on finding out who is behind the gruesome noises.

"Open the door!"

Levon keeps right on yelling. The pitch ebbs and flows between his staggering breath, and the noise filters his ears and leaps off the walls. Gasping for air, dizzy and spent, he remains fixed in his pose and the distinction of his voice for three whole minutes. His belly, once full of fear and betrayal, is lightened by the sounds escaping his chest.

"Levon, this is your father. Open the door right now."

Instead of heeding his father's words, Levon falls to the floor, hugs his knees to his chest, and cries.

chapter 3

Though David was noticeably handsome, he was also humble and unaware of his good looks. Though a star athlete, he was exempt from conceit. Intelligent beyond the scope of academics, his street sense designated him as the go-to-guy when his peers needed guidance along the bumpy road of teenage angst.

These are the thoughts that flow through Levon's mind as he plops himself down on David's comforter. Fleeing the murderous sounds of the bathroom, and his parents' inquisition, he escapes to forbidden territory and the untouched reminder of David's life. Sitting in his brother's bedroom is where he feels closest to him.

This is the first time he's been here since David died. He is resting on his bed, far from the somber crowd downstairs. The quiet is unnerving to Levon: the bat in the corner, the jacket draped across the back of his chair, the computer sitting untouched on David's desk. They all seem misplaced and awkward, stripped of life and void of spirit, abandoned by their owner. The rabbi had said at David's funeral that his life had been stolen, cut monumentally short. That abysmal fact turned his room into a shrine and a sham.

Teachers respected David, his opponents on the field applauded his efforts, and girls were helpless to his boyish charm. That he squired away Rebecca Blake came as no surprise to anyone at their high school. Levon's eyes linger on the picture of the pair that's framed next to the bed. David is in his football uniform after the big win against their rival, the North Miami Beach Chargers. His arm is draped tenderly around Rebecca's shoulder. The sun had kissed his skin that summer—his hair is matted and damp from the game—and he looks proud. Rebecca's hair is pulled high in a ponytail, and her lips form an outline of soft pink around her white smile. How happy they look, the Homecoming Queen and her counterpart.

David hated the nickname Adonis, but it stuck with him to his death. It personified his classic good looks and stature; at seventeen, he was standing close to six feet tall and a slim 165 pounds. Levon memorized both his and David's stats each time they went to their pediatrician Dr. Engle. This fixation became stronger as David grew taller and Levon got heavier.

"It's like this," Bruce once shouted to him as they returned from one of their yearly appointments, "your body's heading east and west, and your boy over here's heading north."

He was right.

Returning to the photo, Levon studies David's features for a sign they may have predicted the future. The walls are emblazoned with plaques, awards, and pictures—David's wrapping around him, grabbing hold of his little brother's heart and choking him of breath.

Levon thinks about how they used to play hide-and-go seek in the house when they were about nine or ten. David always found the best places to hole up. It took Levon hours to find him. When tucked away from sight, David would complete his homework, read a chapter of a book, and write about it in his reading log. His mother would ask Levon why he didn't have time management skills like his older brother.

"It's all about my poor hiding spots," he'd try to explain to her.

"You're saying if you had a better hiding spot, you'd get your homework done more quickly?"

Levon would answer her with indisputable words, "No, no," but in his thoughts he argued, *If I had a better hiding spot, would you like me as much as you like David?*

The shelves in David's room overflow with books. They run the gamut from his favorites, *Catcher in the Rye* and *A Separate Peace*, to volumes of sports almanacs, with a *Sports Illustrated* swimsuit model poking her head out from between the pages. David enjoyed hiking and biking, so there are various copies of *Fodor's Best Trails in North America*.

Levon's eyes grab hold of one of the bookends that Chloe had made for David on his last birthday. Its fraternal twin is concealed from view. Facing Levon is a sturdy, solid black frame that Chloe had decorated with colorful, foam shapes. An assortment of girl-inspired hearts and flowers coat the dark finish. She had colored her name "Chloe" on a sheet of paper, sprinkled it with glitter, and glued it in the middle. She had been so proud of the way she had softened the stark metal her mother had purchased at the store. The complementary twin on the other side—sidled up to *Great Expectations*—is draped in the deep shades of *all-boy*: footballs, soccer balls, and a white baseball clinging for life. She had written *David* in dark blue and green, no glitter. On entering David's room, anyone could easily make out the pink, frilly touch of Chloe's girlieness. When the players from the team came over and teased David about the feminine touch, the *wussy wall*, they called it, he never considered switching its place. David adored his baby sister; the bookends were their bond. It signified solidarity.

The door swings open and Levon knows who it is by the force of the punch.

"What are you doing in here?" she demands.

Her eyes are damp and her nose is red. The bun is nowhere in sight. In its place is a stringy brown mess that Levon hasn't seen loose in years. He cannot believe how long it has grown. It hurts Levon to see her like this—disheveled, aching, and paper thin. It is clear which one of them hasn't been raiding the shiva platters.

Levon pulls himself up from the bed. He can smell traces of David in the air. They pass through his nose at alarming speed. She can smell it too, and the emotions that transform her eyes and splotch her cheeks are easy for Levon to decipher. She is trying not to be angry. She is trying to conjure up a shred of humanity for her son. Much has been thrown at her. Levon bites his lip waiting for what will emerge.

"I didn't want anyone in here," she whispers.

"I know."

"I want…" she stops herself.

What he really wants is to throw up. The screaming has left his throat sore, and all the sweets he had gulped down are rumbling around his stomach at terrifying speed. If the contents of his lunch and the afterthoughts aren't going to tumble out, he knows something else will that is dangerously close.

"You don't understand, Levon," she says, her voice shaking. "You never will."

"I lost him too," he says.

"Parents aren't supposed to lose children."

He had read all about this in the pamphlets the rabbi had given them. When a child dies, a part of his parents die along with him, so, in fact, the death in a way takes their lives. The majority of parents never get over the loss of a child; a good percentage of them divorce.

A lone tear escapes her eye and slowly makes its way down her cheek.

"Tell me again…" she begins, as Levon turns away from her, and she reaches for his sleeve instead of his skin.

Levon answers emphatically, "No." Though in his head, a million follow—life-size, black, bold *No's* that clutter his thoughts, loud and distracting. His arm steers away from her, and he clasps his fingers in a wild attempt to contain thoughts.

"Levon, I need to know, you have to tell me…"

"I said *no*, Mom. I don't want to talk about it."

She wants him to tell her about that night. She wants every detail. He'd already told her. He told her repeatedly in the hospital when the officers were circling around him with their pads of paper and clicking pens. Then he told her again when they went to the police station and officially suspended his restricted license, placing him on probation for the next three years. Then he told her a third time when they were driving home, and they had to pull over to the side of the road so she could vomit. Finally, he said it again, when they went to bed that night, right after she took his cell phone and threw it into the pool.

It was never going to be enough. She wanted to know everything, and Levon couldn't give her everything because in the middle of the story there was David.

She begins to sob again. "I just want to know what he said…"

When Levon ignores her, she reaches into her pocket, pulls out a cigarette and a pack of matches from one of his favorite restaurants, the Big Pink, and begins to blow thick circles of smoke into the air. The senseless inhalation seems to relieve her.

"What are you doing?" Levon asks.

"What does it look like I'm doing?"

"You smoke?"

She collapses onto the bed, whimpering and puffing away. Her long fingers are curled around the thin cigarette. It occurs to Levon that her life has been snuffed out, much like the match she has thrown into the garbage can. She is crying and shaking and going on and on about some kind of trouble she had gotten into as a kid. Levon racks his brain for something he can say that will guide her out of this stupor, something that he hasn't already said in their diluted exchanges. She is delirious and not making sense.

"I never thought you'd be so irresponsible, so careless," she finally says.

Her eyes are fixed, a combination of a watery sadness and a fierce darkness that makes it tricky to spot her pupils. Levon turns away, breaking the connection, and stands up from the bed. He peers down at his mother who has all but melted into David's navy blue comforter.

He didn't want to confront her with a soliloquy of all the things he had done right. He was not a bad kid. He had good values and cared about the people he loved. He wasn't popular, but he wasn't unpopular either.

So he gives her a part of what she wants to hear. "He said, 'Mom's going to kill us.'"

She is thinking about this, silent and somber. The digital clock next to the bed is quiet, but Levon can swear he hears it ticking.

This, she does not expect. *This* does not make any sense. The smoke that infiltrated her lungs earlier, without incident, suddenly has her coughing into her palms. Standing up abruptly, she heads toward the window and opens it a crack. Levon watches her toss the butt through the cramped space and into the waiting garbage can alongside the house. He hopes she doesn't burn down the neighborhood.

"Say that again," she insists.

She heard what he said, but compelling him to repeat it gives her a senseless satisfaction.

"Levon."

"Yes, Mom?" he says, shooting her a look.

This time her words are clear. "What exactly did he say?"

Levon acquiesces.

"He said, 'Mom's going to kill us.'"

Seconds pass when she stumbles toward him and lifts his chin so their eyes are level. Levon holds her pupils in place with his gaze as long as his hurting eyes will allow. When she finally turns for the door, he hears her murmur through the air, indignant, without shame, "Please don't come in here again."

Promises mean everything when you're little
And the world's so big
I just don't understand how
You can smile with all those tears in your eyes
Tell me everything is wonderful now
Please don't tell me everything is wonderful now

chapter 4

Lucy Bell is dancing around her new house, barefoot and tippy-toed. George, her beloved golden retriever, is chasing her, nipping at her heels. Long and leggy, Lucy is ecstatic to be starting fresh. From the minute the delivery trucks drop off her bedroom furniture and clothes, she feels enthusiasm swarming around her.

Atlanta had been a disaster of monumental proportions; they couldn't get out fast enough. As soon as they sold the house, they were heading south on Interstate 75 through the flat, lackluster terrain of the Sunshine State corridor, which, in itself, was ironic, because *Sunshine* was what they used to call her.

That was before.

The house is airy and bright, a sharp contrast from the pictures her parents showed her on the Internet. The images posted on the realtor's website were the size of postage stamps with indistinguishable features, not this two-story home built around what the realtor said gushingly over the phone, was "...a warm, inviting design...French country with an Italian feel..."

Sight unseen, they took it, and when they first walked through the stately double doors, Lucy was mesmerized by the high-beamed ceilings with whitewash finish and the antique oak floors. The windows and French doors were outlined in ivory, and the coated walls were as light and warm as their finishes. Lucy especially loved the lush ivy that draped itself down the weathered lime exterior walls, surrounding the windows and doors, and climbing along the clay-tile roof. It reminded her of Tuscany, and she was obsessed with Tuscany ever since hearing that her mom and dad had gone there on their honeymoon. Leafing through their picture album brought the scenic images of mountains, seashores, and historic culture to life.

"When do I get to go to Tuscany?" she had asked when she was in third grade.

"Soon," they said. It was baffling to Carol, her mom, when she arrived home from an afternoon of shopping in Buckhead to find eight-year-old Lucy packed and waiting for her by the front door.

"Where are you going?' she asked her willful child.

"What do you mean where am I going?" she answered, her tone inescapably sure. "I'm going to Tuscany."

Carol, dropping her bag on the floor, crouched down in front of her child. "Lucy," she said, threading her fingers through the golden strands of Lucy's tousled hair, "What's all this about Tuscany?"

Lucy could tell immediately by the question that there was no chance she was going to Tuscany that day. Her mom tried stroking her hair to console her, but it didn't stop the tiniest of tears from escaping her green eyes. With her shoulders bent forward and her eyes focused on the floor, she returned to her room with her shiny yellow suitcase and began the depressing task of emptying the contents and placing them back in their drawers. Then, she took off the outfit she had especially chosen for the journey overseas—a white cotton dress with pale purple flowers appliquéd along the seams and her brand-new patent leather dress shoes—and replaced them with her worn out blue jeans and a navy, long-sleeved T-shirt that had once belonged to her older brother Ricky. Shrugging her shoulders, the remnants of regret and disappointment fell away.

When her mother caught her walking past the kitchen, she called out, "You okay?" She heard herself cheer loudly, "I'm fine." This display of maturity and awareness was not that of a child who was playing pretend; it was an inherited gift that would serve Lucy well over time.

Lucy is reminded of Ricky, and how odd it felt moving to a new house without him. They had saved him his own room and bathroom, though he was now living at the University of Maryland where he had begun his freshman classes. Ricky was a year older than Lucy, thirteen months to be exact, and even though 390 days and what should have been a school year separated them, their parents—in a flash of impatience and pride—pushed their little boy a grade ahead when he was five. That was why at fifteen, Lucy was in the tenth grade at Beach High while Ricky, at seventeen, was off in College Park, entrenched in Botany 101 and fraternity parties.

It wasn't uncommon for the two to be mistaken for twins—not because of their resemblance to one another but because of their closeness. They were bound by an unusual friendship. Lucy had often heard of twins feeling each other's pain—mining each other's stories—a creepy intuition that transcended explanation. That was what she and her brother shared. It didn't help that in the midst of jubilant, newborn baby bliss, her *I Love Lucy*-watching parents named their son Ricky after the televisions show's lead actor, and when she came along, the awful joke became her namesake. It had always been a source of great humor to hear Ricky come into the house after an evening with friends chiming, "Lucy, I'm home," in the heavily Spanish-accented voice of Ricky Ricardo himself.

Gosh, she missed Ricky. If he were there, they would hop in his car with George in tow and drive through Miami Beach, staking claim to new hotspots. She would find her favorite place to buy vintage clothes; he would find the best peach smoothies in town. Plotting her course and burying her feet in the warm Florida sand would not be the same without her other half, but it was something she would reluctantly have to accept. She reminded herself that this wasn't the same as the last time he wasn't around, the only time, for that matter. Lucy knew all too well how things could go awry when her brother wasn't around.

One two three, step, one two three, step, she counts in her head, while the distasteful thoughts transform her motion into hurried strides. George has gone off sniffing his new abode and Lucy is alone in the empty living room where the massive crystal chandelier trickles from the ceiling. Her very own private conservatory. Floating through the space, powered by a quickening heart and the rushing sound of her pulse, Lucy dives into the air, breathing a shallow pitch. Lucy loves to dance. Having had no professional training or the desire to pursue it, Lucy used her body to help heal herself. When her arms and legs were free to discover the air that enveloped them, her mind followed. *Free, at one with myself, letting go.* These were a few of the phrases she threw around when anyone would ask what she was doing, flying around the house with her arms spread-eagle, her torso moving to a song with no melody.

Escape, her father called it.

When Lucy's mom enters the room, flanked with the last of the movers, Lucy draws her arms to her sides and quiets her legs. A line of sweat has formed above her top lip, and it takes one swipe of her hand for it to disappear. George has returned from his parade around the house and edges closer to Lucy's side. He sits his behind square on her foot and although Lucy loves and appreciates George as if he were her child, and not the year-old puppy they rescued from the shelter, the idea of his butt on her freshly manicured toes rattles her. She gives him a gentle kick, which he obeys, while remaining close. The movers are watching her, leering, and Lucy wishes she were wearing something over her tank top and shorts, but it is dreadfully hot in Miami, far worse than the heat in Atlanta.

Her mother addresses her with interest, "Is everything set in your room, Lucy?"

"Yes," she says, rubbing George's head between his ears, his favorite place to be scratched.

"Are you sure? They're leaving so if something turns up missing, there's no going back."

As if there could be anything in the world to make her go back there. Everything she needs is right here, she decides.

"I'm all set," she says, careful that her eyes stay focused on her mother and not on the sweaty men. George lets out a yelp.

"Where's Daddy?" she asks.

"Out back."

Curious, Lucy excuses herself from the room and makes her way through the wood-paneled hallway that leads to the patio and pool. George follows loyally, a few steps behind her, while she contemplates changing his name to Shadow. His responsive bark, albeit at the lizard he spots sliding across the natural-stone patio, informs Lucy of his opinion on the subject.

Despite the previous owners' attempts to fill their lushly landscaped backyard with trees and plants indigenous to the tropical climate, they failed miserably to shade the confines of the yard. Indeed, the patio area, surrounding the lagoonlike pool with a lovely waterfall, is breathtaking with tropical flora. The sun's glow, though, beaming alongside her face singes her tender skin, and she ducks to avoid the burn. Striding past the crystal blue water and the rock formation that empties the cascade into the pool, Lucy eventually arrives at the fence that surrounds what looks remarkably like a golf course.

Lucy can make out the outline of her father's navy blue shirt where he is stationed against the iron fence with his arms resting atop the finished metal. The sweltering sun has hosed him in sweat, licking the ends of his hair and dripping down the back of his neck. He could easily be mistaken for Ricky; they are about the same height with similar medium skin tone. The two have dirty blonde hair, messy and tangled. It is her mother's one wish to take a brush to both of them. The family resembles one another with the same light hair and greenish-yellow eyes, though the women of the household are softer, lighter versions of their rugged counterparts.

Lucy liked being called feminine. It reminded her that she was clean and fresh and irrefutably innocent. And while she wasn't one to focus on one's physical attributes, especially her own, nothing filled her with more satisfaction than seeing the golden tufts of her hair falling past her shoulders. It had taken forever to grow—five harrowing months to be exact—and when it finally reached the optimal length, long, thick layers framed her face and fell dramatically down her back. It didn't matter that hair was dead. She could attest to the fact that her hair was a sign of life, proof of her growth, and verification of how far she had come.

"Hi, Daddy," she says.

George has stationed himself along the perch of the rocks, making many failed attempts to lure lizards and frogs into his hungry jaws. Lapping at the wetness with his paws, he positions himself for entry while Andy Bell turns to face his daughter.

"Hey, Honey."

"I didn't know we backed up to a golf course," she says.

"It's La Gorce Country Club. They just had it redone."

Lucy situates herself alongside her father where their shoulders almost meet. She watches two older men step into their golf cart and drive away from sight. Lucy studies the wide-open grounds. From her vantage point, there are neatly manicured fairways with the essential Bermuda grass. Her father confirms it is, in fact, an 18-hole course; their house rests on the sixth and seventh holes. Lucy notices how the expansive lawns are checkered in patches of green, giving way to spots of burned gold. The turf appears hungry for water, a reprieve from the unrelenting heat. Even with the renovation, nothing beat the pristine Atlanta courses on which her famed brother had once set records. The thought made her bare feet tickle, remembering the way the lush grass felt beneath her toes.

"Can we play here?" she asks, eager to return to the green, anxious to step on a course again.

"We'll see," he says, which can mean a lot of things, none of which Lucy is sure she can believe.

At one time, they had enjoyed playing golf together. It was the only activity that required one hundred percent attendance of the whole brood. Sure, Lucy had her dancing and her doodling; Mom had her cooking; Dad, his job at the radio station; Ricky, an endless stream of girlfriends. But golf became a group activity for the Bells. Every Sunday morning for as many years as Lucy could count, the family gathered in their father's Denali for the twenty-minute drive to the Dunwoody Country Club. The soulful mornings began at dawn. While the dew dusted the ground, the sun slowly edged itself off the horizon, sprinkling the sky with possibility. Lucy, typically one who relished action, transformed during those afternoons. She was forced to slow down, quiet her brain, and expel the impulses that dared her to run across the velvety green fields and dip into the choppy blue waters teeming with fish.

Gazing at the field in front of her, she muses aloud, "Consider the irony."

Her father flinches at the comment. She should have anchored it down and forbade it from slipping out; her candor, most times, was an admired trait. What neither of them dared to acknowledge was the scathing twist of fate that granted them this view. The golf course was where it began, the setting of why they fled Atlanta in the first place.

"Ricky's gonna freak," she adds, keenly aware of how this coincidence must pain her father.

When he doesn't answer, she follows with: "Let's start our Sunday tradition again. It'll be good for us."

The shrugging of his shoulders is the only response she is going to get, which isn't enough for an optimist like Lucy. Even when her defenses were tried and tested, she soared back to a positive place, healed and strengthened. Dad is less flexible. Discussing the particulars of that afternoon in Atlanta sickened him and distressed the others. Lucy was not one to engage in self-pity nor sweep the shrapnel of that afternoon under the carpet. Malevolence and evil had pierced them all. There was a distinction between what many perceived as denial and the act of forgiveness.

Just because she forgave didn't mean she forgot. Lucy would remember that afternoon and the way the shame engulfed her—

penetrating her—first physically, then emotionally. The damage left her vocal on the subject and much to her parents' dismay, uncharacteristically droll. She loathed those around her walking on imaginary eggshells. Lucy Bell was proud and strong. They could walk on all the eggshells they wanted; she would never crack in two.

"You all right, sweetie?" he asks, slipping his arm around her narrow shoulders, sensing where her thoughts had gone.

"Yeah," she nods, finding his eyes and holding them with hers so he can see that she means it. She was more than all right. And she knew that the move couldn't have come at a more opportune time for her dad. ClearChannel's reigning general manager of Top 40 radio station Y-100 had announced his retirement, and the executives were vying for Andy Bell to take his place. Mr. Bell abruptly accepted the position and immediately put the house on the market. The right offer came through, and Lucy's childhood was packed up in a line of boxes fleeing their gated community. The change in scenery provided a much-needed pardon from the serious events of that May afternoon. Whoever said evil didn't rear its ugly head in broad daylight?

"The house is great," she says, changing the subject. It was impressive and probably very expensive. She wanted her father to know that she appreciated the way in which he provided for them. She thought not being in a safe, fenced-in community like her old house might bother her, though, to her mind, her old security-conscious neighborhood spit out cookie-cutter homes fresh off a suburban assembly line. She was stifled by the likeness of them.

Lucy scans the backyard. She knew she was going to like Miami Beach when they pulled off the interstate and leafy green palm trees dotted the road on either side. And the water, there was so much of it! The pool had once been their only option; now they had miles of beach right outside their front door. When their caravan arrived on La Gorce Drive, the street was lined for blocks with cars, and when they stopped at their address, several of them were spilling out of their next-door neighbor's driveway and into theirs. Her dad had to walk over and ask politely for someone to move a car that was blocking the movers from pulling into their gravel driveway.

Her eyes settle on the house next door. "What's going on over there?"

At first he wavers, though the words slip out, "Somebody died."

"Somebody died?"

"Yes."

She is appalled.

Lucy walks toward the fence that separates the two homes. George follows behind her and immediately begins to bark.

"Quiet, George."

The home next door to the Bells is two story, like theirs, but Mediterranean in style. Lucy finds it fortunate that she could have Italy and the Mediterranean all on the same block. She is sure the house across the street has a distinct Art Deco flair. The diversity attracts her. Lucy peers through a crack in the wooden fence and spots a bicycle resting alongside the house, a boy's bike. She knows it at once. The windows are drawn. The inclination to peek through is fettered by black-out drapes. Lucy's wild imagination is left to wander aimlessly about her new neighbors.

"Did he live here," she calls out to her father, "the person who died?"

He is attempting to roll the garden hose back into its plastic covering, which looks about as easy as folding a fitted sheet. George is growling and braying at a spot in the bushes, nudging the wooden fence with his nose and scratching at something that isn't there.

She repeats the question. Either he doesn't want to tell her or he can't hear her above the cacophony of George's snarling.

"That sucks," she says.

tuesday, october 16, 2007

This is what I know. This is my truth: I will miss David every day of my life.

Better to stick with the truth. I keep telling myself that, keep telling myself.

I haven't written in a few days. Everything has changed. Today, I buried my brother. I kept looking around, waiting for him to walk up to the casket and tell us it was a sick-and-twisted joke. A crazy thought because I know better than anyone that he is gone.

I want to write down the truth since I find I'm caught up in lies. Truth. What exactly does that word mean? Is it what I believe? Or is that perception? And isn't perception merely what I want to see, what I want to be true, not what's actually in front of me?

I was there that night. What I saw will remain embedded in my memory, written with permanent black marker, the ones my mother forbade me to use, especially near her white walls and floors. Marked in indelible ink is the memory of David's demanding eyes, David's lifeless body. I can't seem to shake seeing him. It obstructs everything else. When I try to think about the future, life without David, the images that come to mind are no longer in color, only in black and white. Like how when you take a picture with your camera and your finger gets in the way of the lens, and you see the developed print with a blurry shape in the way of the image you meant to shoot, the details obscured. That's how the future comes to me, in fits of grainy shadows. I don't think I'll ever get past that night; I don't think I'll ever get past that smudge that's impeding me from focusing and seeing a clear picture.

This morning I listened to Rabbi Adler talk about David and all his accomplishments—everything we know and loved about him— and I couldn't help think about the things the rabbi didn't say, the things about that night that play in my mind. I can't rewind them, undo them, hit erase. Mom keeps asking me for details. Dad can't handle any more. I heard him in the bathroom with the door closed. He was crying. He was moaning in a way I'd never heard before. I've let them down in so many ways, but more than anything, I know this one truth: I've let myself down.

Rebecca was at the house today. I inhaled her when she gave me that feeble attempt at a hug, and her smell stayed with me the rest of the day. I kept sniffing my shirt like a lovesick puppy until the scent disappeared entirely, taking with it everything but the lingering look of her eyes, the unspoken question I know was on her tongue. Maybe I will call her tomorrow. Maybe I will ask her if she wants to go to a movie. We were the closest to David. It wouldn't be unusual for us to gravitate toward one another in our time of sorrow, kiss longingly, and fall in love.

David, I don't know if you can hear me. My thoughts, they're so loud I think you must. Or maybe you're reading this over my shoulder.

Why did you have to leave me here to think lecherous thoughts about your girlfriend? Is there even a name for a widowed girlfriend? A bold and brash word for someone left behind? You were always there for me, always, and look how my being there for you has destroyed everything. Who will get me through this shitty time? And don't go laughing at my use of the word "shitty" even though we've always agreed that people resort to curse words when they have limited vocabularies. I'm a wordsmith for God's sake. I study thesauruses and dictionaries like I plow through bestsellers.

Why can't I find a word that encompasses this sick, broken feeling inside? Seems there's no word for my suffering and pain. I am so sorry, David. I'm so sorry for you.

Change is all around us. The new neighbors moved in, and I am sitting outside listening to their voices. They are talking about us and the death that has crept onto their property. Their dog must have spotted me through the holes in the fence because he has positioned himself on the opposite side of where I am sitting and has begun to bark incessantly. Can you hear it, David? Can you smell his animal scent? Can you see his drooling jowls?

I've always wanted a dog, and Mom with her litany of excuses—Chloe, allergies, the shedding, unexplained odors—has diminished significantly the odds of our ever getting one. It's about as probable as Rebecca noticing me as someone other than her boyfriend's younger brother.

Did I mention fat?

Well, I meant to say her boyfriend's younger, fat brother. Not to be confused with the skinny, younger brother that doesn't exist. Since the accident, I've done nothing but gorge myself on cookies and cold cuts from Arnie and Richies. I must have gained five pounds in as many days, and the excess weight has stripped me of my last shred of dignity.

I just stole a peek at the mutt's face through a hole in the fence, and he's pretty cute in a gangly, yellowy, sloppy puppy dog kind of way. He sniffed so close I think I felt the wet of his nose on my cheek. I caught a glimpse of our new neighbor. Her face is hidden by the small opening in our adjoining fence, so what I see are her legs that go on for miles. She is moving from one length of the backyard to the next in hurried strides. My eyes zero in on a tattoo on her right ankle. It looks like Chinese. What it means, I'm not sure, though I'm copying it down so I can look it up later on the Internet. She's yelling at George the dog to quiet down and stop barking. Her voice sounds like music. She sings her words, even the insistent chastising. Then she says, "That sucks," and the words manage to float above our dividing wall and land in my lap. I cling onto them with both hands.

As she moves farther away from my spot on the grass, I am able to see more. Her back is to the fence, and I observe the long blonde hair, the way it tumbles in tune with her words, falling in a playful rhythm. Shit, it's starting to rain. The skies have opened and a sunshower is coating the block with a glistening moisture. Is that you, David? Out there crying? Something tells me it's not. You're never coming back. I keep reminding myself of that.

The girl is mindful of the drops landing in her hair and face, though she doesn't seem to care. Instead of running inside, she frolics along the grass, swaying her arms and swerving her hips. I follow her movements and try to make out the color of her eyes; I'm sure they match the lightness of her hair. Her lips curve into a wide smile, and I can almost hear a giggle escape her mouth. I know by the fluidity of her arms and the grace in her stride that that's what I want to feel inside—everything this girl is portraying on the outside. She is lit from within, and that's the person I long to be.

"Lucy," her father calls out.

Lucy.

chapter 5

Levon remembered the day he found the yellow-covered pads of paper in his mother's closet. They were stashed inside a large cardboard box with other school supplies. Lifting the front flap of the one that sat on top, Levon was drawn to the blank pages. An urge to write stirred within.

Grabbing a pen from the drawer and racing off with the pad tucked under his arm, Levon entered into his sunlight-colored room. And without any intention of starting a ritual that would last the course of weeks, months, and years, he began to write. At first, what he wrote was mundane: the weather outside (always grueling), a grade for each day at its finale (usually B's and C's), what he ate (various things that his mother need not know about). After a few entries, he noticed a pattern: the days lengthened into an accumulation of nothingness.

The transcribing of data progressed to all kinds of superfluous lists: far-fetched fantasies, people he strives to be like, people he does not, recent crushes, and so forth. There was a compulsion that led him to the pages of the pad each night that made any pen or pencil a missile for criticism and complaint. It was a habit that once begun, he couldn't stop. The thought of ending this memorializing of useless data scared Levon, even had him believing that the failure to record insignificant details would mean he would no longer exist.

Over the years, the illogical inventory ripened into sensible sentences and private paragraphs. Levon trusted the white paper with its cerulean lines for thoughts he never dared speak aloud. With the exposed pages, there was always the chance that someone would stumble on his secret stash of revelation and confession; nevertheless, he wouldn't deviate from the standard-lined pads he took from his mother's drawer. Levon had amassed stacks of journals that traced the beginning roots of his expansive writing ability. The journal had matured from a basic keeper of monotonous facts to a complex, richly woven story that deftly described Levon's young, impressionable life. It was there, at thirteen, that he wrote his first poem:

To lie awake in the cold swelling night,
I hear the darkness, smell its impervious scent
And then I realize
It is morning
And the only chill is of my heart.

There were other poems over the years, scattered thoughts and secret streams of consciousness. Their watery rivers of association drift from page to page. These private writings gleaned from Levon's sadness, their themes irrefutably the same. It was therapeutic for Levon to share his fears and thoughts and truths with a confidante who didn't criticize or pass judgment, and so the *Annals of Awareness*, as Levon had so aptly named them, became the source for private, untouched feelings.

David found it thoroughly amusing that his brother kept a journal. When Levon's parents finally put a lock on his desk drawer, it was in response to David having stumbled on one of his earlier editions. Like a trained editor for his novice writer, he redlined his edits with commentary: *"Levon, your diary is pretty damn interesting. Ask Jack if Casey Schwartz is a good kisser."* This in response to Levon's depiction of the night he witnessed the prettiest and most popular girl in the sixth grade kiss Jack Kaplan during a game of truth or dare. Levon had a huge crush on Casey that year—evidenced by her name listed successively at the top of each page of his journal entries for weeks. Levon's portrayal of their first kiss was youthful and desirous all at the same time.

David's commentary bounced off Levon. Even in the breach of confidence, Levon giggled at his big brother's sense of humor. After that, Levon used the desk drawer with its own special key to safeguard his secrets. The remaining pads, having evolved into college-lined notebooks with five hundred pages of scribing, were locked in their storage unit in Hollywood. They marked the years of profound passages—both written and of time—of a gifted writer hidden from sight.

"Whatcha doin'?" comes the voice from the hallway. As an afterthought, she knocks lightly.

Levon is lying across his bed, sprawled on his stomach with his feet swaying in the air. He looks up to find Rebecca standing in his doorway. Closing the journal, he abruptly rises, tucking his polo into his jeans.

"Nothing," shoots out of his mouth.

It is the last day of shiva, the seventh day since they buried David. He thought everyone had left; the house is frighteningly quiet. The two stand there silently in their shared sorrow.

"That goes on your right," she says, pointing to the black ribbon that has been cut by the rabbi and Levon has pinned to his shirt. "The tear should be on the left for a parent—over the heart so you can see it—and on the right for siblings, children, and spouses." She pauses before adding, "…And it doesn't need to be visible, if you don't want it to be."

"How do you know so much about this stuff?" he asks.

Her hair is pulled back today, showing off a pallid, sullen face. A wisp of brown escapes its roots and she is twirling it around her finger. "I don't know." There is reluctance in her voice, which slows her words and makes sentences stilted. "I'm trying to make sense of it all," she adds.

Levon is on a similar journey. Imagining Rebecca Blake sitting at a computer googling their traditions and customs so that she can properly mourn and honor the boy she loved, moves him. Their searches might have surely crossed paths on the information super-highway with Levon busily looking up Chinese symbols of the girl who lives next door.

Throughout the last week of shiva, he had seen her a number of times walking her clumsy dog down their street. Something about the tattoo simultaneously pacified and baffled him. He had already drawn the following tacit conclusions: Her parents must be super cool (how else could she get away with a tattoo?); she is somewhere near his age; she has the propensity to talk to herself in an animated, cheerful way; she favors wearing white. This preference in color he found particularly intriguing. Having studied her comings and goings in the early morning and again when she returns from school and before bed, it is evident that white is the hue of choice for her entire wardrobe.

"Levon, I'm talking to you."

"Sorry," he mumbles, unaccustomed to anything distracting him from staring at Rebecca's face. It is Monday, and she is talking about how technically the last day of shiva should be Tuesday, not today, because Saturday, the Sabbath, is not included in our count.

"I don't think the rules really matter when you bury someone so young," he tells her.

His honesty takes hold of them; he senses the air, the floor, everything around them moving.

"I can't believe we're talking about David. I can't believe he's really gone," she answers, her voice waning.

Levon had flung dirt on his wooden casket. He saw them lower him into the ground. David was gone. His eyes start to well up.

"I keep wanting to pick up the phone and call him. I forget

sometimes. How could I forget?" she asks.

"I called his voicemail this morning just to hear his voice."

"Did he seem strange to you that night?" she asks.

Levon can't possibly know where she is going with this. He doesn't want to delude himself into thinking she is in his bedroom because she might actually need his comfort and support, yet there's an implication in the tone of her voice that makes him think she might.

"He was off, not really himself," she says, searching the floor beside his bed.

His heart starts to move from a safe, steady rhythm as the worry rolls off his tongue. "How do you mean?"

Forming her thoughts and words wasn't coming easy, and the extended silence that followed was still worse. Rebecca Blake, captain of the cheerleaders, most popular girl in their high school, had gone mute. Levon was rapt. Should he sit down next her? Did she want him to pat her lovingly on the back?

"Rebecca, what are you trying to say?"

The quiet is palpable. Her lips clamp shut. She is standing there, knees kicking into the side of his bed, *thump thump*, a wordless hush—she is faceless, too, as she stares at her sneakers, and then an explosion of tears. First, the thick moisture descends down her cheeks followed by a torrent of sounds— part-animal, part-human. Her body sinks onto his bed, limbs and flesh falling solemnly against his pillows and sheets. Levon stands over her, speechless, while a current of electricity triggers stealthlike messages through his hands and fingers: reach in for a touch, get close, pull back. Her cries are deep, soaked in a numbing pain. Levon thinks he might break down also, but then his thoughts return to his brother and how David would have wanted him to rise to the occasion—be brave—and so he bites his lip and keeps the violent storm from rising to the surface.

When she softens, becoming quiet and spent, her body ceases to quiver and shake, and she settles herself at the foot of his bed and says, "I think he was cheating on me."

Levon's exhale releases into the air. "That's ridiculous." Because it was. David worshiped Becks, as he had taken to calling her. They were soulmates, not only connected by their shared elevated position within the social caste system but also connected by time—they had been together since they were thirteen. For the last four years, there was no David without Rebecca. Conversely, there was no Rebecca without David, and that was made abundantly clear by the ghostly remnants of what used to be Rebecca and the despondency that had wrecked her.

"David would never cheat on you. It's not in his personality."

Rebecca shrugs and lets the pain fall around her.

Levon shakes his head in disbelief. He knows how important it is for him to be convincing. David made mistakes, but cheating was not one of them. He was moral and good and kind to animals and small children. David would never betray Rebecca, not like this.

"Becks," he hears himself say, borrowing the endearing nickname and calmly reaching for her open hand. Words, though, were nowhere to be found. Could his words have gotten singed by the heat of her hand pressing against his?

"Gross!" chimes Chloe as she steps into Levon's room and finds him and Rebecca holding hands. "You two are gross and disgusting."

Levon jumps from surprise and the allegation lingering in Chloe's reprimand.

"Don't be ridiculous, you twerp," Levon laughs.

"And don't go trying to kiss her either," she giggles. "Yuck, gross, and double yuck."

Levon grabs her gently at the nape of her neck and pulls her close to him. He is ruffled by her instinct and wonders if she, too, has been snooping through his journal. "Hey, kiddo," he smiles at her. "You doing okay?" he asks.

Chloe reminds him so much of Punky Brewster. Not only the short brown hair and freckled face, it's her wholesome smile and impish eyes. She is a fireball and a clown and Levon's hero all rolled up into one genetically imperfect but spectacular body.

Chloe knows the seriousness of her disease. This wise, precocious child spends hours every day composing lists of what she wants to accomplish—and she always does. Clearly, the whole family is bordering on obsessive-compulsive disorder. Yet, Chloe remains a champion. She never complains about the needles and the injections, and she never cringes when she's told she will be hospitalized and will miss big chunks of school. Rather than exhibit impatience and annoyance by her mother's cloying reassurances and pervasive doting, Chloe handles her mother with ease. Levon would have punched her by now.

Chloe knows what death means. And because of her fragile condition, it doesn't confuse her to learn that her loving older brother has been taken away. Having learned of a fellow GSD patient—the one she befriended at the lavish fundraiser in Boston last year—pass away from complications, the contradiction of children dying wasn't foreign to her. Not experiencing apathy or denial, Chloe has spent the last week traversing between Levon's bed and her parents', where the physical closeness made David's absence less imposing.

Chloe is giggling. Once she starts, she usually can't stop. Levon knows all her secret tickle spots and wiggles and jiggles her until she is vibrating with laughter. These belly laughs are potentially dangerous since Chloe's feeding tube is located in her stomach. "Don't make me laugh so hard, Levvy," she says, jumbled words that come out in bursts of snorts and gurgles. His fingers are tickling the back of her neck and under her arms and behind her knobby knees where the pale patch that never sees the sun is the most sensitive to his touches. Levon begins to laugh, and Rebecca does too. This is a good sign because Levon was convinced that he had forgotten how.

"Stop it, Levon!" she shrieks. "I'm going to pee in my pants…"

This is no joke. She has been known to do that. She's done it before. Levon lets her go, and the three of them are staring at each other with great anticipation.

"I'm going to go," Rebecca says, breaking the silence and standing up.

"You don't have to," says Levon.

"Yes, I do," she says.

They were all there, except for David. Levon wanted her to stay.

"Bye, Chloe," she says with a smile, leaning down to kiss her on a speckled patch of cheek, patting her head with fingers that had minutes before sent risky signals throughout Levon's entire body.

"Bye, Levon," she says with a shrug, unable to meet his eyes.

Levon doesn't answer. He has said goodbye to too many things he loves this week: reading the sports section aloud to David at the breakfast table; watching *Friday the 13th* marathons late into the night; playing boxball in the street. He's incapable of forming the words that will mark her leaving. And without those words, the finality of their dismal reality will transform into a sleep-induced nightmare where Levon will be roused to find David smiling up at him, having listened to their voices through the air vents.

"*Good going, bro,*" he'd say, taking him by the shoulders and lightly shaking him. "*Way to defend your brother's honor.*"

Levon would swell with pride.

"Mommy says I have to go to school tomorrow," says Chloe in a tone that is neither pleased nor objecting. Levon leads his baby sister toward his bed and positions her by his side. The opaque skin on her arms hides the mess that is complicating her insides. GSDIa, Chloe's form of GSD, is most prevalent among individuals of Ashkenazi Jewish descent. There is a test that parents can take to determine if they are carriers. Oddly, the genetic panel given to the Kellers did not include GSD. All the markers were in place (both Madeline and Craig were carriers) for the disease to take root in any one of their unborn children. That it infected one of them was the luck of the draw, and both Madeline and Craig had conflicting emotions about the way it played out. On one hand, Madeline was pleased that she was ignorant to their being carriers, as it may have barred them from having children at all. On the other hand, the absence of Chloe in their lives was unthinkable.

"It's probably good for you to go," Levon finally answers his sister, although he is wondering how his mother expects her to be ready to re-enter normal life.

"Are *you* going?" she asks.

He didn't know. His mother hadn't rendered her decision. He spent most of the afternoon avoiding her and making small talk with their friends and extended family, and he was sure she wouldn't mind his absence during the day. Besides, he would do just about anything to escape this hellish purgatory.

"Maybe I will," he answers, throwing his arm around his sister's narrow shoulder and hugging her.

The dog next door begins to bark, and his raucous sounds prompt Chloe from the space beside him toward the open window. Over the last week of being homebound for shiva, Levon had become a little obsessed with watching the dog and his new neighbor, the beautiful girl with the tattoo. He was now able to set his watch to the girl's dog walking schedule—6:30 a.m., 3:00 p.m., and 8:30 p.m.

"What is *that*?" Chloe inquires, wide-eyed and peering into the night sky. She is so at ease in Levon's space it's as if she knew it was meant to be hers.

"That's George."

"*George?*" she annunciates, "Who's George?"

"Our new neighbor's dog."

"We have new neighbors and they have a dog?"

Should he go on to explain in detail how cute the animal is and how infatuated she will become with him? Should he tell her he is creamy gold with big, droopy eyes and a frenzied tail that could swat butterflies and bees right out of the sky? Chloe wanted to be a veterinarian, for God's sake! A dog living next door was going to tantalize *and* torture her.

"How do you know his name is George? And George can be a girl, you know, short for Georgie."

"This one's a boy, Chloe, trust me."

"Will you take me there tomorrow, Levon? Please, please, you have to take me!"

Her eyes are beseeching—insistent and full of longing. How could he say no?

The lights are out, and Chloe is asleep in her room. Levon is feigning sleep when his mother opens the door and pokes her head inside. Whether she decides to send him to school or not is of no importance. He has already made the decision to go. Besides, what good would he be to them at home, sulking around and getting in the way? Since shiva, his mother survived on delirium and histrionics before taking refuge in her darkened bedroom where she lay lethargic beneath a forest of olive sheets. Levon saw the prescriptions on the counter in their kitchen for the drugs that would sedate her and restrain her from throwing herself in front of a moving bus. He wasn't sure how they mix with the bottles of wine she was consuming. His mother was unrecognizable—inconsolable—and school was a welcome distraction.

"Levon," she whispers to deaf ears, "are you sleeping?"

Questions like this always give him a good chuckle.

He would have laughed in the past and replied, "Yes, Mom, I'm sleeping," but their life no longer allowed for witty humor.

"Levon."

He ignores her again and senses her coming close. It is dark in the room. Levon smells something so unfamiliar to him he has to hold in a gasp. It is her, and she is nothing like the woman he breathed in before. If not for the stale odor, he would never know she is sitting there on his bed, her weight so unobtrusive that it does not make a dent.

Levon thinks about his grandparents, his mother's parents—Sid and Lyd to their friends. They had moved to New York three years ago to escape the heat. When they received the disastrous phone call, they were on the first flight back and holed up in the downstairs guest bedroom. Grandpa Sidney, a robust, handsome man with crooked teeth encouraged Madeline to eat, declared that she's "too skinny," while skeletal Lydia and her "proper nose" turned a blind eye to her daughter's rapidly diminishing frame. Levon overheard them when he carried their luggage from the car. Grandma Lydia said, "This is just terrible, Sid, terrible." Then she added, "But Maddy looks good without those extra pounds."

Levon seethes inside.

His mother says his name again.

He thought she would have given up by now.

Then she does something unexpected. When his mother lays down on the bed beside him, curls her arms around his body, and hugs him, the touch of her body leaves Levon in a swell of tears and confusion. He forgets the stench and concentrates on the feel of her arms around him. It's better than any Shalimar hug he's ever had. He closes his eyes and prays he isn't dreaming.

chapter 6

High school students are bursting with insecurities left over from junior high, and Levon had a menagerie that he carried around with him through the ninth grade and the beginning of tenth. Some kids worried about being liked, some worried about their bodies, some worried about the secrets they kept from their parents, while others worried about grades, fitting in, saying no, and the opposite sex. Levon, in his ability to be fair and indiscriminate, worried about all of the above.

David's death sparked a whole new set of uncertainties that his presence had once prevented. Without David, who was he? When kids directed their blaming fingers his way, who would defend him if not his gallant brother?

Levon mulled over these questions while he brushed his teeth and got himself ready for school. His mother and Chloe were in the other room quarreling over her feeding tube, which Chloe felt entitled to be irritated about. She said it didn't fit into her clothes, and it was especially annoying when she and her friends went swimming. Their bodies were changing and maturing. The girls of ten noticed and talked about things like a plastic tube that protruded from one's belly button.

Levon half expects to run into David in the hallway that connects their rooms when he steps out of the bathroom. Always, in the mornings, they would meet by chance—or on purpose—at the top of the stairs, and race down the steps for breakfast. Instead, Levon is greeted by his mother's voice wafting through the empty corridor repeating to Chloe the reasons why her feeding tube is essential to her health. Chloe doesn't relent until her mother promises to talk to Dr. Gerald about any new developments in gene therapy that might make arguments over the feeding tube moot. Taking the steps two at a time, Levon greets his father at the breakfast table.

The kitchen is Levon's favorite room in the house and not because it's where he receives his daily ration of food. The Kellers had recently completed an extensive renovation, and Levon found the newly designed area his favorite place in the house. This was where they ate all their meals; holidays and special occasions were reserved for the formal dining room. The most noticeable difference is the absence of the wall that had once separated the room in two and has been knocked down, leaving an airy space for the family to gather.

Madeline had fought Odalys, the designer, and unassuming Odalys won. They were proud of Odalys. Besides, her eye for architecture and design was spot on, and the room that Levon has grown to love is tied intricately to his fondness for its creator. During the six-month reformation, she practically lived with them, and her warm disposition always followed her around the house. It was her idea to fill the room with state of the art appliances, throwing in an antique, leaf-laden chandelier. And by bordering the space with floor to ceiling windows, she knew she was forever changing the landscape, pulling nature through the glass and allowing sunlight to kiss them each morning.

The focal point of the room was the butcher-block-topped island, adorned with mahogany wood drawers. Three wooden stools stood adjacent to the island. No one dared sit in the lone seat reserved for David, choosing instead to have a seat at the custom-made banquette, which spanned the wall and held seating for ten.

Levon loves the bright view of their backyard from this vantage point, though today the blinds are drawn. The Ralph Lauren tapestry green cabinets are darker than usual. When Odalys and his mother chose them, they were intended to catch the light that came in through the windows.

"How are you doing?" his father asks without looking up from the paper.

The table is too large, he thinks. Maybe Odalys was wrong. They would never sit there comfortably again.

"Okay," he lies.

Levon glimpses the headlines—"Garbage Truck Slams into Hialeah House Killing Family of Four" and "Violent Death of UM Student a Mystery"—as he takes a bite of an apple from the bowl of fruit on the table. Newspaper headlines, in general, used to appall him, and the *Miami Herald*, with its prolific accounts of the dicey, deplorable truths invading its city doors, is full of frightening captions. Nothing Levon would ever read in the paper would upend him again. Once a tragedy has pierced you, you're numb to someone else's pain.

The silence this morning is louder than usual, and Levon studies his father's fingers on the crisp paper, the stubs of his nails, and the gold band on the third finger of his left hand.

"Did Grandpa Sid sneeze this morning?" Levon asks. It's a private joke they hadn't shared in over a week, and he hopes it will break the quiet.

At precisely 6:15 a.m. every morning, while Craig Keller sips his morning java and reads the paper, he has a succession of sneezes—three to be exact—and Levon blesses him, and they giggle at their theory that newspaper ink infiltrates noses and induces sneezing. They have cited at least seven other people who have been prompted to do the same.

"I haven't seen him today," he says, dropping the paper and clasping his hands together. He waits for Levon to say something, and this only amplifies Levon's edginess.

Craig Keller has always been a handsome, youthful man with a strong face and clear, gray eyes. Even though his thick ebony hair has patches of silver woven throughout, his smile and charm shave years off his age. One of the things that really gets his mother's goat is when people assume they are the same age. Ten years divide them. A week after David's death it shows. Today, Levon's father is a ghost of what he was last week. Deep, dark hollowed-out holes have taken the place of his vibrant eyes, and the golden hue of his cheeks and forehead is faded. Accompanying him at the overgrown table and going through the motions of normalcy has got to be the most excruciating task Levon's father has ever undertaken.

"Are you going to work today?" Levon asks.

His father shakes his head no and throws him a sidelong glance.

This is my fault, he tells himself. *This is not my fault* he counters. The inner debate persists. Even if David independently crashed the car while Levon slept innocently in his bed, there would be no making sense of the aftermath. Having someone to blame was much easier than allowing the crushing truth to sink in—he was never coming back.

"I'm sorry, Dad," Levon whispers and before the words escape his lips, he knows they are insufficient.

A tear drips down his father's left cheek. He doesn't wipe it off. It continues until it lands on the newspaper in a splotch of black ink.

"I know you are, son," he says.

Levon wants to remind him, *"I'm here. I'm alive."* but he decides it's best he not draw any more attention to himself.

His father rests on his elbows and hides his face behind lean fingers.

Levon says, "I miss him. Everyone's so angry. If I could change anything about that night, you know I would."

"Levon…" Craig slowly lifts his head.

"When is she going to stop punishing me? When are you all going to stop punishing me?"

"Levon," he says it again, "it's been a week. Give her some

time. Give me some time. This isn't easy for any of us."

"And what about me?" he asks, his voice rising with each unanswered question. "What about me who's going to school today, and everyone will be looking at me like I'm some kind of murderer?"

He flinches at this. The word, which had lain dormant, made the atmosphere around them boil.

"We told you, you don't have to go if you're not ready."

"I have to go," he says. "I have to get out of here."

"It's not going to be easy."

"Maybe," he agrees, "but I can't sit in this house one more day with the two of you loathing me."

This is the point in their exchange when Levon's father slowly comes undone. The timing is apropos because Chloe and his mother are stepping into the room.

"You should have thought of that," he scolds Levon in a controlled, quiet voice that breaks under the pressure of emotion. As the accusation floats around them, so, too, does his anger. "You should have thought of that before you took the wheel of a car without a driver's license and risked your brother's life as well as the lives of other people on the road. Hell, you're lucky you didn't kill yourself. How would it have made you feel leaving your mother and me to bury two sons?"

"It was a mistake," Levon shouts, "a mistake I'll live with the rest of my life." He stops to catch his breath. "Don't you think I know that? Don't you think never seeing David again is punishment enough?"

Madeline is bawling into the palms of her hands, and Chloe has shrunk into the corner of the room.

"You should have never left this house…you should have never left your sister!" his father hollers at him, the disdain coloring his words. "What were you thinking? What the hell were you thinking?"

"You did bury two sons," Levon interrupts, his voice hoarse and shrill, caught between a cry and a shriek. "I'm here, but you treat me like I'm not. I may as well have died in the accident. I was trying to help David that night. He needed me, and I was trying to help. I would never hurt David…"

"Help him?" his mother wails. "Help him?"

"Mommy," Chloe screams, "Daddy, please stop. Please stop yelling at Levon." Her hands are covering her ears, and she has closed her eyes to shut out the sounds of their shouting.

His mom is in a state that borders on complete loss of control. She is shriveled up in a ball on their porcelain floor. Chloe is begging for her to stop. Craig is staring at Levon, as if to say, *See what you've done. See what you've done to us.*

She is calling out his name, screaming *David* as if her pleading will bring him back, make him appear. The long week of suffering has come to a close, and what she has held back in the company of family and friends is exploding on the brand new marble tiles. *I want my baby back, I want my baby. Please God, bring him back to me, please bring him home.* She is punching the floor and shaking and writhing. Her hair is scattered in clumps, hiding the tears that are staining her face.

"Mommy, stop it," Chloe cries, before running to Levon and throwing her arms around him. "Daddy, make her stop."

Paralyzed. That's how they all react to Madeline's wild outburst. Levon eyes his father, trusting that he will take the first required step in calming her down, but he sits there, trancelike, not uttering a word.

Last night must have been a dream.

"Mom, you're scaring Chloe."

This appears to knock some sense into her, or it is the sound of their doorbell cascading through the room and disbanding her torment. Her screams soften into whispers, and she slowly begins to wind down. The doorbell rings again and no one moves, afraid that anything might send her back into a state of abandon. After the fifth ring, Levon walks away from his second meeting with disaster in less than two weeks and approaches the double doors leading into their home. Peering through the peephole, he finds two familiar eyes staring back at him. He opens the door and greets his grandmother who is dressed in a head to toe neon pink jogging outfit. His grandfather is not far behind.

"What the heck took you so long, Lev?"

She is breathless from her morning jog and whips past Levon in a cloud of baby powder, hairspray, and some other pungent odor. Grandpa Sid is panting, holding onto the doorframe before slinking off to his bedroom.

"God damn dogs." She is pulling off her white sneakers with one angry tug.

"What's wrong, Gram?" Levon asks, although he already knows by the strong scent.

"Dog crap, that's what's wrong. All over the front yard."

Levon stifles a laugh.

"What happened to people cleaning up after their animals? What's this world coming to?"

Grandma Lyd is a feisty, old devil. He remembers her most memorable line when she called during Rosh Hashanah. Levon answered the phone in a blistery tone, and she said, "What's a matta, someone blow the shofa' in your ear too loud?"

Levon silently thanks her for the intrusion. She is heading for the kitchen, a sneaker in each hand, and Levon follows closely behind. He knows what she will find when she steps into their new kitchen—his mother on the floor in a ball, Chloe crying in a corner, his dad with his head propped on the table.

"What's going on?" she asks Levon.

"You've just stepped from one pile of shit into another."

chapter 7

As expected, returning to school is an ordeal. Levon's attendance is met with scorn and speculation. Although his teachers, classmates, and various friends of David's make admirable attempts to hide their chatter, there is no mistaking it fills the hallways.

Rebecca is conspicuously absent—her helm outside the gym doors vacant—and it occurs to Levon, in the shadow of the sweeping space, that abandoning his family to return to the social populace may be premature. He walks through the tan hallways in a catatonic daze with his head folded down low and treads his sneakers along the white tiled floors.

Clusters of students traipse by him, some knocking into him, others clearing a space for him to pass, and though their mouths are moving in audible tempo, Levon can not make out any discernible words. If they are averting their eyes or if they are whispering into the palms of their hands, he is unaware. He is focused on the sterile floor in front of him. With his folders and textbooks held close to the buttons on his shirt, his academic armor buffers him from stares and glares.

Levon moves from period to period in slow moving, languorous motion. By the time the bell signifies the end of the day, he has a thundering headache and can barely swallow. It takes all of his strength to push through the metal door leading outside where he is greeted by a plume of warm, fresh air and the realization that David is not there to drive him home. That David will never be there to drive him home again is the scary truth that marks the unsettling journey on a smelly, city bus.

He had googled the bus route from school to his neighborhood and knows that the journey is twenty minutes. Travel had always meant family trips or exotic locations seen on the Travel Channel, not the seven-minute walk, four-tenths of a mile to be exact, from Prairie Avenue to Dade, Meridian, the Miami Beach Convention Center, and the #117 bus.

The air is moist as the bus deposits him on the southeastern corner of Sixtieth Street and Pine Tree Drive. Levon loves Pine Tree Drive, the street that runs parallel to his own, La Gorce. The palatial homes on the water have grand entrances with sweeping driveways and countless bedrooms. His house is only a block and a half away, two-tenths of a mile according to MapQuest, and what awaits him there sends him walking in the opposite direction. He is not ready to return. His legs pounce on the unfamiliar footpath, each step a punishment, a vigorous attempt to squash something that Levon wants to dispose of. His shoulders hunch forward, and his eyes train on the ground below.

"Look up," a voice calls out from over his shoulder. "If not you can't see what's getting you down."

It is her voice.

"Hey, wait up," she says from behind, following him in the wrong direction. "Aren't you gonna turn around? I'd call you by your name, but I don't know it. We were never properly introduced. I'm 5955, your neighbor."

Lucy. He knows her name is Lucy. He hadn't seen her on the bus.

She has caught up to Levon and is keeping in step with him.

"You are 5945, aren't you?"

Levon will remember this moment for a long time because it is when he first realizes how his new neighbor can be physically present in many places at once. They are strolling side by side down an endless block of cement. Lucy is on Levon's right—he is sure of it because every few steps her left elbow brushes into his—though he'd swear he can feel her circling around him, swirling around his neck, his legs, and nipping on his ears. Maybe it is the way she walks with her arms flailing at all degrees and how her legs don't step, they waltz. She bounces, he decides, and her vibrations leap around him, ricocheting off trees and the sidewalk and into the sky. There was something wraithlike about her, and if he touches her, she might disappear.

"Do you have a name 5945, or do I have to refer to you in code?"

Levon focuses on the ground in front of him. Without looking up, he acknowledges his new neighbor with, "Your dog crapped on our lawn."

She tosses her long blonde hair to the side and laughs.

"Your Dog Crapped on Our Lawn. That's your name? Do you have a last name?"

"Yes, *Today*," he answers. "Your Dog Crapped on Our Lawn Today."

Levon thinks his attempt at humor is moderately funny.

"I'll have a talk with George. That's his name, by the way. I'll make sure he steers clear of your lawn."

"There are rules you have to follow in our neighborhood. People pick up their dog's poop here."

"I'm sorry," she says, "usually I'm pretty good at cleaning up after him."

"My grandmother's shoe and George now know each other intimately."

"Yuck," she says, apologetically. "Unless you want to talk about dog poop all the way home, I'm Lucy," she says, brandishing her hand out for him to shake.

Levon studies the friendly palm that sends a signal to his legs to halt their concentrated march. The day had been so tense. He is having a hard time thawing out. He doesn't want to be rude to a new neighbor.

"I'm Levon." He hands her his chubby fingers and finds her eyes beneath tortoise-shell rectangular glasses. On her, they are impossibly cool, and the gray of her eyes, or green, he's not sure, is a maddening combination of mischief and mystery.

"Levon?" she asks.

"Yes, Levon."

"I think I liked Mr. Your Dog Crapped on Our Lawn better."

Levon doesn't know what to make of this. Whatever cynicism was there earlier has suddenly been zapped away.

"Were you named after the Elton John song?" she asks.

Levon considers his parents' hasty decision to name their least favorite child after a great uncle six times over.

"And he shall be a good man," she begins to sing.

"Who?" he asks.

"Levon," she answers. "That's the song. Are you a good man, Levon?"

He takes a breath and feels his legs go weak. "I'm all right, I guess." It is an effort to take the next few steps, and he knows he will have to tell her soon that they are going the wrong way. The sun is beating down on their backs, and he feels a line of sweat dripping down his shirt. Here is someone who knows nothing of the damage he's caused. Here is a person he can be someone else with. Except next she asks about the bandage across his face.

"Ice hockey accident."

"Tough sport," she says. "I bet it hurt like mad."

"You have no idea."

What did she care anyway? She was gorgeous and blonde and light and dreamy and no one like her had ever paid any attention to him unless they wanted to get access to David. She had to be blind, he thought. She *is* wearing glasses. He is unsure of what to say next. He's never had idle chatter with such a luminous creature.

"Okay, seeing how I have to pull information out of you, and you're reluctant to ask about me, we're going to play a little game. I'll give you the answers, and you tell me the questions."

Levon shifts his backpack from one shoulder to the other. Lucy circles around him, stepping up her pace until she is directly in front of him walking backwards. Their eyes are level with one another, and with each backward step, she hurdles an answer into the air.

"Fifteen."

"That's easy," he says. "Your age."

"Atlanta."

"Presumably where you used to live."

"Two points," she smiles.

"White."

This is high school and uniforms are a thing of the past, so perhaps Lucy has her own dress code that dictates her flair for all things white. White linen pants and a white cotton T-shirt. The only hint of color is a pair of beaded necklaces in turquoise and gold that fall down the front of her top and clatter when she sways.

"Your favorite color."

"Is that your final response?"

Levon doesn't answer. He should reply with something clever and sarcastic, but the sentences and words are jumbled by the thrill that has tickled his nerves. To refrain from any further embarrassment and to ensure that their exchange continues—because he enjoys being near her—he explains that they need to turn around because they are walking in the wrong direction.

"You don't think I know that," she says, turning around and continuing her backwards walk. "You were the one who looked lost."

He doesn't know how she manages to know everything, walk backwards, and not fall on her butt.

"Okay," she says, "let's move on to level two. This is where it gets infinitely harder. And thank you, by the way, for making this two-minute walk a marathon. Ready?

"Ricky."

"Your boyfriend?"

"Nope."

"Your sister?"

"Close," she tells him.

"Your brother."

"I gave that one to you," she teases.

"One-hundred and twenty-two."

"How many boys have tried to kiss you?"

"Eh," she buzzes, "try again."

"I give up."

"All the Facebook friend requests I've ignored."

"Wow, you're not nice."

"Thirty-one."

"Flavors at Baskin-Robbins?"

This gets a laugh. "No. Are there really thirty-one?" she asks.

He would never tell her he actually tried them all on a dare from Bruce two summers ago. "No clue," he says.

"The number of times I've read *The Alchemist*." Then, she says, "Watch it, Levon, don't step on that cute little caterpillar," at which she bends down and picks it up gingerly before returning it safely to a patch of grass.

"Gabriel Byrne and Andy Garcia," she begins again, resuming her position in front of him.

"Your favorite actors."

"Those old men? Hell no, they're my mom's. Mine are—"

"Let me guess," he teases. "Vanessa Hudgens and Zac Efron."

"You obviously have me mistaken for one of the local cheerleaders. Didn't you see Don Cheadle in *Hotel Rwanda*? Unbelievable performance."

"And the other one?"

"That's easy, DiCaprio, of course. Ready for your next challenge?"

"The suspense is killing me."

"Football, basketball, baseball," she says.

"Words that end in 'ball'?"

"Wrong, try again."

"Your favorite sports?"

She rolls her eyes. "No, dummy, sports with grossly overpaid athletes. Golf is my sport of choice."

She is smiling at him, a full-toothed, genuine grin. "You like this game," she teases. "You could've just asked me questions yourself. That's what neighbors do. Here's one of my favorites. 'They're afraid of something, they love something, they've lost something, and they're dreaming of something.'"

Levon says, "It sounds like a riddle. What does it have to do with you?"

"It has to do with all of us," she quips. "You should know this, Levon. Think about it."

He thinks about it and draws a blank.

"Think about you, think about me, think about strangers meeting."

When she says this, she points at him with her fingers, and then back at herself. It is a signal of alliance. "You lost me," he says.

She takes a break from walking backward, which is a wise move, because they are about to cross the street.

"If you want me to tell you, I will," she taunts him, "but I think it's something you should think about."

Levon believes it would bring her great pleasure and satisfaction to blurt it out. "I think too much already," he says. "Just tell me." But she's off, galloping across the street, leaving Levon in her wake.

"Catch me, first," she yells, taking off along the tree-lined streets and expecting him to follow suit. Levon admires how she maneuvers across people's front lawns with her bag tucked in the fold of her arm. She cuts back and forth under trees and over flower bushes, darting left and right. She is approximately two blocks ahead of him before she turns and realizes that he hasn't even begun a fast walk. He is meandering down their street watching her fly through the air like a butterfly let out of a cage and though he wants to run—wants to be near her again—his stiff legs hold him back.

"Run, Levon, run," she shouts, this time perched outside his house with her bottom against the hood of his mother's dark Mercedes.

Levon takes his time getting to the house. She patiently waits for him to arrive. He is flustered, less from the heat than by her being there.

"I so hope that's not the fastest you can run," she deadpans.

Levon is panting. He is out of breath when he asks her, "Are you going to tell me the answer to your little riddle?"

"No," she says, sliding off the car and heading toward her house. "Master George awaits," she calls out over her shoulder.

When she is halfway up her driveway, she stops abruptly and turns around. Levon watches her glide through the air, planting her feet directly in front of him. He's not sure what to expect; anything can come flying out of this girl's mouth. Then she asks, "Who died?"

The question is as daring as the person asking it.

"You don't have to tell me if you don't want…but I would tell me if I were you."

"Don't be so sure about that."

"Was it someone you were close to?"

A line of loud, sporty cars coming from the direction of their high school roar down the street and break the wordless silence. The radio blares Ne-Yo complaining how he's sick of love songs, and the assertion along with the hum of their engines drown out the tidal wave that is building in Levon's mouth. When they finally pass, the silence strangely resumes.

It's the despair in Levon's eyes that prompts Lucy to change her mind. "You're right," she says, "it's probably none of my business." He watches her turn again and head up the driveway. Her steps are not hurried; her arms are flat by her sides. Levon wants her to stay. When she is almost out of earshot and takes the first step up the stone stairs leading to double doors, Levon shouts, "My brother."

Lucy's fingers are on the handle; they remain still.

"Did you hear me? I said *my brother*."

Lucy's lithe movements are replaced with rigid ones. She and Levon are joined in their awful clumsiness. For Lucy, letting go of the brass handle is a laborious task. Her body has been seized by revulsion. Levon wonders what she is thinking while she stares at her front door. She finally releases the knob and begins the journey once more across the grass that borders the two homes. The sun's glare on her glasses hides her eyes, though Levon can see something slipping down her face from beneath the frames.

"I'm really sorry." She straightens herself and is close enough for him to touch. "I don't know what to say."

Levon tells her many things without opening his mouth. She apologizes for asking. She says if she had known it was his brother, she would have never been so insensitive. She was only trying to be friendly.

"It's okay. You didn't know."

"I always put my foot in my mouth."

"There are worse things," he says.

They stand like that, awkward and broken, until Lucy asks if he wants to walk George with her.

"I can't today," he replies, "but Chloe, my sister, wouldn't mind an introduction. She loves animals."

"I'm really sorry, Levon," she says again, and he nods his head. He can tell that she means it. "They're the four things you need to know about someone when you first meet."

Levon doesn't understand. "Is this another of your riddles?"

"It's the answer to the first," she explains. "When you meet someone, remember they're afraid of something, they love something, they've lost something, and they're dreaming of something. I had no idea your loss was so huge."

Levon says, "Yeah, it's a big one."

"I'm sorry," she says.

"It's an interesting insight."

"I ripped it right out of my *Life's Little Instruction Calendar.* Have you ever read it? The guy's a genius."

"It's good, even for a plagiarist."

"There are tons of books on life instructions. I have thousands of stolen ideas on how we can live fuller lives. I've even come up with some of my own. You'll just have to wait until tomorrow."

Levon laughs, thinking she can't possibly be serious.

"Thousands," he repeats, "can't wait."

"So I'll see you tomorrow?" she says.

Long after his mother's tempered interrogation about school, and even after the family eats a silent dinner from Epicure, while Madeline hides in her bedroom with the curtains closed and shades drawn, Levon escapes to his room. It is almost time and his body senses it as much as the telltale chimes of the clock. The pull is real, not something he imagines, and it leads him to the window and a starlit night.

Her lively stride—she is crossing over to their property. Levon can't make out her features in the darkened night, though he would venture to guess that she is smiling the same bright, beautiful smile that captivated him hours before. In a fleeting second, she passes from sight. Lucy Bell's version of fifteen is baffling to Levon—an incongruous age—part childlike, another part old soul. She is a mixture of temperaments: strong and sarcastic, wholesome and grounded, honest and withholding. She is air and light infused with darkness and thunder, an array of contradictions.

Levon had never given thought to the mystical world of ghostly phenomena, and now something about Lucy's existence has him doubting everything he once believed to be true—she appeared on the very day they buried his brother; she took from Levon his heaviest sorrow and replaced it with glimpses that levity might be possible.

chapter 8

As is the custom, Rabbi Adler pays the Kellers a visit. With shiva officially over, he explains that the days and weeks immediately following will be the hardest. During shiva, the house is full of people and distractions; the mourners are rarely alone. In his experience, families hold it together in the presence of company. When left alone to face their solitude, the real grieving begins.

The rabbi encourages Levon's father to join him upstairs in the bedroom where Madeline is swathed beneath the covers in her eternal malaise. Madeline isn't buying into the notion of their talking through their anguish and finding strength in prayer. Her anger and refusal incite Craig who storms out of the room, slamming the door so hard that the windows rattle.

Levon is holed up in his room down the hall, unloading his recent thoughts onto a blank page. He cannot go back to school. Unbeknownst to his parents, he calls his guidance counselor who offers his condolences and gives permission for him to stay home another day. "It was probably premature for you to come back so soon," Mr. Hayes says. "See how you feel tomorrow." Levon, who drifted through calculus, Spanish, and biology, in a coma of thick fog, is coming apart. What should have ruffled his mother's already tattered feathers and been a noticeable sign of her son's emotional unraveling, instead left Madeline unaware and disinterested.

Levon's own feelings of bottled-up rage and dismay are so closely linked to his mother's strife that he has become obsessed with her depression. He hears every word of their conversation through the air vent.

Today's conversation is an improvement from the last. His mother had gone ballistic when Rabbi Adler handed her the bereavement books with titles such as *Death of a Loved One*, *Coping with Grief and Loss*, and, the unspeakable, horrific, *Grieving for Your Child*. Levon is positive they are still strewn haphazardly on the living room floor where she had thrown them, missing the rabbi's head by less than an inch. His mother would rather die than read anything that acknowledges the hole that has desecrated her heart.

Levon feels sorry for Rabbi Adler.

The young rabbi with his clean-shaven face is out of his league with the maniacal Madeline Keller. Levon pictures him in her room in his freshly pressed slacks and lavender dress shirt. Today he is wearing a matching purple yarmulke. If only it could protect the gentle man from the stabbing insults of the woman under the covers. Her resistance hits him harder than the books might have.

The rabbi's voice tumbles through the vent, loud and clear. Here is a man accustomed to filling a room with words. "No one's telling you not to feel this way, Madeline. I cannot tell you whether God knows or understands your pain, only that Jewish tradition offers you time to heal from this tragedy."

Madeline Keller is devastated. Levon can't make out sentences, but he can make out phrases and a harangue of boundless suffering.

"…I don't want time…there is no God…God wouldn't take my son…"

Though her thoughts are disjointed, to Levon they make complete sense. Anger and agony are laced together and form the fabric of her soul.

Levon hears the bedroom door open and close and the tapping sounds of the rabbi's shoes on the hardwood stairs. His father is waiting for him at the landing where they whisper in hushed voices. "I've left the name of someone I think you should talk to when you're ready. Levon especially. This is quite a burden for a young boy to carry."

Levon hears Chloe playing in her room. She is supposed to be resting, and Levon knows she is fiddling around with her iPod so as not to hear the sounds coming from her mother.

Last night Chloe woke up at around two a.m. and started throwing up. His mother was convinced it had something to do with the food she ate at school. GSD patients experiencing vomiting and the resulting dehydration run the risk of their blood glucose levels dropping. Chloe's sickness led to Madeline's hysteria. "Everyone's out to destroy my family!" she screamed to nobody in particular and loud enough for all of South Beach to hear. It confirmed to those within earshot that Madeline Keller had become a very sick, scary woman.

"What did you pack her for lunch?" Madeline balked at Levon, who was now in charge of preparing his sister's perfectly portioned meals while his mother slept. "It wasn't his fault," intervened Craig. "I spoke with the school, and everything was in order. Dr. Gerald thinks it was probably stress-induced. There's no way we could have prevented it."

Levon likes Dr. Gerald and doodles a picture of him in his journal. In the fear-based bubble they've lived in since Chloe has been diagnosed, he has always been the voice of reason. The forerunner in GSD study, Dr. Gerald's dedicated research has made generous strides toward a cure, and he has recently left his post at Boston Children's for a position at Shands Hospital in Gainesville. To have him so close will provide a sense of security—however faulty—and Levon believes that if familiarity breeds contempt, then perhaps proximity will breed a cure.

There is no known cure for Chloe Keller's disease, and few people living with it are older than forty-five. With less than a thousand people afflicted, hardly any philanthropists and no pharmaceutical companies have put their dollars or research funding behind this orphan disease, which is the lonely stepchild to its big sisters and brothers, cancer and heart disease.

Thoughts collect and multiply in Levon's head. He writes:

Some diseases are tricky. Take my mother's grief. It's not a disease you find on WebMD by plugging in symptoms. Where is your discomfort, the prompt asks? I type in: my heart, my lungs, my wrists, my toes, my stomach, my knees. There are too many places to name. Can't I just click on the entire body, front and back, inside and out? Sure, grief is not a classified illness like depression or diarrhea, but it is a persistent disease that plagues its victims with clusters of acute pain and nagging symptoms. Though one can treat the side effects and numb the pain, there is no known cure for grief.

Levon is droning on in his journal. Although what he's expressing is important, he's not writing about those potent seventy-two hours. He is unable to entrust them to the page. And then there's Rebecca. He wonders what she might know about that night. Why does she believe David was cheating on her? What was wrong with David the evening of the accident? Levon doesn't dare write down the scary questions. Words have ways of being misconstrued and scrutinized.

He writes: *I've gone over it in my head a dozen times, and there is nothing I can do to change the story, the players, the ending. I grapple daily with the facts: the should-haves and the could-haves. David had so much more to lose than I. If only there was something else I could've done.*

Levon drops his pen and rolls over onto his back, trying to remember happier days. He returns in time to when his parents surprised them with an overnight stay at the famous Fontainebleau Hotel. He closes his eyes to take in the details of that glorious afternoon in their cabana by the beach. He smells the salty ocean mixed with the pounds of sunscreen his mother smeared on his face; he hears the splashing waves; he tastes the sweet cherry flavor of his then-favorite drink, the Shirley Temple.

Levon feels the warm sun beaming down on him, and he can hear Chloe's giggles as she frolicked in the ocean.

The doorbell sucks him out of his Fontainebleau bliss. It's a rush of Madeline's friends who have made a pact not to leave her alone. They come in pairs throughout the day, carting an assembly line of home-cooked meals. The house is filled with an endless stream of women coaxing her out of bed, persuading her to eat, urging her to shower, to change her clothes, to brush her teeth. The women take minimal interest in Levon, and whether it is their loyalty to their pain-stricken friend or their inability to find a pleasant word, a quiet permeates the house and banishes Levon to the safety of his room.

No one even mentions the fact that he is not in school.

chapter 9

Lucy finds it inconceivable to comprehend the loss of a brother. And while the school day is washing up around her, instead of immersing herself in the gloriousness of her newfound anonymity, she is desperate to talk with Ricky, hungry to hear his steady voice. Her new neighbor, Levon, is absent from the bus. She hopes she hadn't scared him off with her prying. She can only imagine how hard it must have been for him to utter those words, *my brother*, when she asked who died.

Lucy fingers the cell phone in her pocket. It is early morning on Wednesday. Ricky goes to the Cornerstone on Tuesday nights, once the infamous Vous, which means he's holed up in his dorm room, nursing a mild hangover. She is crossing the halls between second and third period, and it's a dreadful climb from literature to Spanish. Lucy cannot get over the amount of Spanish she is expected to learn in such a short amount of time. The demographics of Miami Beach had shifted over the years. Once the home to snowbirds from the northeast, it was now an international hub that has attracted a largely multicultural populace. Hardly *anyone* speaks English, that much she has noticed. Spanish is both required and a necessity here, and Lucy, with all her self-imposed visions of sophisticated worldliness is tripping over the words, lost in a flurry of conjugated Español. She had no command over the language.

As she approaches the door of Mrs. Arnold's class, a hand brushes against her back and she jumps. She hopes it's her new friend, her only friend, but it is not. She watches as the perpetrator walks passed her, scampering toward a group of fellow students. They appear to be normal teenagers leading typical teenage lives, though Lucy knows that normal can be deceiving. Hugging her bag closer to her body, she notices the way they are appraising her.

"*Hola*," she calls out with a friendly smile. "*¿Como esta?*"

The joke is lost on the group. They turn away from her and race each other down the hall. The best way to get people to stop staring and talking about you is to get right in their face and say *hello*—it was a method she had perfected time and time again.

Mrs. Arnold's door is beckoning. Her thoughts return to Levon, how he's an interesting study—shy, overweight, not cool by American teenage standards. He reminds her of Ricky, though they look nothing alike.

She senses depth, mild humor, and she is sure if she peels back some of the many layers, she will find a friend that can speak to her soul. Where Ricky has left a gaping hole, Levon enters to fill it. He hides his humanity in a naiveté that can be mistaken for aloofness. Lucy sees it in his sweet brown eyes, and she is sure no one has ever told him that he has dreamy eyelashes. She doesn't dare tell him that. It might send him running—not necessarily a bad thing in his condition—and she wants to meticulously strip away those layers.

Ricky was always telling her she was a magnet for lost puppies. What he meant was that she liked to be needed.

Lucy takes a seat in the crowded room where Mrs. Arnold has already begun an open dialogue. Lucy is lost and it shows. She searches the eyes of her classmates, native Miamians with years of Spanish under their belts, and finds that none of them are as puzzled as she. When the bell finally rings, she decides she's had enough school for the day and saunters out of the bulky building. Finding the cell phone in her bag, she dials Ricky's number en route to the bus stop.

Her brother answers on the first ring. "I was just thinking about you."

"Hey," she says.

"What's wrong?" he asks, sensing her mood across the miles. "And shouldn't you be in class?"

"Spanish Heritage Day," she quips. And then, "I miss you."

Ricky knows his connection with his sister is strong, and he also knows that her call is prompted by more than the geography that separates them. "That bad?" he asks.

"*Mas o menos.*"

"Tell me what's going on."

Hearing his voice is always enough. Even with the traffic blaring on Dade Boulevard as she crosses the street, his words inch her closer to inner peace.

"I'm good," she says, this time more convincing

"Have you made any friends?"

The mere mention of the word has her thinking of Levon. Friend. So many different interpretations. "Did Mom tell you about the new neighbors?"

"It's terrible," he says.

"The brother goes to my school. It's awful."

"Someone to fix," he says. "That should keep you busy."

"He could use some sprucing up."

"Watch yourself, Lucy. The boy is in mourning. Not everybody finds your magic endearing."

"He's sweet."

"Sweet like nice, or sweet like I've found my pulse again?"

Lucy doesn't bite. "No, nothing like that. I hardly know him."

"Then let me rephrase the question. Is there any chance you could like him?"

The question surprises her. He hadn't asked about her interest in the opposite sex in a long time. Five months if anyone were to count.

"You should see the memorial they have here for the

Holocaust," she answers instead, approaching the somber sculpture on Meridian Avenue. "It's really beautiful."

"Are you sure you're okay?" he asks.

She chews on her lip thinking about her neighbor missing his brother. After what she has survived, nothing rattles her more than death: the forever aloneness, the stark finality. She slows down her pace and takes in the tranquil beauty of the circular colonnade. "It wasn't how I imagined getting to know our neighbors, with all those cars parked outside and people lining up the street in tears."

"Are the dreams back?" he asks.

Lucy is quiet. They hadn't returned, and the mention of them flusters her. Only her dear brother could bring out the feelings she had buried deep. She swallows and starts to preach, "Can't dwell on the past. The future is full of possibility. No better present than the present. Rule #517."

"Oh boy, new boy has no idea what he's in for."

This makes Lucy smile. It feels out of place as she passes through the open-air structure that memorializes six-million Jews. For her, the giant hand reaching out of the ground signifies hope. "When are you coming down?"

"Thanksgiving."

"I can't wait," she says. "I love you, Ricky."

"I love you more," he replies.

It serves as a reminder of how troubling the Atlanta exodus had been for him. Loving her *more* was tied up fiercely in regret, having let her down with his absence on a day when she needed him most. Lucy never blamed him, but he blamed himself. When they hang up and Lucy sticks the phone in her back pocket, she is standing in front of the sculpture entitled *The Beginning*.

Two frightened children nestle within the safety of their mother's arms. The expressions on their faces are of unspeakable fear and worry; Lucy can hear them begging, pleading with their eyes, *can this really happen to us*? The stone wall behind the sculpture reads, *"...that in spite of everything, I still believe that people are really good at heart.* " She does not have to read the name below them to know whose words they are. Since May, she has pored over Anne Frank's diary so many times she can recite the most poignant quotes by heart. If anyone can illustrate resiliency with unflappable bravery, it is that of the thirteen-year-old girl who was forced into hiding by the evils of anti-Semitism. For a period of time, the insightful teen survived one of the worst horrors of prejudice with her will to live and unbroken spirit. It was a lesson that crossed generations and gave Lucy a renewed sense of self. After all, Atlanta had been her personal horror.

She steps back from the statue—its warm glow brushing against her cheeks—and sees her bus turning the corner. She thinks about Levon. It will take some time, but she is sure she can help him. George will be her accomplice; George will wheedle him along. She will walk him when she gets home. Something tells her Levon will come to her.

chapter 10

"How about taking a ride with me to my office, Levon?" Craig is standing in the doorway reminding him of how going to his office as a small child was once a huge deal. Levon doodles on the page, acutely aware that Lucy Bell has infiltrated his thoughts. He slams the notebook shut.

"Sure, I'll come," he says and places the binder in his knapsack so he can tote it along and write whatever comes to mind.

They make the drive to his office in downtown Miami in minimal traffic. It is a glorious fall day, the heat and humidity had been wiped away by the thunderstorms earlier in the morning.

Idle comments about the weather ("The temperature must have dropped ten degrees since yesterday.") to sports ("Do you think the Dolphins have a chance against the Patriots this weekend?") fill the car. Levon tries frantically to remember the last time he accompanied his dad to work. The filing cabinet in his brain remembers the disappointments.

There was "Bring Your Child to Work Day," when Levon dressed in his best khaki pants and white oxford button-down, only to be told that Chloe had a fever. Since his mother had jury duty that day, his father had to stay home and monitor his sister's vitals. Levon resentfully went off to school. He was in the third grade, eight years old, and one of only three children in the class. The other two were givens: Harry Framer's dad lived in New York City and Lily Davis' dad was dead.

"I'm sorry about yesterday," his father finally says. At first, Levon thinks he can hear his thoughts, that he's taking responsibility for the earlier disappointment. Craig continues by saying, "Your mom's having a tough time. We all are."

As if Levon didn't know that. They all were.

They are on the MacArthur Causeway passing the exclusive, pricey mansions of Star and Palm Islands on the right and the deserted Port of Miami on the left. This is one of Levon's favorite stretches of road where the turquoise waves kiss the shoreline and the palm trees line the median. As a kid, he would stare up at the cruise ships—massive floating cities—that lined the port's seawalls. Today they are all at sea. If he acknowledges his dad's remark, he is admitting blame. If he ignores the comment, he stands to offend, and that is not something he wants to do.

"How are we supposed to get through this?" Levon asks.

His father doesn't have the answer and he tells him so. "A lot has been broken, Levon. Some of it will never be fixed."

"Will you ever trust me again?" he asks, in need of the man's forgiveness.

"Give us some time," his father answers, and Levon notices at once how he uses the word, *us*, and not *me*—proof that the man who is supposed to be his hero can't make a unilateral decision. Levon wants to right the wrongs, and his father is unable to disassociate himself from his mother to have a one-on-one conversation. Why must she always be in any space with them? His thoughts are a tornado of disdain and neediness churning at an uncontrollable speed.

Time. It always came down to time.

"We're here," his father says, as if Levon wouldn't recognize the parking structure that led to his father's office high above

Brickell Avenue. Levon follows behind him toward the elevators and watches while he hits the button for the Penthouse.

"I won't be very long," he says, while Levon studies his face for any genetic similarity.

The door opens and he is greeted by the modern offices of Keller Development. Levon feels a rush of pride for his father and how hard he has worked over the years to maintain a successful, prestigious company. As President and CEO, the demands on him are great. Levon has become accustomed to his father's absence. And he has never acclimated to the shift in Craig Keller's personality when he passes through the steel and glass doorways of his flourishing corporation. At home, Craig Keller is a yes-man, adhering to his wife's regimented code. At work, he transforms into an autonomous, creative force whose brilliance and vision has shaped much of the Miami real estate market. As soon as they are ensconced in his corner office with breathtaking views of Fisher Island and the Biscayne Bay, the transformation has begun; the poised, commanding persona emerges.

"I am terribly sorry, Mr. Keller," marks the murmurs of his staff and his flaxen-haired secretary, Jane. They are clamoring around him with important documents that need to be signed and papers that have been waiting for his approval. Craig Keller grows in stature as he assumes his position of authority and begins attending to important paperwork. Envelopes conveying sympathy cards cover his desk. Grief is like a bolt of lightning, and everyone around it recoils. Levon takes a seat in one of the leather chairs and spins to capture the view his father had once described as a tropical paradise.

The picture of the three of them is prominently displayed on a shelf, and Levon reaches for it at once. Chloe was eight, Levon thirteen, and David fifteen. It was taken in November. Levon knows this because the photo would become their holiday card for the coming year. His mother had it blown up to an eight by ten for Craig's office, and Levon remembers how his father beamed with pride when he saw their broad smiling faces.

When Levon focuses on the upturn of Chloe's nose and the handsome symmetry of David's features, and even his own jovial pose, the unity captured by the photo surpasses each child's glaring differences. Individual and unique, together they form a family.

Three sets of eyes beckon Levon. Scrutinizing their youthful faces, he searches for the improbable fix to what's gone wrong. How can he mend the hole where David stands? Levon's eyes settle on his own, but tears make him blurry and invisible.

When his father draws near, he wipes his eyes and abruptly turns the evidence of crime facedown on the shelf.

During the next hour, Levon watches as his father sifts through emails and legal documents while firmly dominating the phone. When he says goodbye to the designer in Milan, he stands up from his chair. "I have to look over some renderings for a new building."

Levon asks if he can join him. When his father refuses, it sends a pinprick through his belly, puncturing him in one snappy gasp. Levon takes out his notebook, rests comfortably in his father's chair and continues to write.

Glossing over the last entry, his thoughts are laced in obsession and paranoia. He finds that his fingers have no control over the fancy pen he finds in his father's drawer, and sentences pour out of him in a phonetic frenzy. He's thinking about Lucy Bell and her shiny lips. His lips have never tasted the sweet strawberry that girls use to coat their mouths. The pen records his desire, the stirring from within that lately he has not been able to tame. Shiva and a sensual kiss do not go hand in hand. He closes the book to go to the bathroom. His father's loyal employees move out of his way as he walks down the lead-colored hallways, like the parting of the Red Sea, making room for him to pass as they share their heartfelt sympathy. Sounds coming from the office at the end of the hall—the one directly across from the bathroom with the door slightly ajar—cause Levon to stop.

Peering into the crack of the door, Levon sees the back of the black shirt and jeans that belong to his father. He is sure that's what his father was wearing when he left his office twenty minutes before.

Arms are wrapped around his father's waist. Levon moves in closer, concealing himself from view. His heart is racing, and his palms are sweating. When the two untangle themselves from each other's arms, Levon abruptly backs up to the wall, and although he can't see them, he can hear every word.

His dad is crying.

Okay, Levon thinks, this is what people do in times of death.

She is asking his father what she can do, and by the sound of her voice, Levon envisions her cradling him in her arms and stroking his hair like one might a small child.

"I wish I could be there for you," she says. "I didn't know what to do…if I should call…I wasn't sure…"

"It hurts…"

"I'm so sorry," she says, in a tone that carries into the hallway and soothes Levon as well.

Levon is caught, suspended between disbelief and actuality. He hightails it into the bathroom, his entire body shaking from the clandestine scene he's just witnessed. He's not sure he can go to the bathroom; instead, he uses it as a refuge to wait out the trembling that has besieged him. He stands in front of the vanity and steadies himself by resting his shaking hands along the white porcelain sink. He is hunched over so he doesn't see his reflection in the mirror. David has been gone eleven days, and he has not once seen his parents console one another.

After a few calming minutes, replete with denial, he splashes his face with cold water and escapes the bathroom.

Timing is everything.

There is no such thing as a coincidence.

Levon has heard these phrases from time to time. No one knows their implication better than he. Coincidence is something he studied very recently in physics class.

The story was remarkable and not everyone in the class was a believer. Mr. G.— short for something long and unpronounceable— was introducing the concepts of coincidence and synchronicity when he cited an inexplicable, extraordinary incident that happened in Beatrice, Nebraska in 1950. Levon always liked Mr. G. He reminded him of Rick Moranis from the *Honey, I Shrunk the Kids, Dog, Cat, Neighborhood* movies, the affable, well-meaning scientist whose experiments always went awry. To Mr. G., teaching was an experiment of sorts. He was the quintessential professor who documented probability by the range of colors the students wore each day and studied the impatient sound waves of those who sat through the fifty-minute class without uttering a single word. If you spoke, you would have seriously come close to electrocution. This reminded Levon of the time he introduced static electricity to the class, and for roughly twenty seconds, the entire group's hair stood up straight in the air. They looked like a family of porcupines, and Levon has a photograph, courtesy of Mr. G., to prove it. Mr. G taught valuable lessons in a most unconventional, interactive style.

Levon recalls how Mr. G. detailed the story of the church in Beatrice that had a scheduled choir practice for fifteen of its members at 7:30 p.m. For reasons both unbelievable, yet plausible, not one of the members made it to the church on time. "And the irony," he began, "was that five minutes later, at exactly 7:35 p.m., the furnace of the church exploded, destroying the ill-fated building. Was it fate?" he asked, "Coincidence? A spiritual message from a higher power? No one denies it is astonishing and that it raises the possibility that coincidence is proof of another dimension. Personally," he added, "I find it rather befuddling"—a word he liked to use from time to time—"that coincidences that are this systematic and this purposeful could be the result of random probability."

By then, the class was split into two: the believers and the skeptics.

"Mathematician Warren Weaver and author of *Lady Luck: the Theory of Probability*, 'calculates the staggering odds against chance for this uncanny event as about one in a million.'"

Levon was beginning to lean toward the believer's side.

Next, Mr. G. introduced synchronicity in relation to coincidence. You would have thought he was retelling the story of man's first steps on the moon the way his words escalated, inflating the incredulousness of the account. Most every head in the lab was leaning in closer to hear about the string of coincidences that occur frequently and appear to have some significant meaning to the observer. "Perhaps," he said, biding his time for a momentum-building pause, "they see these occurrences as a signal for change…"

What would Mr. G. make of the latest "coincidence"? How he ended up with the urge to pee at the exact moment his father was succumbing to a show of grief with a woman other than his mother?

"You hungry?" his father asks, interrupting Levon's meditation on a higher power, an infinite universe. He has returned to his office, absent any sign of the emotion he has just poured out down the hall. Maybe Levon was seeing things. Perhaps, his ability to decipher truth and fiction had been compromised in the accident. Or, maybe it wasn't such a big deal that his father found someone to talk to.

Consider the possibilities! Mr. G.'s voice was saying, one finger pointing to the sky.

Levon nods and grabs his notebook from off the desk, hugging it close to his chest.

"Is something wrong?" his father asks.

A period of mourning, like chronic disease, is not the most advantageous time to ask someone if something's wrong. Did Craig Keller expect his son to respond with the truth?

"I'll have Jane get us something to eat. Anything in particular you want?"

Roast beef on rye with deli mustard and a pickle. A Sabrett hot dog. French dip. Two burritos.

The secretary waltzes into the office twenty minutes later with two healthy turkey sandwiches and diet cokes. By then, Levon is challenging himself to a diabolically difficult game of Sudoku on the

Internet while his dad is reading through the last of the mail. This is anything but comfortable silence, more like a deafening herd of stampeding feelings, halting abruptly at the cage door that holds father and son captive.

Like so many meals before, they eat in silence with a pitiful number of interruptions. Levon takes careful note of each of his father's bites into the oversized sandwich. He does not want to finish before him. He does not want his dad to see how ravenous he has become.

They eventually discuss the future—bypassing what's painful— the immediate weeks that include Thanksgiving and Chanukah. Long-range plans are more tolerable—*Does Levon have any interest in architecture or real estate? Has he given thought to college?* His grades are decent, though they never came easily. David rarely picked up a textbook; his intelligence was innate. Levon, on the other hand, spends hours a day studying. Levon is a visual learner; reading explanations and facts ingrained the information into memory, which was probably why he enjoyed Mr. G.'s class so much. David was an auditory learner. He listened to NPR every morning and could recite to the family, verbatim, the details of the war in Iraq—naming the principals, the number of casualties, and the differing policies of world leaders. He was a great debater, prompting a number of family arguments fueled by diehard libertarian beliefs, which opposed his father's conservative, Republican perspective. Too young to be a card-carrying Democrat, David had looked forward to voting in the 2008 presidential election. Levon had trouble following the hostile milieu of war and politics. Despite his bewilderment on the subject, he was ready for change.

"Out of state is a good option," his father says when Levon tells him he's always wanted to go to the University of Miami like his parents. "Not because I want you far away, Levon. It's a great opportunity for you to see beyond the four walls of Florida, to expose yourself to a different part of the country."

Levon is bowled over that he's even considering sending him to college. He was convinced they would send him to a local university and keep him under lock and key on La Gorce Drive until he was thirty. The discussion is somewhat premature since he is only fifteen, though maybe talking about a future for his living son lessens the other loss.

"I haven't given it much thought," Levon says, which translates negatively to his successful, goal-oriented father.

"You have to start thinking about these things. A career isn't going to happen for you; you have to make it happen. There must be something you're interested in."

He loves to write. He thinks that is obvious.

"Craig?" a voice interrupts, and the two Keller men look up to a nice-looking sinewy figure with a cascade of auburn curls. She is unsure of herself—hands fiddling with a folder in her nervous fingers—and the indecision leaves her stranded in the doorway, uncertain if she should enter.

"Levon, this is Olivia; Olivia, my son, Levon."

"I've heard a lot about you," she says, remaining in the doorway.

"Olivia is one of our talented, new architects," he explains at the same time she blurts out, "I'm so sorry about your brother, Levon."

Levon thanks her because he doesn't know what else to say. *Me too?* It's not like a person sneezing, and you know to say *bless you.* There's no script for condolences.

"You left this in my office," she says to Levon's dad, offering him the green folder that, up until this point, was holding her upright. "I thought you might need it…I'm sorry if this is a bad time."

"Thank you," his father says. "We're finishing up here. Why don't you give the file to Jane. She'll know what to do with it."

Is it irritation that Levon hears in his father's voice?

Or is he afraid that his son might suspect that the two of them were wrapped around each other in a corner office down the hall, which gave credence to Mr. G.'s theory of nothing happens by chance?

Levon thinks that maybe the interruption will lead them off the subject of college and his future—it does not. His father bombards him with questions and ideas. Levon senses he is being *helpful* more to distract himself than out of interest in his son's future. Levon, though, is not one to toss back attention being thrown his way. When the subject of writing comes up, Levon's dad asks to read some of his work.

"You've seen the articles I've written for the newspaper," Levon half asks, half tells.

There is no mistaking he has not. "I'd like to read them sometime," he says.

The excitement tricks Levon into thinking his writing means something to his dad. There's so much he wants to share with him. He sees this as a window to fly through. Maybe he can talk to his father about the magnificent mystery of girls. He would tell him how he's never actually kissed one, and he would ask him what it's like, what he's supposed to do to ensure that it's memorable. Maybe they will go fishing together or to Heat games, like other kids his age with their dads. Maybe this tiny opening will expand into something fuller; they will grow close and have a special bond. Levon assumes his father can read the thunderous claps in the air around them. But his dad is licking his lips and crumbling the paper that had covered their sandwiches. He deflates when he sees that his dad is giving the wadded up wrappers the same amount of attention he's giving him.

chapter 11

Lucy Bell is walking George when they arrive at the house. Since she does this every day at the same time, Levon is not going to record it in his series of strange and unusual events. Though she is holding on to the gawky beast's green leash, the dog is clearly in charge, tugging Lucy across the lawn.

"Hey, Levon," she calls out, pulling George's collar and shouting *heel* toward the dog's deaf ears. "This dog obedience thing isn't working out for us," she says.

"Having trouble keeping up with your own life's instructions?" Levon asks with a smile.

"They did say it would teach you and your dog a lot. The only thing I'm learning, though, is impatience. Hey, is this your dad?" she asks, already extending her skinny arm to Levon's father who is making his way to the other side of the car.

"I'm Lucy Bell," she says with a smile, "the new neighbor."

"Nice to meet you, Lucy Bell. How are you enjoying the house?"

"It's awesome," she says, stroking George along his back. It is his reward for sitting still by her feet. "Right, Georgie?"

"I'm glad you're enjoying it," he says with genuine pleasure. "It's one of my favorites. Which room is yours, the one with the spiral staircase and the loft?"

"How did you know?" she asks.

"We created the room with a teenager in mind."

Lucy turns to Levon.

"He's a developer," he tells her. "He built your house."

The afternoon sun is peeking over her shoulder. Lucy frees one of her hands from the leash to shade her eyes from the sun. "We plan on staying for a while," she says. "The house is perfect, better than perfect. I love every inch of it."

Levon's dad thanks her with a warmth and generosity Levon hasn't seen in weeks. "It really is a special one," he adds, and instead of turning to leave them alone and head up the circular driveway, he initiates amiable conversation with Lucy about Miami Beach history and architecture and the bricks and mortar that inspired the Italian-style home with French finishes. Levon detects the change in his father, however slight, and it renders him speechless. His work is his passion. The ease with which he explains the evolutionary changes in real estate clearly fascinate Lucy, and have apparently bored poor old George who has given up on chasing the birds flying overhead and plunked his lithe body onto the cool grass for an afternoon snooze.

Levon observes his dad and Lucy Bell with mindful indecision. Lucy is a mystery of multiple proportions. His dad towers over Lucy, and it's the first time Levon realizes she's not wearing shoes. She would later tell him about the tickle between her toes when she runs through the grass, how it is a guilty pleasure. Levon has many guilty pleasures, none of which involve naked toes.

She is saying something to his dad, and Levon hopes it isn't one of her silly games or quotes of the days. His parents are fragile; Lucy's uncensored breeziness may not be welcome. It was one thing for them to discuss his father's work, something that lives on and endures in time and hopefully through a few Florida hurricanes, but if she brings up David, which Levon fears, who knows how his father might react.

"I'd like to see what you've done with the place," he says to

Lucy, appreciatively.

"My parents would like that."

"It's nice to meet you Lucy Bell."

"You too, Mr. Keller."

After Levon's father's departs, George is rolling onto his back, flexing his legs, with an invitation for one of the two-legged, less hairy creatures to tickle his tummy. He is whimpering, demanding Levon's attention. Simultaneously, the front door opens and like a jack-in-the-box, out shoots Chloe, shouting, "Puppy dog!" George, startled by the commotion, stands up on all fours and runs toward the miniature doll that closely resembles one of his tug toys. Levon, grabbing the leash of the unwieldy beast with both hands, is throttled forward at full speed across the drive and lands face down at his sister's feet. George is licking her from head to toe, and she erupts in giggles, falling to the grass. George has found a new playmate.

"Levon!" Lucy shouts.

Chloe is stretched out flat on her back and the pooch is mounted atop of her, licking cheeks and remnants of lunch. His paws are tickling her tummy and she is laughing, irrefutably happy. The earlier signs of any frailty have all but vanished. Levon, still holding on to the mechanical bull named George, pulls himself together, wipes the dirt and grass from his jeans and stands upright.

"Come on, George," Lucy says, taking the leash from Levon, giving it a tug. "Gentle," she orders, but George is having too much fun with his new pal. To George, Chloe is another one of his toys, although with cooler sound effects.

"What is that?" Lucy stops, giving George one aggressive tug. Chloe is having the time of her life, wiggling and jiggling, while George nips and paws and licks.

"What?" asks Levon, moving forward to take a closer look.

"*That*!" she exclaims, pointing to a blotch of red that is staining the front of Chloe's *Life is Good* T-shirt and leaking down the skin along her side.

"George, off!" Lucy screams. "Off."

Somehow, whatever is wrong, is going to be his fault.

With George by Lucy's side, Chloe is able to survey the damage, and at the sight of the crimson river pooling in her belly, she begins to panic.

"Levon, what is it?"

George, with his animal instinct, begins to pace back and forth, and it is then that Levon sees the object that's lodged between the dog's gnarly jaws. When Chloe begins to sob, he drops it to the floor and unleashes a high-pitched howl. How is the innocent pup supposed to know that the plastic device hanging from his mouth is not a snack?

"Levon!" Chloe is hollering his name while swatting at the protruding mass of skin and tissue surrounding her upper right abdomen. Her eyes are tricked into thinking she can swat away the gushing blood like a bug.

"What can I do?" begs Lucy, gripping George, unaware that what he had in his teeth came from Chloe's stomach. "What the heck is that?"

The scene brings the accident to the forefront of Levon's mind. Decisions have to be made in order of importance—life, death, protecting the gift—and this is not the time for Levon to remind himself that his hasty, altruistic response has failed him in the past. Levon reaches for the feeding tube and lifts his sister off the ground. Chloe's animal-like screams have prompted his father to bound out the front door and run toward them. "What's wrong?" he shouts. Reactive and unable to wait for a reply, Craig sees the blood and steals Chloe from her brother's arms, throwing her into his parked car. Levon realizes when they are halfway down the driveway that he is still holding the tube.

"Dad, wait!" he yells, running after the car, but they are gone, a streak of black and silver careening down the street to Mt. Sinai Hospital.

"Levon, I'm so sorry...so sorry..." George is whimpering and resting apologetically at Lucy's feet. Chloe's blood has painted the fur of his paws.

It had all come to pass with excruciating speed. "What was that thing in her stomach?" Lucy repeated while Levon flipped back through the pages of his mind. Something so innocent, so unforeseeable, was bound to lead to questions and varying degrees of blame.

"It's Chloe's nighttime feeding tube."

"Her *what*?"

Lucy's insistence leads Levon to sum up the last ten years of living with a sister who could die at any minute.

"Cornstarch?" she asks, "That's the cure?"

"There is no cure," he dryly answers. "The cornstarch maintains her blood sugar levels. If she misses a dose, she will die."

"I've never heard of it before."

"Most people haven't. Why don't we sit?" Levon suggests, noticing that Lucy's entire body is trembling. "Or let me put George back in the house."

She shakes her head no and holds the leash in her hand tightly as she thinks about what she just witnessed. "I'm freaked out, Levon. I don't typically get freaked out. That was crazy freaky."

"Welcome to my world," he replies.

"Really?" she says. "You're going to make light of this?"

"Never," he says. "But it's my life. Our life."

"I feel horribly. How could I have let this happen?"

Lucy's barrage of questions doesn't end there. Frantic and frightening, her questions solicit the information she needs in order to tame her hysteria. Agreeing, finally, to sit down, the two perch themselves on the thick grass while George rests his head in Lucy's lap. She strokes his fur as a method to soothe him and herself.

Levon takes note of how Lucy's temperament shifts as she learns more of the facts. The answers, although senseless and sad, swaddle her in their steady facts, and her hands seem to lose their tremor. None of his friends has ever shown this much interest in Chloe. While everyone politely treats the sick girl as though she is as delicate as glass, they conveniently avoid the details, as if they might catch GSD through its explanation.

"Your family's been through a lot." Noting Levon's breadth of knowledge on the subject—the statistics he blurts out, the enlarged liver, fatigue and chronic hunger he explained with medical precision, and the tremendous strides Dr. Gerald has made with gene therapy, she says, "And you manage to keep track of it all and hold it together."

This makes Levon proud and embarrassed. "I love my sister," he says. "Who do you think gives her the cornstarch while she sleeps? My mother has no concept of what day it is, let alone the time. My dad and I have been taking turns."

"Your parents are lucky to have you. Chloe too."

"Whatever."

"Whatever, according to my sources, is a bad method of changing the subject," she says. "Rule #921."

Levon wants to tell Lucy to remind him of that when his mother learns that his foolishness permitted a dog to maul his sister. Chloe's hopes of ever getting a dog—hypoallergenic or mini—have just gone out the window along with a dozen or so of her other wishes that his mother had stripped away.

"And when someone compliments you," she continues, "the only response necessary is a polite *thank you*. Rule #610."

Levon does not find her life bites even a bit encouraging right now.

There is a white hair clip stuck to her belt loop that catches Levon's eye. In one sweeping movement, she snatches it from its place, twists her hair in a knot, and fastens it behind her head. Levon is spending more time studying her face, her fingers, and the stray wisps of hair than he likes.

"What happens now?" she asks.

The question makes him tense. He is scared that something even as minor as a displaced feeding tube could take a sudden turn for the worse. He remembers back to how, after they had hit the tree,

David seemed okay, he and David had been talking. There *was* a definite exchange of words. He *was* alive then.

His silence unnerves her. The apprehension returns. "She's not going to die, is she?" Lucy asks, her voice cracking. "This isn't going to kill her, is it?"

Thinking it best to keep his uncertainty to himself, Levon shakes his head and tells her, "No, they'll replace the tube. She'll be fine."

"You're so calm," she points out.

Levon is coming out of his skin. She doesn't need to know that.

"What can I do?" she asks. "You have to let me explain to your parents."

"No," Levon insists. "It's best if you walk in a direction away from my house. My mother holds serious grudges. If she sees George, it'll set her off. Who knows what she'll do."

This seems to placate an ordinarily obstinate Lucy, and the afternoon draws to a close. Night washes over the sky, and steals the final rays of light. It is one of those early fall evenings in Miami when darkness vanishes the day's heat. This is the time Levon feels at peace. If it were possible to close his eyes and breathe in waves of air that haven't been polluted by misfortune, he would fill his lungs with the fresh mist and pretend that everything that had transpired over the last two weeks was a dream.

He is worried about Chloe. He is heartbroken about David.

Gazing along his stretch of street, Levon sees lights illuminating kitchens and dining rooms where mothers are preparing dinners for their families. The streetlights are caught between the faint light of dusk and the approaching curtain of nightfall. The stars above are winking. It is the hour when Levon would hear the growling of the car engine outside his window and watch as David bundled his books and equipment into sweaty arms, home from football practice. He would be wearing the school's white practice uniform, and Levon could see the dirt and grass stains, muddy and green. His hair would be damp, and sometimes David pushed it behind his ears and away from his face. Their mother loved it that way; she could see the outline of his eyes, the smooth jawline.

He was always excited to see David. To Levon, their friendship was so important. In his playful way, David always rang the doorbell whether or not he had his key. He said he liked the sound of the chime. It reminded him of the ice cream truck that used to drive down their block when they were kids. Levon would run to the door to let in his brother. For him, after school was comprised of a conscientious round of studying and an abundance of Yodels. The lack of extracurricular activities stopped mattering when the bell marked an end to his cramming sessions and a foray into David's world.

When Levon would open the front door for David each evening, the family dynamic would immediately change.

"What's up, bro?" he'd say to Levon, jabbing his little brother with his fist and dropping his dirty things to the floor—his mother would inevitably ask him, for the hundredth time, to leave his things anywhere else but on her expensive Persian rug.

Nothing was ever *up* or *happening* until David stepped through the threshold of their home. Much hinged on his presence. And while Chloe unnerved them, David was the center of all things hopeful that could be.

"Levon, are you all right?"

Lucy's voice is pulling him from his memory. She has laid herself flat against the grass and is staring up into a grayish half-lit sky. "Lie down and stare at the stars. Isn't the universe an incredible thing? Think about it. Look how big the sky is. It goes on and on until infinity."

Levon looks up and sees a depressing shade of gray hovering over their block.

"What do you think's up there?" she asks.

Levon answers, "Stars, some meteors, JetBlue."

He doesn't say *David*, though the word is on the tip of his tongue.

George is resting his head on her belly. He has been chastised into silence and restraint. She is petting him the length of his back while she speaks. "Do you believe there's anyone up there watching us?"

"What do you mean?"

"Like people or spirits?"

"I'm not sure what I believe anymore," he says.

"You don't feel a connection to something bigger than us?"

"No."

"You have to believe in something."

He is pondering a mountain of thoughts. He hates not knowing where David is. He wants to believe he's up there watching, perched on his shoulder, though what about the times when he doesn't want him there?

"I think we're all here for a reason," she continues, "that we're connected in some weird, cosmic, magnetic way. All the choices we make route and re-route the course of our lives. It's like circuitry. The components of an electrical system rely on each other; if one breaks down, the others can't do their job."

"You don't happen to have Mr. G. as your physics teacher, do you?"

"Mr. who?" she asks.

"Never mind." And then he adds, "What does any of it matter if we're these microscopic specks with no lasting impact?"

To Lucy, it mattered. Lucy believed in karma and the power of the universe. "Everything in life happens for a reason. We don't always understand it at the time because we accept things at face value, but, believe me, nothing happens by chance. Rule #215."

Levon interrupts, "Explain Hurricane Katrina. All those people losing their lives, or if they lived, their homes and families?"

"It's part of the greater good, Levon. That's what I'm trying to tell you; the world is huge. We're a small component of a much greater existence."

He doesn't understand why he's arguing with her. Hadn't he

turned into a believer after hearing the story of the church in Nebraska?

Levon closes his eyes. He can feel his brother's hands, smell him in the open doorway, hear his voice, but he can never touch him again. He can never talk to him again. He can never share the same air.

It sounded like she was saying his brother had to die.

How could that be true?

Chloe.

They didn't get back from the hospital until way past midnight.

It should have been as simple as popping in a new feeding tube and sending her on her way, but the emergency room doctor recommended she stay for a few hours so they could monitor her. I bet he was amazed to see a medical condition as rare as GSD and just wanted to spend some time with it. Dad's demanding pleas forced Mom out of bed, and Mrs. Bell drove her to the hospital. I don't know. I wasn't afraid, at first. Lucy kept calling the house throughout the night. I kept telling her that everything was fine, but she was having a hard time believing me, and by then, I was having a hard time believing myself. Every time I told her that things were going to be okay, she argued back, projecting some horrible outcome. After a while, I started to think she was onto something. Maybe something terrible was going to happen.

I waited up. When my parents and Chloe walked through the door without a word of dreadful news, I called Lucy's cell phone and let it ring once, our agreed-on code that things were okay. I would have liked to have texted her—something about us having our own private cyber-language enthralled me—but my cell phone remains at the bottom of our pool where my mother so graciously flung it. I wouldn't even consider asking for a replacement. I could just hear her now, the way she'd rip my head off with some cutting remark about the word "replacement." We'd both know right away what she was referring to, though neither of us would allow the words to escape our mouths. As if humans can be replaced. As if David could ever be replaced.

I went into Chloe's room and sat with her for a while. She was chattering away, playing with the ponytail that one of the nurses braided for her. I studied the freckles on her face, half-listening to her tell me about the IV and the doctor with the bad B.O. I was trying to count the coffee-colored dots. It was something I did often when I was afraid. Tonight, I got to fifteen before she hollered at me, "Levvy, are you listening to me?" I never lie to Chloe, so I told her the truth. I told her I was half listening. She didn't understand. Either I was or I wasn't. I told her I was counting her freckles. "Again?" she asked, which took me by surprise because I had no idea she knew that I'd ever done it before. "What number are you at? Break it to me gently," she demanded, throwing her fingers up to her face, hiding from my stare. Sixteen. Seventeen.

"Eighteen," I said aloud, "and that's good luck, so I won't count any more tonight."

With that, she let her hands find mine, and she squeezed them hard.

Then she looked up at me with puppy dog eyes and asked about the puppy dog George.

"Is he in trouble? Is mom going to make them give him away?"

I told her George was fine and, no, George wasn't going to have to move. Then I reminded her that the only thing that really mattered to any of us was that SHE was fine. She shushed me, not one to revel in the constant attention thrown her way.

"Did he actually swallow the tube? Is he going to have to have an operation to take it out or will he have to poop it out? That's gonna hurt, Levon."

"He didn't swallow it," I reassured her. I didn't tell her it was mangled and bloodied and that I gave it a proper burial like one

might a pet hamster. I couldn't just throw it in the garbage with her blood on it.

Mom and Dad were in their room. Sid and Lyd were downstairs watching All in the Family *reruns. It was quiet, so I relished the time I got to spend with Chloe without interruption. I was waiting to be punished, scolded, or yelled at—it didn't come. I was more curious than relieved.*

I turned the lights out and tucked Chloe into her hot pink, dimpled blanket. Then I knelt down on the floor next to her bed and took the braids out of her hair because she said they were starting to give her a headache. Amazing. She complains about a headache and nothing else!

"You know, Chloe," I told her, while brushing the strands of her hair with my fingers. "You know what all these freckles mean, right?"

She was beginning to fall asleep, so her words were quiet and slow. "Yes, Levvy, I know."

I watched her falling sleep, and she whispered, "Tell me again."

So I did. I told her what the eighteen plus freckles meant. They were kisses. They were the kisses from all the angels who were watching over her. "And that new one," I added, "right there, right by your ear—that one is from David."

chapter 12

"How are things at home, Levon?" Dr. Lerner asks.

Levon takes his time answering. He is studying the walls of her office and wondering which chairs his parents sat on when they came the other day. He wonders if it was *their* idea or *her* idea that he needed to come too.

She mistakes his quiet for having thoughts too painful to voice and silence ensues.

Dr. Lerner is a tall, sturdy psychiatrist whose formal certification includes marriage, family, and child counseling. Her cozy office, high above Biscayne Bay, is oceans apart from her homeland of Israel, and when she speaks, a hint of the textured accent and culture slips through her sentences.

Levon begins with, "I don't know what to say. I've never been to a shrink's office. Is that okay to say—a shrink?"

She laughs, which puts Levon slightly more at ease.

"What comes to your mind when I ask the question?"

David thrashes through his mind like the wind and rain beating against windows. He tenses. If he starts talking about David, he may not stop.

He asks, "Did they tell you how he died?"

"Who?" she asks.

"You know who," he replies. "Isn't that why I'm here?"

"Is that something you want to talk about?" she replies.

Levon goes silent again. He can't tell by her frizzy hair and sympathetic eyes if she knows the whole story. The whole community knows the details of the accident. There's something threatening, though, about this smart, refined woman thinking the worst of him.

"Do you think it would be useful for our work in here to talk about how he died?"

Levon scratches at his head. His hands are clammy, and he wipes them on his jeans. He doesn't understand the way this works. He imagined she would ask him questions, and he would give her answers. Instead, she is being evasive, mysterious. The stillness is getting to him.

Dr. Lerner stares at him. He had memorized the three moles on her cheeks. Her lips are turned up, not a full smile though not a frown either.

"You're very serious," he says.

"What makes you think that?"

He doesn't even bother answering.

"I understand this is very painful for you, Levon."

Finally, he has a response, "No, actually, you don't."

"Don't what?" she asks.

She is good, he must admit. The question fills him with sadness. If he risks speaking aloud, the grief will pour out. His eyes well up, and he fights the urge to rub the wet from her sight. The clock on her desk says 1:15. He's been here only fifteen minutes, and it feels like an hour.

"Do you think he had to die?" he asks.

Dr. Lerner's piqued interest doesn't go unnoticed. She swipes at the lively ringlets of curls that have fallen across her forehead, framing a nondescript face and unusually large nose. She backs up in her chair and her hands clasp around her knee. The elicited response doesn't come.

"Are you the only one who gets to ask the questions?" he asks.

"Tell me more about David having to die."

Lucy and her stupid words flood his brain. "It's nothing. I just wondered if you believe that 'everything happens for a reason' bullshit."

"Do you believe it?"

"I don't know what I believe. One minute David was alive, and we were talking, and the next minute he was dead."

Levon begins to cry and she gets up, tall as a giraffe, and hands him a box of tissues. After she sits back down, she crosses her legs and clears her throat as if she's about to speak. Levon is on to her antics and knows she's not going to say a word. He shares with her the next sentence that passes through his mind.

"He was such a good person. He really cared about people. Me, Chloe, he always took care of us. He made everyone feel special. He made them feel good about themselves."

"He sounds like a likeable boy."

"He had it all. He had everything going for him…"

"How did that make you feel?"

Levon looks up from the wad of crumbled tissues and raises his voice. "I didn't want him dead."

"Who said you did?"

"You're implying. You're tricking me into saying things I don't mean to say."

"I never said anything about you wanting David dead."

Levon is beginning to feel the seeds of hysteria planting themselves in his stomach. "You have no idea what I've been through. You have no idea what it's like to be me and live with this…this…"

"This what?" she asks.

"All of it. I'm so alone. I'm so alone in this."

"I'm not sure what that means, Levon. You are not alone. You have parents who love you, a sister who needs you."

"*They hate me!*" he yells across the room. "They blame me for everything. They wish *I* died and not perfect David."

"Your parents are in pain, Levon, and I can assure you that they don't wish for anything to happen to you. Do you think maybe you wish that for yourself?"

"What, now you think I'm suicidal?"

"Have you thought about it?" she asks.

"Great, my parents think I'm a murderer, and you think I'm suicidal."

"You're very worried about what I think of you. Is it always that way with you?"

Levon shrugs his shoulders. He worries about a lot of things when it comes to her. Can she read his mind? Can she tell when he's lying? Does she know, like trained lawyers, that a criminal averts his eyes when he's not telling the truth? Did she already hear that he let his sister play with an actual live animal that almost killed her?

"I'm here to help you, Levon. I think you're in a lot of pain, and I'm your ally. My job is to work with you to help you get through this."

His parents told him the same thing when they dropped him off in front of her office building. They even went as far as to explain the differences between a psychiatrist and a psychologist. This was their way, he assumed, to prepare him to be put on some drug like Ritalin or Prozac, so they can blame his shortcomings on a chemical imbalance.

He asks, "Is it very common for someone to die the first time they try a drug?"

Dr. Lerner uncrosses her legs again. "Is there a particular drug you have in mind?"

Levon's head shakes back and forth. "No."

"My experience with drug use is that our bodies are all unique. Like anything we put into our systems, we never know how we might react. That goes for food, alcohol, drugs, especially drugs," she adds. "It happens, but not nearly as often as food allergies."

"Aren't you going to ask me if I'm doing drugs?"

"If you want to tell me, it's privileged information."

"Are my parents exempt from being told?"

"Whatever we discuss in here stays between us."

"Anything?"

"Anything. Unless, I feel you're a danger to yourself or to others."

"That's actually funny, considering why I'm here in the first place."

She asks, "Why is it you think you're here, Levon?"

This time, Levon's silence lasts longer than before. He's thinking and thinking, and the noiseless room swaths him in a breeze that is more prickly than soft. It's weird to be sitting across the room from someone and staring at each other without speaking a word. His thoughts are loud and scattered, and he studies Dr. Lerner to see if she is someone he might be able to trust.

Here is what he knows:

She thinks he may have wanted David dead.

She thinks he may be suicidal.

She thinks he is a murderer.

She thinks he does drugs.

She knows he's in a lot of pain.

She knows how to trick him into feeling things he's been trying to avoid.

Here is what she doesn't know:

He's smarter than she is.

He's scared shitless of drugs.

He's not a murderer.

He's not suicidal (although the phrase *better off dead* makes some sense to him).

He loved David too much to want him dead, and the feeling was mutual. David loved Levon too.

And as far as the pain, well, maybe she got that right. He was swelled up with pain. One poke and he would deflate, loudly and violently.

"You just went somewhere," she interrupts. "Would you like to tell me where?"

"This therapy thing just isn't working for me."

"How do you know that?"

"Maybe because when I'm looking at you, I'm thinking about how grating it is being here."

"That whole time you were quiet you were thinking about me?"

Levon nods. Geez, he was stupid. She's a trained psychiatrist.

"Sometimes when things are too painful for us to talk about, we focus on something benign to cover the pain. You asked me at the beginning of our session if your parents told me about that night. Why don't you tell me what happened."

She starts to write notes on her pad. Levon's irritation grows and mounts into fantasies of swatting spitballs in her face.

"I can't," he says, while his hands drop in his lap. He wishes he could drop, too, down on her couch.

"Why do you think you can't?"

She thinks it's because he'll break down and cry and the pain will rise up through his throat and he will lose control and all the *feelings* will come to the surface and that would frighten him. But that's not it.

"I can't."

"It's that hard?"

Levon isn't sure if hers is a question or statement of fact.

"I just can't. Let's leave it at that." His eyes burrow into hers, and he's probably imagining it, but he swears she can read his mind and she knows he's hiding something.

"Why don't we talk about you, Levon," she begins again. "Let's start over. Tell me about yourself."

Levon lets out a laugh.

"You're not used to talking about yourself?"

"Usually about Chloe or David."

"How does *that* make you feel?"

Levon sits on her question. "I don't know." And then he pounces, rude and snippy. "How do you expect it to make me feel?"

Then, he quickly apologizes. "I'm sorry, I'm really not such a bad person."

"I would agree with that," she says.

"But I don't feel like myself in here. I'm distracted. I'm annoyed."

"Yes, you said that. Have you considered that you might be angry, Levon?"

He asks, "At who? My parents? My brother? Chloe?"

She answers for him, "Maybe all of them, including yourself. I'd be mad if I didn't get the attention I wanted and my siblings were receiving it instead."

"I wouldn't want the attention Chloe gets, and David is another story. I'm prouder of my brother than anyone. We were best friends. He was my only true friend. I could never be angry at him."

Something about those words make Levon want to cry again.

"I'm sure you miss him," she says.

Confusion begins to settle as she peels away his layers and probes into topics he had earlier tried to avoid. He was getting confused about what they were actually discussing. Who is he supposed to be angry at? What is he supposed to be angry about? He shakes his head back and forth. It can't be. He doesn't feel anger; it's something else, something deeper and scarier that's lurking inside.

"I miss him every second of the day."

A moment passes as she looks at him. He thinks he might cry again.

She says, "Levon, I know this isn't easy for you. I know you're worried about expressing your feelings in front of me, maybe even admitting them to yourself. I do believe I can help you. In fact, I know I can help you."

This grabs his attention. How could she know anything about him? And yet, the bandage for all his bruises buoys him in such a way that he almost feels guilty for the fleeting absence of melancholy. He has no right to be happy anymore.

He's in Dr. Lerner's office and they're talking about his

feelings, though his mind drifts to a football stadium. He is five years old, and he and his father are watching the Miami Dolphins play the New York Jets. Mom is home, pregnant with Chloe, and seven-year-old David is at a birthday party. His father thought he might be a tad young to sit through the three and a half hour game, but Levon proves him wrong. It is one of the top-three best days of his life.

The weather was in the seventies and the day was a bright, clear blue. They had club seats on the fifty-yard line. It's picture postcard perfect, though what mattered the most, what left Levon spewing in his journal years later, was the closeness he and his dad felt. They tailgated hours before the game with colleagues from the office. They tossed a ball back and forth, and his father remarked on what a strong arm he had. "Little Marino," he called him. When they got to their seats, their togetherness didn't end. Levon was bursting with questions about the yellow flags, the downs, and the multiple penalties that had the crowd going wild. His father could have easily tuned him out and focused on the field. He was a diehard Dolphin fan, talking aimlessly about the '72 champions and how the 'Phins were the team none other could rival. Bob Griese. Don Shula. There he was, watching hall of famer, Dan Marino, toss bullets across the field against the nemesis Jets; nevertheless Craig Keller had only one person on his mind, and that person wasn't wearing the number thirteen on his back. It was Levon.

The memory was carved into the walls of Levon's mind and remained there for years. Sitting on his father's lap—that cannot be undermined. Consider football and the effort that goes into bringing your opponent down. Ultimately, the game concludes with a W or an L. The Dolphins and their Marino got a big W that November afternoon, as did Levon. However, the memory was bittersweet. How can a child not feel some sadness when remembering the last time his parent held him close?

"Levon, can you tell me where you were just now?"

Levon was starting to grasp the whole Q & A thing. When she

asked where he went, she wasn't referring to a physical location.

"It's stupid," he says.

"It may feel stupid, but it's not. It's important to our work in here. You need to learn to trust me."

"I just want to be happy," he said. "I just want this shitty feeling to go away."

It was really stupid to say because now she was likely scribbling on her pad that he was definitely depressed. He'd already decided that he wasn't going to take any medication. He'd pretend to take it like they do in the movies, and then he would spit it out and flush it down the toilet. He'd show them who was depressed.

His head was beginning to go murky and dark. A cocktail of emotions he couldn't make sense of were diluting specific memories. Was he missing David? Was he missing Dan Marino? Or someone else?

"Our time's up for today," she says.

Levon exhales.

He is out of the chair and across the room reaching for the doorknob to freedom.

sunday, october 14, 2007
12:43 a.m.

Seargents Gerald Goldstein and Dan Branson are the first ones at
the scene. They are cruising along the Sunset Islands where the
slumbering suburban neighborhood meets Alton Road when the faint
blinking of taillights come into view.

"What do we have here?" Dan grumbles to his partner, straining
his neck to get a better look. He is tired and anxious to get home to his
new wife. The eleven-hour shift ending with the raucous crowds on
South Beach has him drained. The streetlights on this particular strip of
road in Miami Beach are out, and Goldstein has already called into
headquarters to have Florida Power & Light dispatch a crew.

"Doesn't look good," says Goldstein, the burly officer with a
record of forty years on the force. "Call for some back-up and the
EMT. This ain't going to be pretty."

Steering the car to the side of the road, he turns off the ignition,
grabs a flashlight, and steps out of the car.

"Can't tell you how many accidents I've seen at this corner," he
continues, grabbing onto his belt, preparing himself for the damage
he's about to face.

No matter how many years you spend on the force, it doesn't get
any easier to see mangled, torn up bodies, lives ended at the snap of a
finger. "How many times do we have to complain to these guys about
the lights? I thought they were coming up with a better way to mark

this street?"

The quiet, residential community just north of South Beach is unaware that a car has wrapped itself around one of its sturdy trees. As the officers approach the demolished vehicle, Branson could swear he hears muffled voices coming from inside.

"Can anybody hear me?" he asks to the empty air.

Silence.

As he draws closer, the voices he's intent on hearing turn out to be the car radio humming a hip-hop song that is more a rant than melody. "They say these cars are built to last," he quips. "The only lasting part looks to be the darn radio."

The two officers lean forward for a look inside the tangled vehicle. Goldstein stands on what is left of the passenger's side of the car, and Branson stands on the remains of the driver's side. The car has split into asymmetrical pieces and amazingly, the two bodies are still in their seats, thrust against the inflated airbags.

Goldstein sees the blood first. He follows the trail with his flashlight until it leads to an undistinguishable body part. Then he sees the crimson shirt with white lettering and the seal of Beach High's football team. He catches his breath. All four of his children passed through the halls of Beach.

The sound of blaring sirens fill the air. It is a matter of seconds before the EMTs have evacuated their truck and sprung into action. Adrenaline pumps through young Branson—he is unsure if the person in the driver's seat, the one intimately attached to the airbag, is moving.

"What have we got here?" the female EMT, Sheila, asks. She appears not much older than Goldstein's youngest daughter.

Goldstein responds bleakly, "Looks like two kids." He wants to tell her they're probably not much older than she is, but time, in a crisis like this, is as valuable as oxygen. Besides, she's already on the driver's side with her back to him.

"We've got a live one, Louis," she hollers to her partner, a gangly man who could pass for a car salesman. He surprises Goldstein and springs into action. "Can you help me with the kid?" he asks Branson. "He's a meaty one and he's really wedged in there."

That's a nice way of putting it, Goldstein thinks to himself. He himself has been called whale, buffalo, all variations of things one might eat; meaty had a kinder ring to it. He sympathizes with the boy at once.

After lying the boy's body on the stretcher, a battery of tests are performed. His eyes open with caution and the boys asks for his brother. Across from him, Sheila reaches for the other boy. His pulse is there though weak.

"We don't have much time," says Sheila to her partner. "I can't get a blood pressure. Could be internal bleeding. We've gotta move this kid out of here fast."

chapter 13

"Levon?"

"Yes?"

"Can I ask what happened to your brother?"

"You just did."

"Really," Lucy says, with a gentleness that eclipses her tendency to pry.

Levon does not take long to answer. Firmly, he says, "No," leaving no doubt as to his conviction. He had enough therapy this week.

A few days have passed since they've spoken, and they are riding together on the rickety bus that delivers them to school. *Rickety* was a word he used to argue with David about all the time. David used the word to describe his peers who had little confidence. "Why not call them *insecure*?" Levon would ask. But David refused. "Everybody says *insecure*. It's grossly overused." This ultimately began a debate on popularity and self-esteem, both of which Levon personally had no experience with, though had many opinions about. Levon laughed when he heard David use the term on more than a handful of occasions to describe the big, burly football players on his team. To Levon, *rickety* was something physical, like the bobbing, clackity-clack of the oversized bus.

"You're going to have to talk about it one day," Lucy says,

interrupting the chain of thoughts linked to his loud, firm reply.

Once Levon discloses the details of that night to his nudging neighbor, he fears she will rethink their strange, unique association. He's actually amazed that the refusals haven't been upended by the snarky gossips at school. He is sure everyone is talking about the accident and that the assumptions will trickle down to Lucy Bell's thirsty ears. He can tell his rejection has silenced her, which is unusual for someone so typically chatty. Usually, she can go on for hours about the most inconsequential, random things.

"Be persistent. You never know when your tenacity will pay off. Rule #121."

"You think that's going to make me talk? Your ridiculous motivational quotes?"

"Tell me about Chloe. Is she doing all right? Were your parents pissed?"

He thinks about telling her his parents are always pissed, that they had been pissed for almost a month now, preceded by years of misdirected anger, and that it will continue until hell freezes over. But he stops himself, the analogy likely to spark a diatribe on global warming. "She's perfect." He also doesn't tell her how his father is astounded by his "flagrant capriciousness" and "unreliability." His mother went right for the jugular. In the absence of words, she basically avowed to him that he was useless, invisible, and altogether a failure.

The bus is teeming with people today. Levon and Lucy are forced to share a seat and their knees knock against each other's through the stop and go of the jittery machine. Lucy is positioned on Levon's left side, closer to the window, and the striking tattoo along the outside of her right ankle comes to view. He must have copied it wrong because on the Internet, he read the symbol means *rice cake*.

Levon doesn't know much about Lucy. Theirs is a *predestined* meeting, she declares, when by happenstance and exact alignment of the stars, they land at the bus stop at the same time that crisp Monday morning. Levon doesn't have the heart to tell her that their meeting had more to do with their attending the same high school, living next door to each other, and the predetermined Miami-Dade County Metro bus routes.

"You're very intense, Levon."

That was something he was used to hearing, even before the recent tragedy. The few acquaintances he had—Danny Riggins, Harry Tolz, Jonathan Rothenberg—chided Levon for his silent reservation. The four of them had been friends since junior high where they had worked on the school newspaper together. Writing was their shared passion that initiated creative stories and articles for their classmates. Levon's personality shined on paper; he came alive through unabashed candor. Decidedly the most talented of the group, with an irreverent sense of humor that exploded onto the page, his gift unfortunately did not translate to conversation.

And because Levon's social skills never developed, his cherished group of friends grew away from him, got caught up in girls and parties and the social nuances that typify high school.

The bus comes to a screeching halt, jolting the pair forward in their seats. A truck passes to the left with HVAC Services written along the side. *Fabrication and Installation*, interests Levon. Fabrication's dual meaning lingers in his mind. In the writing world, fabrication is a cock-and-bull story, and his first reaction when he reads the black letters on the white truck is to balk.

It is the last stop before they are deposited at their destination and the four-tenths of a mile stroll to school. Levon wants to immerse himself in Lucy, but he is depressed today, more so than before. He doesn't feel much like talking. The rumination has eaten away at him and leaves an empty pit in his stomach where his breakfast used to be.

"Can we just not talk?" he pleads, which is like asking a small child to walk, not run.

She doesn't say anything, though a deep, exasperated sigh escapes her lips. Levon manages to squash his guilt, and then notices Lucy's busy fingers reaching inside his backpack.

"What are you doing?" he asks, grabbing the black sack and prying her fingers loose.

"What have you got in there, a weapon? You're not going to take your aggression out on our unwitting classmates, are you?"

The reference to heinous acts that have marred schools all over the country perturbs Levon, and he shoots her a look that tells her so.

"Well, you guard it like it's an explosive," she adds.

Tucked among the worn-out trigonometry book and the MLA handbook is his turquoise blue, 2007, college-lined journal. The year is coming to a close, and the dwindling number of remaining pages has him concerned. Leaving it at home is no longer an option. He is convinced his mother, with her duplicate key, will find her way into his secret cache. His fear is unfounded. It stands a greater risk of being discovered by a nosy teenager with clammy hands like Lucy.

Not one to readily take no for an answer, Lucy wrestles the backpack out of his grasp and starts rifling through the contents. Levon can't possibly raise his hand to a girl or use physical force to push her from their seat, although it's tempting. He doesn't know any other way to grab the vinyl bag away from her clawing fingers.

"Look what we have here," she mouths to Levon, lifting the spiral notebook that says *Private, Keep out! That means YOU!* scribbled across the front cover. "Is this like your diary?"

Levon reddens under the flame of Lucy's teasing words.

"Oh my God!" she says, "You actually have a diary. That's so cute!"

"It's a journal," he shouts at her, failing to grab the notebook from her intrusive hands.

"I stand corrected," she says. "A journal suggests sophistication. What do you write about?"

"None of your business."

Her fingers graze the pages and Levon flinches, pulling back. "You are relentless," he says, "and a meddlesome snoop."

"Come on," she teases, "what can be can so private that you can't share it with me?"

The robust green and white metro bus is about to round the corner. The new Beach High with its modern glass and concrete architectural design is coming into view. The palm trees lining the entryway remind Levon to breathe. Claustrophobia has taken its toll on his body, fueling his arms and legs, which are about to erupt into flight or fight. Once he's off the gurgling vessel and away from Lucy's leering stare, he assures himself he'll be able to shake this menacing feeling. She's too close, he thinks, in ways more invasive than physical contact.

"I see words..." she taunts him, flipping quickly through the pages. "I see sloppy handwriting and I see..."

The pages are turning, and he is fighting her. She, though, is fast and merciless, and the shuffling sound drowns out the whirring buzz of the bus engine.

"C'mon Lucy," he says, careful not to sound as if he's begging.

"Is that...is that my tattoo?"

Of the hundreds of pages, she hones in on the one where he has doodled about her intriguing and permanent marking.

"That *is* my tattoo," she says with astonishment, holding the notebook upright and peering at the illustrated page that couldn't have been any less obvious had it called out her name. "Or something like it. How cute...you tried to copy it. You could've just asked," she says, tossing the journal back as though she has won some battle.

"You could've just minded your own business."

"You are my business, Levon," she says. Then she proceeds to explain how they are neighbors, which categorizes them above friends, though a notch below family. "I guess you can call it an extension of family," she says, "which means, in essence, that I have to put up with a lot of crap from you, and you have to put up with a lot of crap from me that we wouldn't necessarily have to put up with from friends. There's not much we can do about it because we're stuck, unless you move or I move, which, based on my calculations, won't be for a while."

The way she tied up their cozy alliance left no room for Levon to recant what was factually true. He was already putting up with an insurmountable level of crap from her, both of the figurative and literal nature. The *extension of family* business actually appealed to him in his needy, desperate attempt to latch onto something meaningful and long-lasting.

The bus pulls up to their stop, and Levon is already sliding his body off the seat and shoving the journal with its folded-down, wrinkled pages back into his bag. Hiding the words and sentences won't obliterate the image from view. Lucy would always know how he scribbled something of hers onto his private pages. The passengers on the bus file out one by one, slower than Levon can tolerate. He is frustrated at the pace which leaves Lucy positioned directly behind him, lingering over his shoulder, like a hungry mosquito salivating before taking a bite. She whispers in his ear, "Forgiveness."

Levon's humming to himself, so he doesn't have to hear her breezy voice circling around his ears. "That's what the ideogram stands for," she says, again, "forgiveness." He is stepping off the bus counting the seconds until they are free from the confining odor, a stale dinginess reminiscent of a summer he spent working in a bagel shop on Alton Road, wearing mildewed sneakers. *Forgiveness.* The word grazes Levon like a bullet. It slows up, speeds forward, entirely unsure of its target. He has thought about forgiveness many times over the last several weeks though not for the typical reasons. His forgiveness meanders down a long and convoluted path, one he chose to take alone. In that moment, the short-sighted, reckless decision to save David was easy. The outcome, however, could never have been predicted. Her *forgiveness* falls on deaf ears.

Passing the memorial on their right, Lucy is once again drawn to the sculpture of the hand at the end of the towering arm. She stops to appraise it while Levon complains that they're going to be late. He shuffles past her unaware of the other tattoo, the one scribed on the outstretched arm that erases identities. Crossing the street, she runs to catch up with him. Together they head toward the crowd of students filtering into the cream-colored buildings. Lucy is swirling around him in her circular Lucy style. "Come on, Levon. Don't be so melodramatic. It's really not a big deal. It's kinda nice you find my tattoo interesting enough to give it a blurb in your journal. Most people think it's appalling, that I'm too young for anything that permanent."

Voices creep around them as they step into the busy hallway. Levon considers what she has said about permanence, and he wants to write it down before the words slip from his memory.

We all have inscriptions, whether visible or hidden. Though some are easy to see with the naked eye, others are concealed deep within and leave a lasting impression—a permanence on our souls.

Levon is well aware that he has to respond to Lucy. She knows enough about him that his refusal to acknowledge what she's saying might infer that he cares—he's not sure if he does. "I'm glad it means something as substantial as *forgiveness* because I thought it meant *rice cake*."

"You looked it up?" she asks.

"I tried."

"Levon Keller," she begins, grabbing him by the shoulder, insisting that he stop walking. The bell is about to ring and hordes of kids are passing, knocking into them. She's about to say something profound. Levon can tell by the way she wrinkles her nose and stares him in the face. She even manages to stand still, something he's almost certain he's never seen her do. But before the words come tumbling out, a tall, pretty cheerleader steps right in between them.

"Hey, Levon," says Rebecca.

Lucy takes a step back and lets Rebecca take her place.

"Who's your friend?"

The girls wait for Levon to make the introductions while he stands there speechless, cheeks growing redder by the second. A month ago, no one would have ever believed Levon Keller, the boy who resembles Drake's brother Josh in the Nickelodeon tween show, would be surrounded by two of the school's most beautiful girls.

"I'm Rebecca," she says, and before Levon can stop himself, the phrase that he has repeated so many times rolls off his tongue, and he blurts out, "David's girlfriend."

Lucy stares at Levon while Rebecca looks to the ground.

"Lucy's the new neighbor," he begins again. "She's a sophomore." Turning to Lucy, he continues with information she probably could care less about. "Rebecca's a senior, captain of the cheerleaders."

The girls exchange niceties, and Rebecca tries to persuade Lucy to try out for the junior varsity squad. "There's always room for more girls," she says.

Levon can hardly wait to hear Lucy's response. She is gorgeous with a killer body, which automatically makes her a contender for anything obnoxiously popular and cool by high school standards, but Levon knew early on that Lucy had no interest in the social class pecking order or in their afterschool clubs.

"I'll have to think about that," Lucy says with a smile. "I've never really considered being a cheerleader." Levon assumes she is mocking Rebecca, but she doesn't seem to be. The smile is real.

"I'm really sorry for your loss," she says to Rebecca.

Rebecca nods, and the swell of tears forming in her eyes is hard to miss.

"Levon, are you doing okay?" Rebecca asks. "When are the stitches coming out?"

"I'm all right," he answers. "I think two more weeks."

"You know, you should probably start putting Vitamin E on your skin now. It helps it to heal."

"I'll take that under advisement," he says.

"I'm glad you're back at school," she says. "Last week was hard. I really want to talk to you. Can I stop by after school?" Lucy watches the two of them with growing interest. "Or maybe I can give you a ride home? I heard you're taking the bus."

"It's not so bad," he says, unable to formulate words or find an affirmative answer. If she knew he was taking the bus, then everyone in the whole school knew. Rebecca was considerate, patiently awaiting his response, though she knew his answer. No one in his right mind had ever turned her down.

"Meet me by my car after school." Then she turns to Lucy and asks her if she would like a ride too.

"And miss the bus and all its glamour? No thanks," she laughs.

Levon can barely swallow and shoots Lucy a look. Just when he's convinced himself that being around Rebecca Blake and her fruity scent doesn't send a shiver down his spine, he feels a fluttering, and Lucy, with her expression as smug as ever, gets to watch.

A loud bell echoes through the busy corridor. Rebecca disappears from sight leaving Lucy and Levon the last to get to their classes. Everything about the two girls, from their coloring, to their sense of humor, to the bold branding on Lucy's ankle, distinguishes the two girls from one another. Rebecca is a goody-goody, the sweetest kind. Tattoos are for naughty girls. Somewhere in the middle of the vastly disproportionate range of virtue is where Levon finds himself.

"What were you about to say to me?" he asks, remembering the look on her face before Rebecca walked over to them.

"Your dead brother's girlfriend?" she asks. "Say it isn't so."

He raises a hand to stop whatever it is that is bubbling over in her brain.

"The plot thickens."

Levon turns and begins to walk away. If he doesn't make it to English class in the next thirty seconds, he will have to face the humiliation of Ms. Seward's scolding. He doesn't need to draw any more attention to himself.

"He didn't know about it, did he?" she yells.

Lucy's reference to David as a measly pronoun, depersonalizing him as if he weren't a real solid presence, incenses him.

Levon turns around. A couple of feet separate them. Lucy's arms are hugging her books. She is staring Levon down, waiting for him to speak. She has no concept of the time, nor does she care if she's late.

"His name is David," he says, his voice rising while fingers clenched his language arts folder. "It *was* David," he begins again, "until I got behind the wheel of a car, and we ended up wrapped around a tree."

He pauses. "You want to know about me? You want to know about my brother? I'll forever be the kid that killed him. How's that for your stupid game of Jeopardy?"

"Levon…"

"No, Lucy, you asked, and I'm gonna tell you. I shouldn't have been driving. I shouldn't have left my sister home. I knew better, but I did it, for him, for David. Are you satisfied now? I'm a frickin pariah in this town. I was a loser before, and I'm a bigger loser now. You can thank me for sparing you the trouble of a friendship based on lies and hypocrisy. You would've figured it out sooner or later."

Lucy is stunned into silence. She is facing him, and her mouth drops—nothing comes out of it. The hallway is barren and Levon's self-inflicted battering resonates in the air around them. "It wasn't ice hockey…I had no idea," she says.

"Of course, you didn't," he spits at her. "How could you? You wanted to believe we were kindred spirits connected by coincidence in a paltry Kevin Bacon game, but we're not. We're very different people. I'm not who you think I am; I'll never be that person."

"We all have our demons, Levon," she finally says. "You're not the only one who makes mistakes." She starts to move away from him, and Levon sucks in his breath ready for a reprimand. She says, "I decide who my friends are, not you, and not Miss Florida over there either. *Me. I decide.* You want me to feel sorry for you? I don't. I told you things happen for a reason, and do you know why I said that? *Because they do.* It's the reason you did what you did, and if you can find some truth to that, you might be able to forgive yourself. Stop waiting for everyone around you to do it for you."

"My truth will never set me free," he quietly utters.

"We all have secrets, Levon."

"Not like this," he says.

"How do you know?"

"Because I do."

"You don't know," she says to him, before turning her back and heading down the hall. "That's why they call them secrets."

chapter 14

Lucy dumps her books on the kitchen table and finds her mother preparing dinner. A self-described foodie, Carol Bell can whisk up a gourmet meal with her eyes closed and with whatever may be in the pantry. The Bell women have inborn skills and talents; their fluid motion, precise timing, and keen awareness make them masters at their gifts.

The older woman's gaze is fixed on her daughter while she sprinkles a handful of spices into the simmering pot on the stove. She asks what's on her mind, and Lucy says *nothing*, while all she has been able to think about is the Keller family. When she had intimated that big things were going to happen, she hadn't expected blood and a visit to the hospital, or the news that Levon was driving the car that killed his brother.

Carol Bell holds up the wooden spoon to her daughter's open mouth and offers her a taste of her famed marinara sauce. Lucy savors the rich blend of tomato and garlic, careful not to drip on her white T-shirt. Her mother often brags about her secret ingredient, though Lucy is well aware of the bottle of Chianti that she generously poured into the pot, which she keeps hidden in a cabinet.

Lucy hears the car pull into the driveway next door and pretends not to care. Witnessing Levon trip over his words around that cheerleader girl made her want to puke. He was not turning into the best protégé. There are weaknesses they need to work through, especially when it comes to cheery pink lipstick and pom-poms.

"Something's not right," Lucy says, licking her lips.

"What do you mean? It's my usual recipe. I haven't changed a thing."

"Not the sauce, Mom. The sauce is perfect. I meant next door."

Closing the lid on the simmering pot, she responds, "That's putting it mildly. What happened over there is tragic. Nothing right about it at all. I brought some fresh, baked challah to them the other day. The mother was worse than I had imagined."

"Challah? I didn't know you knew how to make it."

"George and I ran into the rabbi leaving the house. I thought it might help."

Lucy observed her mother and her gentle displays of thoughtfulness.

Levon rarely spoke of his mother, and when he did, it was with fear and mistrust. She didn't know if it was a result of the accident, or if he had always felt this way. Levon and Chloe needed their parents during this unstable time. Something was nagging at her that she hadn't quite put her finger on yet.

"Have you ever heard of glycogen storage disease?" she asks her mother, who is chopping into a large onion. The tangy scent infiltrates their matching eyes, and simultaneously, both women dab at their tears.

"Please, no more bad news," her mother begs.

"It's Levon's sister. She has it. It's like the opposite of diabetes."

"That poor family. They've been through so much."

"I wish there was something we could do for them, a way we could help."

Carol Bell stops cutting and wipes her hands on her apron. "You're doing everything you can possibly do. Grief is a process. You know that better than most. All you can do for them is be there and listen. Unless you've been in their shoes, it's impossible to fully empathize." She reaches across the granite island and tucks a strand of Lucy's hair behind her ear. Lucy doesn't need her mother to stroke her hair. She has read between the words and clichés enough to know what the gesture means.

Peering out the kitchen window, she watches Levon and the cheerleader in her shiny red car. *Attention seeker*, she grumbles under her breath, detesting the words and what they imply. "I'm going to walk George," she says.

"He was just out back."

Lucy shrugs her shoulders. Levon and pom-pom don't know that.

George comes pouncing toward Lucy when he hears the rattle of the chain. "Sit," she tells him, and surprisingly, he listens. "Good boy. Listen carefully," she begins, grabbing his puppy face in her hands. "It's very important that you steer clear of the big red toy out there in the driveway. Get it? No leg lifting, no poops, nothing within five feet of that car. Understand?" George stares lovingly at his boss and lathers her with his tongue. "I'm going to take that as a yes." He tongues her again to clean away the salt from her onion tears. She lets him do it some more.

George is as excited as she is to be outside. His tail wags in the breeze and his pink tongue hangs out of his mouth. Lucy smiles down at her buddy, refusing to look in the direction of the car. She is convinced the two of them are huddled together without any idea she is nearby. Rebecca is probably applying Vitamin E to his stitches.

George's pace quickens and Lucy's slow, languid steps increase with his. She pats him on the head, "Good boy," when they make it safely past Levon. The car's engine is running; she is relieved to see they aren't holed up in there with windows closed and no fresh air. Lucy exhales.

Girl and dog walk around the block, and Lucy embraces her new surroundings. It's hard not to compare Atlanta with Miami Beach. She vaguely remembers being told by one of her friends that the very best parts of Miami were better in Atlanta, and the very worst parts were worse in Miami. She didn't see the distinction. Miami had beaches and palm trees; Atlanta was a five to six hour drive to any sand. Maybe it was Los Angeles her friend was talking about. She couldn't remember.

The sound of her cell phone ringing shuffles away the past. Fumbling in her back pocket, Lucy retrieves the phone and reads the words *Natalie McFadden* across the screen. Natalie's persistence feels like a hailstorm. The girl is relentless. She has called every day since their departure and during the weeks before the imminent move. Once Lucy's friend and confidante—that changed when trust was broken and alliances torn in two. Lucy is not ready to answer the call. It makes her feel sorry for the friend who is trying so hard. She wishes someone would tell her to stop, to leave it alone.

The friendship is over. It's that simple.

Natalie had been in love with Nathan Brady since they were five. In her mind it was always Nate and Nat, Nat and Nate, or some derivation of the two. She wasn't able to see his lack of interest. "We're going to get married," she'd say, naive and dreamy. What struck the group of friends was Natalie's mélange of denial and overzealous hopefulness. Her faith was what impressed Lucy the most, even after everything was destroyed in their once idyllic Atlanta community. All the misguided fantasies fell by the wayside when their tight-knit group of friends, and their loyalties, were tested.

The call goes to voicemail, and Lucy knows that Natalie is leaving the same message that she left thirty-five times before. "Lucy, please call me. We need to talk. I was wrong. I'm sorry. I miss you. I'm sorry I didn't believe you. I'm so, so sorry. Please forgive me. Please, can we talk?"

Lucy can recite the message verbatim, including the singular sound of Natalie's nasally voice. And sometimes she did. While drifting off to bed at night, when the darkness engulfed her, she echoed Natalie's pleas.

It's not that Lucy couldn't forgive Natalie. They had all been through such sadness; she had forgiven her long before her finger first pressed ignore on the string of phone calls. The first was surprising; the second, sad; the third through the tenth came at a very hectic, complex time; the twenty or so after that boiled down to Lucy's defiance. She did not want to speak with her. She knew she would eventually have no choice but to answer. She would eventually have to tell Natalie the words she needed to convey. The friendship was over, and for no other reason than this: that part of her life was over.

George pulls hard on Lucy, as though he knows where her thoughts have gone. They have circled the neighborhood and are approaching the shiny, cherry chariot. George lets out a yelp and starts chasing something on his tail. The circular motion has Lucy tangled in his leash, her legs lifting up and stomping down in resistance. She tries *heel, stay, stop,* and *sit* to no avail. George is twirling her until she is dizzy with embarrassment.

"Really, George? Now? You pick *now* to mess with me?"

The extra pull on his lead doesn't help. The tight grip further entangles her and forbids her from escaping. She knows her fair skin is tinged with red. She can feel the humiliation creeping up her back, behind her neck, and splotching her face. *Great, just great,* she thinks. *Levon and fancy face get to see me lasso myself with my own leash.*

chapter 15

A question often asked of the residents of Florida and other tropical climates is "Which would you prefer, a hurricane or a tornado?" For the residents of California, a variation on the theme is "...an earthquake or a hurricane?" Having lived in Miami all of his young life and accustomed to unpredictable, inclement weather, Levon had thought about his response countless times. Indeed, Hurricane Andrew did slam into southeastern Dade County packing a punch that transformed neighborhoods into piles of haphazardly strewn matchsticks. But even the loss of electricity, flooding, and irreparable damage to his home does not dissuade Levon from his answer.

His answer was always unequivocal: a hurricane is much easier to deal with than an earthquake or tornado.

The key is preparation.

Levon did not like surprises of any kind. As often as he had watched renowned meteorologist Max Mayfield at the hurricane center assert his projected storm paths, Levon had defended his stance to anyone who would listen to his stories ripped from the news: "See that, those people in Oklahoma had no time to prepare for a tornado. And look at that cone," he continued, referring to the colorful projected path splashed across television screens indicating a looming storm in the Caribbean. "We've got *time* to prepare."

With mathematical precision, meteorologists and hurricane specialists (seasoned, yet dimwitted veterans who fly jets into ferocious storms) tracked the daily coordinates and barometric changes that resulted in the shift over several days from a "watch" to a "warning." During such periods of hurricane activity, everyone in the community became mesmerized by the periodic updates of the National Hurricane Center and its cone projections.

David would take a swipe at Levon's logic. "I'm definitely not coming back to Miami after I finish college. Remember that storm," he said, referencing Hurricane Wilma on her pilgrimage toward Miami a few years back. "And look at us, we're the schmucks sitting here watching this thing come at us. The rest of the country must think we're morons living here, a peninsula waiting to be swallowed."

Levon would argue, vehemently defending his view. "But we can go to the store. We can stock up on supplies, hunker down. Prepare." These were the words he stole from Jeff Weinsier on Channel 10 as he reported live from an area that was expecting a direct hit. "The people in the Midwest get sideswiped unexpectedly by a raging wind funnel." The threat of earthquakes caused Levon paralyzing fear—that you could be shaken from sleep while your home slips down a cliff into the ocean.

Levon liked to be prepared. Even if a hurricane hit and flooded communities, uprooted homes, and devastated land for miles, *they were geared up!* He clung to the notion that they had done the best they could, and the rest was up to fate. The alternative, to be caught off guard, was just too scary. And like a tornado, when Rebecca Blake parked her shiny red Volkswagen bug in Levon's driveway that afternoon and confessed to Levon that she was pregnant with his dead brother's child, Levon was anything but prepared.

"It's impossible," Levon professes. He is having trouble breathing. Her words hit him hard in the stomach, knocking the wind out of him.

"I was there, Levon. It's possible."

She shifts uncomfortably in her seat.

"Why are you telling me this now?" he asks. "Why didn't you tell me the other day?"

Levon can't understand how he had lived in a house with his brother, shared meals with him, a bathroom, and had not known he was about to become a father?

"I don't believe it," Levon repeats, unable to accept the preposterous probability. Wilma had trekked through Miami; La Gorce was flooded and school was closed, but at least, they had been ready. How could he have not seen the change in David?

Rebecca is wearing jeans and a long-sleeved black Lacoste sweater. The smitten alligator is eyeballing him, resting on her breast in pure preppy bliss.

"He really didn't tell you? After the funeral, at your house, you looked at me like you knew, like you understood…"

Levon remembered the look, but she had it all backward. It was she who looked at him that afternoon; it was she who hinted to Levon that there was more to the story. Tragedy blurs details. Recovering from the accident was a means of survival. The details were a convergence of collateral damage.

"Where were you that night?" he asks Rebecca. "Why didn't you drive him home?"

She is picking at her cuticle with persistent might. "We'd had a fight. We were trying to figure out our options. He was upset, so upset."

The picking persists, and Levon sees blood form around her nail and Rebecca's tongue come down on the crimson liquid.

"I wanted an abortion," she whispers. "Quick and quiet. David did, too, but he struggled with it. I told him I wasn't ready to be a mom. I told him I was going to go through with it."

"How do you know for sure?" he asks, in need of facts, cones, barometric pressure.

Rebecca leans across the seat and finds her purse on the floor by Levon's sneakered feet. Reaching into the oversized leather bag, she pulls out a black-and-white photo with a fuzzy mess in the center.

"My appointment is tomorrow."

"Becks…," Levon begins, and his fingers reach for her hand, forcing the picture to fall through the crack between the seats. She wriggles away from him, cowering in her seat like his little sister. David's baby is growing in her stomach that very second. He has to stop himself from reaching across the seat and touching her belly.

"My parents dropped me off late to the party. At first, I thought David wasn't there yet, so I hung out with the girls, and after about an hour, I walked outside to the pool area and saw him sitting on a lounge chair next to Shelly Kaligeris. They were pretty close to each other. It looked all wrong, and I knew something was going on." Here, she stops and takes a deep, wistful breath.

"David loved you. Everybody knew that."

"Have you seen Shelly Kaligeris?" she declares. "She has humongous boobs…"

"And a face to protect them. David would never…"

"I'm not finished," she says. "There's more."

Levon sees Lucy Bell sauntering down the sidewalk toward her house and feels the immediate pull in her direction. Never in his life had he been more torn; he feels like racing out of the car, away from Rebecca's confessions, and bolting toward Lucy and her jocular steps.

"She's pretty," Rebecca says, following the path of Levon's eyes. Levon knows that shortly Lucy will be walking George, and she will find them there. "I'm glad you found a friend, someone you can talk to."

It's not lost on him that Rebecca doesn't consider him a possible suitor for the hot girl who lives next door.

"We're friends, too, aren't we?" he asks. It is a question that comes out pathetic and stupid. She is fiddling with her hair, taking turns holding it up behind her head and patting it down flat with her fingers.

"I guess I never saw it that way, though you're right. I suppose we're friends."

The significance of this admission has Levon calculating his popularity. He lost his big brother, his only friend, and he's gained two new ones instead. A heavy price to pay for a couple of companions.

"You don't have to admit it to anyone," Levon jokes.

"I won't," she says. "And you can't tell anyone about the baby."

Levon must have appeared deflated and bruised, because Rebecca leaned toward him and shined her famous smile. "I was kidding, Levon. Don't take everything so literally—except the part about keeping your mouth shut about this. That you can't repeat."

Levon gave her his word, and Rebecca continued to tell more of the story: A fight ensued by the pool. Shelly mocked David for casting her aside when Rebecca showed up, something about "little boys being henpecked," and she walked away in a huff. Rebecca wasn't going to let Shelly off that easy and grabbed her arm, accused her of being a slut. Shelly Kaligeris was unfazed by Rebecca Blake. She was hell-bent on enjoying high school, and if it meant dabbling in drugs and other girls' boyfriends, she didn't really care, and laughing at Rebecca she said, "The reason you didn't see David when you got to the party was because he was with me, and let's just say, I was taking care of him in ways you never could."

"He was confused," Levon interrupts, allowing her no time to summon the images that must have bombarded her brain and turned a four-year relationship into nothing more than a bad episode of *The Hills*. There's no way he touched Shelly Kaligeris."

"I keep telling myself that, Levon, but I can't shake it. The thought of him with her makes me want to throw up, and it's not morning sickness."

Outside the car and down the street, George is chasing his tail, which has Lucy tangled in the green leash. He wants to help her, but Rebecca needs him more. He focuses on Lucy's hair blowing in the breeze and the way she raises her legs, one at a time, to try to untangle the cord from her ankles. Her mouth is opening and closing and Levon can't hear any sounds, though he's sure she's having fun twirling in circles while she's telling George off at the same time.

Beside him sits a girl who is speaking to him from the heart, though Levon can't imagine what's going on inside her. He knows what it's like to endure the quiet suffering of keeping a secret that large. He hears her, he empathizes with her, and still he does not trust what she is saying. It is almost as if she is talking about somebody else, a stranger, not David.

"We were so careful," she says. "We were always open and honest with each other. When I told him the test came back positive, he freaked. He wasn't the same after that. Didn't you see him change?"

The thought makes Levon sick to his stomach. Troubled families with botched histories spawned stories like this. Not the Kellers and his deeply principled mother.

As if sensing where his mind has drifted she says, "My parents are going to tell your parents."

Levon is thinking about how brave she is and how everything is now changed. "He should've never gotten in the car," she said. "He should've stayed with me, and we could've worked it out."

Levon sits upright, struck by the dual meaning of what she is saying.

He asks, "Did you see David get into the car with me?"

"What does it matter?" she answers, looking away sullen and apologetic. "When we were outside by the pool, I slapped him across the face and told him I hated him. It was the last thing I ever said to him."

Levon feels as though the same hand has smacked him across the cheek. He is struck by the bitter sadness of their goodbye, while his mind hones in on something else. His heart is thumping wildly in his shirt.

She is saying, "I have to live with that for the rest of my life."

More tears. A baby. A pregnancy. A car door opening.

Levon's volatile mind is racing.

"No," she cries, "I didn't see him get into the car. I never saw him again. That slap was the last I saw of him, the last thing I gave him."

chapter 16

The phone call from Rebecca's mother comes the next day. Levon sees the numbers on the caller ID. There is no way he can save his mother from the impact the conversation will have. So much for burying secrets.

Edward Blake the name reads across the tiny screen.

The house is quiet other than the penetrating ring. His father and Chloe have all but abandoned him for hamburgers at The Charcuterie, and Sid and Lyd were meeting friends for lunch at the Bal Harbour shops, so he and the mad woman upstairs were left to contend with the matter of the phone. Levon shakes his head, projecting the seismic tremors that are about to result from their telephone call. Scurrying up the stairs, taking two at a time, Levon wants his mother to pick up the call before it's sent to voicemail. Maybe they aren't calling about the baby but are checking to see how the family's holding up. They had formed a close friendship over the years through the kids, so it wouldn't be unexpected for them to phone. Levon, though, knows the truth.

One ring. Two rings. Three rings.

If it goes to five, the call is lost. The saccharine-laced recording of his long ago cheery mother would trickle through the phone line, masking a home gone sour.

Without knocking, Levon pushes open the master bedroom

door. The black envelopes him, and he gasps from the cold, putrid air. Four rings. His mother, startled, wraps the covers around her and sits up in the bed.

Hurling himself across the room, Levon lunges for the receiver. "Hello," he says. "Uh, hi, Mrs. Blake." The words are hurried and nervous. Levon pauses before answering, "I'm fine."

"Tell her I'm sleeping," Madeline Keller grunts, lying back down and covering her face with layers of down bedding. Levon is holding the phone in his right hand while his left draws the curtains and opens the window next to the bed. The light hurts his eyes, though the fresh air feels good.

"Shut it," she mutters.

"Yes, she's right here," Levon chants into the phone with more clarity than before. "Let me get her for you."

With that, his mother swipes at him to get out of her room. Her skin feels cool on his arm like vampire flesh. Her frail body can barely squeeze out a substantial shove, and she retreats, glaring at Levon with bloodshot eyes flanked by dark black circles. If Levon didn't know better, he would have thought she had been punched.

The enemy is in Levon's hand, and he is thrusting it at his mother. She is insistent that he help her—to make up some excuse—and Levon is as equally persistent. "Take it," he demands. "You *need* to take it."

This volition in her normally docile son stirs something frightful and foreboding in Madeline. She grabs the phone with such violence that one of the fingernails she hasn't gnawed off stabs at Levon's skin. When her words find their way out of her throat, they are hoarse and gravelly from sleep, nothing like Lucy's conviction that one should always answer the phone with a smile in their throat.

"Hello," she says.

It is not until Levon backs through the doorway and leans against the wall outside her room that he can catch his breath. He realizes that he had been holding it in. The exhale accompanies a quivering that shakes his entire body. His fingers are tingling, a sensation he is unsure if he is imagining. The breaths come deeper and deeper. He hopes he is not having a heart attack.

Concentrate, concentrate, he keeps telling himself. He is determined to hear their dialogue. He stands transfixed outside the door, waiting for the script to begin: the *No,* the *how could you?* the slam when she throws the phone across the room, and it smashes against the wall.

"What can I say?…Yes, I know…"

Levon comes up with variations of Mrs. Blake's part in the dialogue, which elicit his mother's meager responses.

"Now's really not a good time, Marcy."

Pause.

"What do you mean?" his mother asks, her tone changing, the pitch abruptly higher. Levon thinks his heart might jump right out of his chest. The thumping sounds are interfering with his hearing, and the rush of adrenaline is sending swells of sweat down his cheeks and into his armpits. He hopes he remembered deodorant.

"That can't be," she says. "It's not possible." And now she is crying. Her words are jumbled up in her sobs. Deciphering the pain from the confusion is a daunting task. The one sound that is crystal clear is her desperation.

"There have to be other options…She doesn't have to do that…We can take him…"

Levon hears the cries rise and fall. They reach a crescendo until the last coherent sentence Levon can discern is, "Please don't do this. Please…," which concludes with the crashing sound of the phone, the anticipated dissolution to their exchange, thundering through the air.

A fragile silence floats through the doorway. He prepares himself for the storm surge, the aftermath. *How much can one person take?* he asks himself. It is the question that circles Levon while he waits in the hallway. Around him, familiar family photos dot the walls. Their watchful eyes stare him down. Chloe's big brown eyes are hypnotic; David's eyes are teasing. The pictures had changed in the recent months. Or, perhaps, it is his memory of them. Levon's backside is against the wall, and he's counting the seconds until she finds him cowering in fear. Prayer has typically never worked for him, yet he clenches his eyes and the numbers fall from his mouth like frantic pleas. Her movement is slight, though he can hear it sneaking up on him. Whether it is a scolding or an inquisition, he is prepared.

She is in a trance when she walks through her door. This is what Levon observes: her hair is unkempt; her dark eyes are bloodshot and swollen; the thick, white chenille bathrobe swallows her up; her words are sharp as a blade.

"You knew about this?"

They are the same height. Where Levon dwarfs his mother in sheer heft, she makes up for in robust personality. She gets right in his face and starts shrieking.

"You knew about this, and you didn't tell us?" Then, she threw out impossible questions with impossible answers, like what did *they* do wrong as parents.

"I only found out yesterday."

"And you kept it from us?"

Levon lowers his head.

He wonders if she notices David peering over his shoulder, encased in velvet and glass.

He wonders when everything went so wrong.

He wonders if his mother would suffocate if he sits on her.

Levon notes that even while she struggles with unthinkable sorrow, what personifies her most is her all-encompassing rage. It's woven into her frazzled hair, tucked deep inside the folds of her eyes, and is lurking in her crossed arms that shade her chest.

"We should have been told," she says flatly, worn out from her tirade. "There were things we could've done."

"You'd been through enough."

"Does your father know?"

"If he knows, it's not from me."

Nowhere is there acknowledgment of their precious son's mistake. He and David had been warned about girls and rubbers and pregnancy. He was ten when his mother gave him entry into the secret world that David had already inhabited, when she whipped out *How Babies Were Made,* the purple and blue book decorated in cutouts of naked boys and girls covering their privates with their hands. He was heading off to summer camp where it was widely known that sex education was *taught* by teenagers. David was twelve and giggling through the evolutionary explanation that began with illustrations of chickens and dogs humping and concluded with humans having intercourse. The book was entirely outdated, but his mother had learned about sex from the illustrated couplings, and, therefore, it was good enough for her kids.

They had come a long way from that afternoon when Levon pulled his brother aside with questions. "No, bro, you don't jump on a girl's back like a piggyback ride."

Levon is snapped back to the present by the door slamming downstairs. Levon's mom pulls her bathrobe tighter as she heads for the stairs.

"I'm not through with you." She points at Levon. "Craig, we need to talk," she barks.

Levon fears for all of their lives. What if she has really gone crazy? He didn't want to end up as the subject of a *Dateline* special where the seemingly perfect family is shattered by an act of violence. The shiver down his spine is an entirely different sensation than the pulsing traveling down his fingers. Though the confrontation is over, Levon's breathing remains fraught and hurried. He can't seem to catch it. All his parents need is for him to drop dead on the wooden floor outside their room. His fall would shake the pictures from the wall, and the one of David holding a football in one hand and Chloe in another would come sliding down, hitting Levon atop his head, the frame shattering into pieces.

Yet, the image dissipates into something else entirely. He doubts they will care if he dies. She would hear the loud thud of his tubby limbs, and she would run upstairs, tripping over his lifeless body, only to find the shattered glass and David's luminous face staring up at her. Then, she would tuck it under her arm and cry for the frame of her favorite photo.

"Mommy's angry," Chloe sighs when she reaches the top of the stairs and finds Levon panting against the wall.

"Go to your room," he tells her, shielding her from what is to come. When he is sure the door is closed and Chloe is lost in Hannah Montana, he sits at the top of the stairs and listens to the battle waging downstairs.

"Rebecca is pregnant. At least, for a couple more hours."

"What are you saying?"

"Don't act like you didn't know."

"I have no idea what you're talking about."

Levon can't see his father's reaction, but he can taste his lack of knowledge. "Why are you hysterical?

His mother enjoys moments like this. Being in the know gives her unprecedented power. "You don't get it," she says.

Levon crosses his arms and his head finds refuge on his forearms. When he closes his eyes, he is able to see his mother's smirking face. It is full of hostility and distrust.

"Get what?"

She draws out each syllable, careful to annunciate the words as one would for someone hard of hearing. "Rebecca is pregnant."

"Oh," he says. Then, "Oh, shit."

He repeats it again.

Levon is proud of his father for finally figuring it out.

"They want her to have an abortion! An *abortion*!"

"Calm down," he tells her. "What happened?"

"What the hell do you think happened?"

"I thought they were careful," his father says.

Madeline's tone is cruel. "If they were careful, she wouldn't be pregnant. If they were careful, God damn it, what does that even mean?" Her sentences are spilling into one another. Where one ends, another has already begun. She sounds manic. "And I can't even get angry at them for not being careful because I'm fucking *happy* she's pregnant."

"Then why the hell do you sound so pissed?"

"They're getting rid of it. Today. Right now."

A helicopter flies overhead and Levon can't make out the next couple of exchanges. Insults and accusations are muffled by the swirling blades, which sound conspicuously like whimpers.

"This baby is all I have left of him. If they get rid of it, they're getting rid of David."

Levon pokes out his head from behind the banister and sees his parents facing off in the kitchen. His mother's arms are flailing in the air, punching at Craig, while her eyes remain fixed in terror. Tears stream down her cheeks. He's trying to calm her, but there is too much agony for his trembling hands to make a difference. "Don't touch me," she shouts in his face. At this, Craig Keller backs away from the woman he no longer knows.

When the hyperventilating ends, she retreats to the other side of the room with her back to her husband. He says, "We can't ask her to have this baby, Mad. It's not fair to her."

"I'll take the baby," she fights back. "I'll raise it myself. I'll love that baby. You know I'll love that baby."

"David wouldn't want it this way."

The mention of his name settles her down before the next round of tears.

"Maybe I should call Edward."

Madeline Keller shakes her head. "No. It won't change anything."

"I'll call if you want me to," he says, pressing on. "I'll get Rick Mann on the phone. He's the best. We must have some rights."

"We lost those rights the day we buried our son. We lost everything. Really, what's left? There's nothing left. This baby is the last part of David, the last link. And I can't have that either. He's slipping away. How many times do I have to lose him?"

157

Levon hears his father's footsteps moving toward her. Heck, he even feels like running to her and throwing his arms around her.

"I said don't touch me. Please, don't touch me."

"Mad…"

"And don't call me that…Don't touch me and don't call me that."

"I'm sorry," comes out of his foolish mouth. The words crack and split, splintered with humility. There are too many wrongs to right.

Sadness washes over Levon, inhibiting his ability to stand up. He wants to find his journal so he can write the poem he is humming in his brain:

Soil, when saturated in water, grows beautiful, tall flowers.
My human rain, my tears—
I will not sprout powerful leaves or petals.
I am a weed with no direction or hope.

Words have the ability to move him physically through his bedroom door. His journal is not where it should be. He wants to fine-tune the poem. He's checked the desk drawer, in his backpack, and it's not anywhere. His heart booms at an alarming speed. A door slams downstairs, and Levon figures his father has taken off. He is searching under his bed, inside drawers, and behind his dresser. He asks himself where he might have inadvertently left it.

The door to his room comes ajar and in walks Lucy.

She is holding the spiral notebook in her hands.

"Looking for this?"

Levon is speechless; fear has numbed his arms and legs.

He moves toward her and grabs the binder from her hands.

"I didn't read it," she says, "although it was tempting."

Levon is searching the pages for evidence that her nosiness has made her a thief of the very worst kind.

"If you don't want anyone to read it, you shouldn't leave it in plain sight."

"I never leave it in plain sight."

"I went to get a snack out of your pantry, and it was resting on top of the granola bars."

"You just walk in my house and go through our pantry?"

"Your dad let me in. Actually, he flew past me. I think he let me in."

Levon is having a bad day. It feels like someone has taken pliers to his forehead and is squeezing. He rubs at his temples with his free hand.

"Sometimes it can be cathartic to talk, Levon."

He knows she can't understand why he needs to be so protective of his thoughts. He implores her to leave it alone.

"I think you're hiding something."

"What gives you that idea?"

"Why were you driving that night, Levon?"

He drops the notebook on his bed and stands embattled before Lucy. She has passed through his room and stands before him. She shows no signs of backing down. Her glasses rest on the top of her head.

"What are you *talking* about?" he asks, his hands running wildly through his hair.

"You, Mr. Play-by-the-Rules, the boy who lives a repressed life suddenly acts on impulse? There's something not right about what happened that night. You know it, and I know it. That's why you treat that notebook like it's the Hope Diamond. Come on, Levon. It's me. You can tell me anything."

Levon is shaking his head from side to side. Tears are starting to form around his eyes. "I wish I didn't have to say no to you."

"Then don't," she says, her crystal green eyes stripping his defiance from within.

"I can't. Trust me when I tell you that I can't. It's not for my sake. It's for him. It's always been about him."

"No, Levon," she insists, "that's bullcrap. This is about you."

"It won't change anything. He's gone, and everything is the way it's supposed to be."

"With the evil android cursing you, and the remainder of your family falling apart? This isn't the way it's supposed to be."

"I have to protect my brother."

"Who's protecting you?" she asks.

chapter 17

Levon is draped across the sectional sofa in their living room, sipping ginger ale and watching Ellen DeGeneres. Levon loves Ellen. If there is anyone who can help him escape his life and the darting pain in his stomach, it is Ellen's irreverent humor and realistic depiction of modern American culture.

The house is quiet. His grandparents have returned to New York. His mother is sleeping upstairs, something she is doing even more often since the call from the Blakes. The phone rings; his father's not making it home in time for dinner. This, too, has become a norm for their household. Levon slams the phone down on the table with a bang.

Levon remembers a time when family dinners at six o'clock were a requirement, not an option. The family would discuss their day; it was a time for camaraderie and recaps. Levon's mom would cook some tempting recipe she'd gotten off the Internet or from one of her friends, and they would test out new meals like butternut-apple soup and rosemary rigatoni. These days, his mother slept through the dinner hour, and if Levon was unable to scrounge up some leftover take-out or a peanut butter and jelly sandwich, he would simply go to bed hungry.

Lucy showed up one night with a bowl of spaghetti bolognese. Carol Bell wanted to be sure he was eating, confirming to Levon that the whole world knew his family was in need of help. Once it would have pained his mother to have the Kellers' open wound on display—but now there was no way to hide the gash; it was too big.

Ellen is introducing one of his favorite guests, Steve Spangler. Levon settles back on the cushions hoping the science guy will distract him from the headache that is beginning to hammer away at his temples. He is watching with mild interest as Steve conducts electricity using Ellen's arm as a conduit, but not until Steve mentions the word "cornstarch" does Levon perk up. Curious, Levon raises the remote and increases the volume. He presses the TiVo button and rewinds the last few seconds.

"Water and cornstarch...soupy consistency...put your hand in it...you can punch it, trapping the water between the fragments of starch, and, voila, the cornstarch turns into a solid..."

Sitting upright on the edge of the sofa, Levon pays careful attention to the monitor. Cornstarch, Chloe's life-saving mixture, is the climax to Steve Spangler's electrifying segment. Ellen is using her fist to punch at a bowl of cornstarch that has been mixed with water. Spangler explains to the audience how water changes the substance into an unusually dense material that can resist Ellen's punches. Conversely, when Ellen sweeps her fingers through the substance, it slips through them. And if that wasn't enough to satisfy Ellen's already fascinated audience, from behind the curtains emerges a giant tub holding *two thousand* boxes of cornstarch mixed in water and the assurance that one lucky member from the studio audience is going to walk across the cornstarch mixture without sinking.

Levon admits the experiment has piqued his interest, and although he's openly skeptical—body weight is far different from a punch—he can't shake the idea that those two thousand boxes could treat lots of sick GSD kids.

The ache that was clamoring away at Levon's forehead minutes ago is now the fuel igniting his thought processes. Ideas are bouncing around his brain at a ridiculous speed. He thinks he's onto something, but has to slow himself down in order to put together a plan.

The producers have chosen a young, bubbly woman from their studio audience to complete the imminent feat. She springs onto the stage and is instructed to remove her shoes. Levon is watching intently, admiring how the woman traipses over to Ellen as though they are old friends who are sharing coffee in Ellen's private living room and not being watched by gazillions of viewers. If he were in the studio audience, he would be the person praying he didn't get picked. Levon hates to be the center of any type of attention. So why was he hatching a plan that would bring attention to himself and to his sister's disease?

"Levon?" It is his mother.

Looking up from the television, he sees the ghost of her former self. She is dressed—out of the bathrobe that had become her fashion staple—and clad in black slacks and a black silk blouse. Her hair falls down the sides of her face, tousled and matted from sleep. She's makeup free, and there are splotches covering her pale cheeks, which used to glow naturally from the sun. Flesh and bones give the illusion that he's looking at a skeleton. Where her pearl necklace once rested daintily around her neck, the oversized balls stampede across her clavicle. Her mouth is moving, though Levon can't make out the words. In one rapid click of the remote, he mutes Ellen as she cheers the woman across the tub of cornstarch.

She gazes at her watch. "I'm going to temple."

This perplexes Levon.

"I can't sit here anymore…The rabbi said…"

She is unable to finish as a tumult of tears pool in her eyes. She paces the floor in front of him and hides her face in shame. He has never seen his mother so frail and defenseless. Her steely arrogance has always signified strength to him, and this dismal, fragile apparition makes Levon very afraid.

"Do you ever feel him around you?" she asks in a whisper. "They said I would feel him. I haven't felt him."

He didn't have to ask who she was talking about. Maybe he should run to her. Maybe he should offer her his shoulder as a symbol of the olive branch. The urge is familiar, yet her rejection has worn him out. His brain is telling him to get up, but the synapse responsible for transmitting signals to his arms and legs has disconnected—grown weary—and his body fails him.

"Do you remember when he went to sleep away camp that only summer?"

Levon nodded.

"Remember the airport? He was so quiet. I knew he didn't want to go. Do you remember what he said?"

Levon was eight at the time—David ten—and he remembered exactly what his brother said. They were about to step out of the airport's automatic sliding doors when his brother's whimpering voice called out from behind. Levon was a spectator in their exchange that afternoon, though the memory struck him with a throbbing force. His mother sunk down to comfort David who was hyperventilating. The shouts of his counselors flew across the airport. David was holding onto his mother's arms with both hands. When he finally pushed back, he grabbed hold of her eyes. "I'm going to miss you so much," he said.

"I'm going to miss you, too."

Levon refuses to return to that place. Missing someone who was leaving for a few weeks was entirely different than leaving you forever.

"Do you want me to call Dad?"

She is trembling, her shoulders rising up and down. "No, no."

"Is there something I can do?" he asks, tentatively, slowly opening a door, unsure if he can step through. When she shakes her head instead of shouting at him and ranting that he's already done enough, Levon thinks his legs might lift him up, but they are heavy and have no interest in walking.

Levon knows it's sometime between five and six in the evening, and he wonders why his mother is going to temple without his father. The only time they ever stepped foot in synagogue was for Rosh Hashanah and Yom Kippur. Was she suddenly becoming religious in the wake of David's death?

"Dad's not coming home for dinner," Levon says, his voice trailing. "What about Chloe?"

"She's coming with me…" at which Levon turns his head in the direction of the tapping sounds of Chloe's feet heading down the stairs. This was clearly an outing to which he was not invited.

His sister appears in the doorway wearing a white dress with red ribbons and sandals that are crying out to be replaced. Her toes hang over the front, and they are so marred and scuffed that it is hard to identify their natural color.

"Shabbat Shalom, Levon," Chloe smiles up at him, holding a prayer book under her arm that he has not seen since his Bar Mitzvah. *Had they all completely lost their minds,* he wonders? Or is he the culprit, the villain who is in most need of an appointment with God? The thought preys on Levon—how he might pray and repent and wipe the slate clean—though something tells him his mother's forgiveness will not come easily, nor should it. Chloe is unclear on why he isn't joining them and has the good sense not to ask. Besides, he is beginning to look forward to having the house to himself.

"Come on, Chloe," his mother says, reaching for her daughter. The tears have all but vanished. Her composure is back. No one considers how he might amuse himself in their absence. Levon is certain that if he doesn't eat, if he runs away, no one will care.

friday, november 2, 2007, 11:33 p.m.

They return from temple with no idea of what I've done while they've been away. They leave, they return.

Lucy let herself in after she heard their car pull out of the driveway. I could tell the veil of mystery shrouding my time spent with Rebecca bothered her as she skirted around the subject, asking and not quite prying. I was writing a short story about a boy who targets Ellen DeGeneres to save his sick sister. She grabbed the spiral notebook from my hands and read the pages.

"This is brilliant," she told me, her face beaming with Lucy's famous smile. And I thought she was referring to the idea—how the lone boy took on a high-powered television celebrity and got her to support his orphaned cause—but she was remarking on my writing, gushing about how talented I am.

"Really, Levon," she said, "you have a gift."

I copied down what she said, verbatim, quotes and all, savoring the highest praise anyone has ever paid me. By inscribing it onto paper, I can savor it time and time again, and never forget how nice it feels to be good at something.

Lucy and I are nothing alike. She's adventurous and wild, while I am timid and afraid. She's quirky. Artistic. Outspoken. Daring. Those are the words I'd use to describe her. She's the kind of girl that takes out her contact lenses over a sink of running water. She's the kind of girl who puts the earphones from her iPod in the reverse ears. I am overly detailed and careful, comfortable with following directions. I wouldn't be caught dead with the L headphone in my right ear.

After she found me crumpled in a ball, writing pages that I refused to share, she screamed at the top of her lungs how I needed to go out and experience life instead of waiting for life to happen to me. I held my hand up to her face, the universal sign for stop, so there was no mistaking my stance. No one had experienced life as I had. No one.

Grabbing me by the leg, she dragged me off the couch until my bottom slammed hard across the floor.

"What's that for?"

"Get up," she yelled. "We're getting out of here."

I'm writing this down because I'm finding most of it hard to believe. If I pen every detail, maybe what happened will seem more real, less like somebody else's life.

I grabbed a jacket, locked up the house, and followed Lucy to her mother's car.

"Get in," she said.

"You don't have a license," I said.

"Get in," she repeated again. "They won't be home for hours."

Don't ask me where my common sense had gone. I tried, but I couldn't seem to find it. Not with her breathing so close.

She drove north on Collins Avenue passing the Eighty-fifth Street beach, through Bal Harbour, and over the Haulover Bridge. She's only been in Miami a couple of weeks, and she already knew to take it slow through the stately stream of high-rises leading to the bridge—the strip is notorious for lurking cops and their speed traps.

It was a few minutes past six o'clock, and the air was dark and balmy. I had no idea where she was taking me, until she turned toward the sign, Haulover Beach.

"It's a nude beach," I said.

"Are you serious?" she replied in mock surprise.

She parked the car in the vacant lot and said, "Levon, try to be brave. Even if you're just pretending to be. I swear, no one will be able to tell the difference. Rule #412."

I said, "I think the beach is closed; we're not supposed to be here."

Anyone who knows me knows that breaking the law is not my idea of fun. I am the one who actually puts the dime in the Brach's candy jar before digging into the bin of bulk candy. My only crime is how literally I take the word BULK, stuffing dollar bills into the canister and handfuls of candy into my pockets. Besides, I'd visited the police station way too many times already this year.

I panicked. I was afraid of drug dealers skulking in the bushes, waiting to kidnap us and do creepy things to our bodies.

Lucy ran off in front of me, and I had no choice but to follow.

The beach was noisy, waves thrashing against the shore, and I could make out her silhouette in the distance close to the water's edge.

"Haven't you seen Jaws*?" I hollered at her, the words caught in the cool air, echoing along the beach and missing her ears completely.*

She threw her bag down on the sand.

I tried to dissuade her. "I can't get my stitches wet."

She started to take off her clothes. "Come on, Levon, become one with the world, free yourself, free your spirit..."

I was about five yards away from her when her spirit—along with her shirt and jeans—went flying through the air, revealing a modest one-piece. She was off running into the crashing waves before the garments hit the ground.

I screamed for her to stop, but she didn't hear me. The waves were clamoring for her, brash and noisy, wrapping around her like a swirl of creamy frosting.

I could barely make out her shape amid the foamy spray, though I could hear her voice.

She was shouting at me to come in, citing prophetic,

philosophical phrases about living my life to the fullest and how fear is for the dead and the way to actually live is to let go of fear. Then it dawned on me that this might be the first and last time I get this close to a partially naked, hot girl. Was it worth getting mauled by a school of hungry sharks?

I struggled with this question. If I couldn't see the bottom of the ocean, I wanted no part of it. But when I slammed my eyes shut and imagined my future, what it might hold for me, I saw a big nothing. I surely didn't want that. I had been roused, awakened by a slither of gold frolicking in the water. Shark food or the golden ticket?

What the hell, I thought. It was dark and she wouldn't see the folds of skin around my middle or that my chest had no definition. So I stripped down to my boxers, heaped my clothes in a pile next to hers, and ran as fast as I could into the frigid water.

"Levon!"

The way she said my name, I could tell she was pleased. She was gorgeous in the light of the moon with drops of ocean and salt on her face. She was giggling and splashing me and humming the Jaws *theme. I was nervous and excited and thinking if I died at that moment, at least I was doing something adventurous.*

We stood facing each other.

"Levon, there's something I have to tell you."

She said it just like that. I couldn't believe it was actually going to happen to me! A hot girl was going to proclaim her love for me, and she was going to straddle me by the light of a Miami moon and I would finally have my first kiss. She was going to tell me that she didn't care about my extra pounds, that she had been attracted to me since the day we met, especially attracted to my mind, though she needed to take it slow; she cherished our friendship and wouldn't want to lose what we have.

But that's not what happened.

"Levon, I was raped."

I swear the ocean stopped breathing around us. The waves stilled; silence persisted. Shivering, I quietly wished for my clothes, for her clothes. I wanted to move away from her, to tell her to cover up. She raised her tattooed leg into the air, the one with the forgiveness tattoo. There isn't anything forgivable about that.

"We were in Atlanta," she said, bringing the leg down. And then she added, "Nothing's ever what it seems, Levon. There's so much more to a person than you think."

Thank God she didn't pin one of her meaningless numbers to that sentence. She turned her back to me and started walking to the shore. I would protect Lucy Bell from any threatening sea monster, I decided. I followed behind her. I watched her long, skinny legs and pretended she wasn't wearing a flimsy white piece of fabric. I tried not to concentrate on her butt and her legs as they led her toward the pile of clothes. When she bent down to get something out of her bag, I turned out of respect.

Had she looked my way when I walked toward her, I might have cowered in shame, but she did not. If that was her way of garnering me the same deference, I wasn't sure. I do know that I have found my first real friend, and the fantasy of Lucy that I have conjured up has been washed away by her stormy truths.

She didn't get dressed, instead, she laid out her clothes as a place for us to sit. She was so comfortable in her body, though I couldn't get my shirt and pants on fast enough.

I sat down next to her, and she smiled at me. Then she said this: "Levon, you are an amazing person. You, what's inside of you. You hide it under that big body of yours, but I see it."

Kids talked behind my back, whispering and joking about my body, but no one had ever come right out and flatly—and let's not mince words here—acknowledged that I am a tad overweight. When Lucy said what she did, I was hearing it for the very first time.

It's impossible to imagine Lucy as anything other than beautiful and bright, formed and fashioned by good genes and good luck. She was raped on a golf course in Atlanta in broad daylight by someone she liked and trusted. There was a group of them that hung out on the weekends, Lucy and her brother Ricky among them—though

Ricky was absent that day, the first and only time. They were drinking and horsing around, and one of the guys got so out of control that he followed Lucy into the bushes when she had to go to the bathroom, pushed her to the ground, pulled at her clothes, and laid on top of her.

The boy admitted to the crime, cooperated with the authorities, and made several honorable attempts to apologize to Lucy. He claimed he had no recollection of the incident. He had used cocaine for the first time and was out of his mind. Formally charged, his wealthy family had connections, so, after showing remorse, chalking it up to bad judgment, and a brief stint in rehab, he walked away with Lucy's pride, virginity, and a slap on the wrist.

Ricky was racked with grief for choosing that afternoon to be away. He wanted to kill the kid.

Their whole group dismantled, one by one, alliances and loyalties pitted against each other. But the boy, despite avoiding jail, was not free at all. Overcome with self-loathing and hopelessness, having become the community's pariah, he swallowed a bottle of his mother's Valium, went to sleep, and never woke up. There was so much blame going around. The lines between victim and villain were unclear. Confused, Lucy cut off all of her hair.

Then the Bells sold the house, packed up their belongings, and headed south.

Lucy told this story as if it were an ordinary day she was describing and not the one in which her soul was ripped into pieces. "That's why I chose forgiveness," she said with a sigh. For the record, I will never ever understand her forgiveness. Then she asked me about my secret.

Being around Lucy makes me want to confess to all kinds of unspeakable thoughts and tawdry secrets; one in particular, how I was falling in love with her.

But what if I told her a different secret?

What if I told it to everyone?

Would they be able to forgive me?

Would it help them heal or make things worse?

The rest of the night is blurry. I was teetering on the brink, pushing down my secrets so they couldn't escape. This wasn't a time for the focus to be on me. I wanted to be there for Lucy, to take care of her. She begged me to tell, but I was strong in my conviction and remained tight-lipped.

We walked off the beach toward her car. I wasn't ready to go home yet, so we took a drive to South Beach. Lucy parked in the garage, and we walked a few blocks to a tattoo parlor. Daring me to get a tattoo, I vacillated between getting a permanent versus temporary one. I wanted to be brave and daring like Lucy. I picked the Chinese symbol for courage. Lucy actually decided for me. It stung like hell, but the symbol already has me feeling different, stronger. It's on my ass, and no one will ever find it there. It hurts to sit, a small inconvenience I have to bear for the relief of knowing my mom will never see it.

It's hard for me to imagine Lucy's slender body harmed, violated. Her flaws and blemishes are no different from mine. I think we are all start out as beautiful, and then our pain and problems stain us. I saw Lucy tonight with new eyes. Lucy has forgiven the boy who wronged her. Even though he took something sacred from her, she has made her peace with the loss. It is her resilience and acceptance that inspire me to be a person who can right a wrong and survive chaos and turmoil.

We went to Jerry's Deli and ate matzo ball soup and potato latkes in honor of Shabbat. I thought about my mom and sister at temple and even though they were probably already home, I said a prayer for them, for all of us, a prayer that we would survive this. Lucy and I talked for hours and laughed and shared stories of our childhoods. Both of us had markers that divided the before from the after, the then from the now.

She told me I had beautiful eyes—honest eyes.

Was that her way of letting me know what was expected of me?

When I got home, the whole family was in the living room,

oblivious to where I had gone, to what I had done. Yes, I branded my bottom, but more importantly, I swam in the ocean after dark, and I rid myself of clothes that hid my burdensome body. I was revived. Although I am the same Levon who woke for school this morning, when my head hits the pillow in a matter of minutes, I know that nothing will ever be the same.

My mother smiled at me. Whether it was because she was happy to see me or for some other dubious reason, I can't be sure.

The rabbi offered her some writings he thought might be beneficial to her, to all of us, and this one I read over and over:

It Is Never Too Late
The last word has not yet been spoken
The last sentence has not yet been written,
The final verdict is not in.
It is never too late
To change my mind,
My direction,
To say no to the past,
And yes to the future,
To offer remorse,
To ask and give forgiveness

It is never too late
To start over again
To feel again
To love again
To hope again.

It is never too late
To overcome despair,
To turn sorrow into resolve
And pain into purpose.

It is never too late to alter my world,
Not by magical incantations
Or manipulations of the cards
Or deciphering the stars.

But by opening myself
To curative forces buried within,
To hidden energies
The powers in my interior self.

In sickness and in dying, it is never too late
Living, I teach,
Dying, I teach,
How I face pain and fear,
Others observe me, children, adults,
Students of life and death,
Learn from my bearing, my posture,
My philosophy.

—Rabbi Harold Schulweis
In God's Mirror: Reflections and Essays

Suddenly, in the midst of commotion and blame, everything is beginning to make sense. Tomorrow, I will begin again.

sunday, october 14, 2007
12:50 a.m.

The ambulance is shuffling though the nighttime air. The boys are positioned beside one another. The EMT, Louis, asks the one who is conscious if there's anywhere in particular that hurts. He looks over at his brother and asks, "Will he be okay?" He is panicking inside; his lips are sore and caked with blood. To speak is an arduous task.

The boy is alarmed because minutes before, in the wake of screeching brakes and flying debris, his brother was alert and talking. Did it matter who formed the words when together they had agreed on a plan?

Louis ignores his inquiry, which sends the boy into a spiraling frenzy. He has to talk to him. He has to figure out what they are supposed to do.

He calls out to his brother; the name—so familiar on his tongue—lingers, full of prayer and promise, though his brother doesn't answer. Instead of his brother's soothing voice, he hears the shattering signal from one of the emergency medical devices. The monitors emit loud beeps, haunting rhythms that echo the boy's wild, erratic heartbeat. He is sure he can't feel his fingers and toes. He is sure his arms and legs will fail him if he attempts to flail. He is numb, everywhere, yet, his entire body is wired to explode, and he can't stop it.

Sheila says something that she probably says every day. For the boy, though, they are the words that will set the stage for the unfolding of events that will forever alter his young life.

"We're losing him," she says.

"No," the boy shouts out. "He's my brother! You have to save him!"

The man and woman are working on the brother, pushing, pulling, breathing, coaxing him back to life. Lights are blinking, machines are buzzing—a symphony that will climax with dreadful silence and a flatline signifying one's worst fate. The silence stretches, first seconds, then minutes.

The boy is crying, "Please don't leave me."

It's too late. His brother is dead.

What had they done?

chapter 18

Lucy can barely sleep. The night exceeded her expectations in more ways than one. Noting the date, it was the first time she was able to get into a bathing suit and jump in the Atlantic Ocean since moving to Florida. Granted, it was a one piece and it was dark out, but she finally did it.

Although he doesn't know it, Levon has guided her through her disrobing. His own unwillingness to get undressed had eased her inhibition. It was a rite of passage they tackled together. Although, his passage was painstakingly slow.

He had asked her how she could strip into a bathing suit in a public beach after such an act of violence. One eavesdropping on their conversation might have thought he was insinuating, or suggesting, that she had asked for it. Lucy knew that Levon saw too much good in her to intimate that. It was an appropriate question, one her parents would have abhorred had they known what she had done.

Lucy can make out the shadows and light of their neighborhood coming through the skylights on the loft's ceiling. She is in her shabby chic bedroom, resting atop her white comforter and lilac sheets. Rising from bed, she descends the spiral stairs, one at a time, to get a closer view. A seat has been carved out beneath the window, and she hurls herself onto the soft cushion and rests her head against the pillows. It's her favorite spot in the room. This vantage point provides a clear view into Levon's world. Lucy knows he is busily writing every detail of their night together in his journal. He had all but admitted it to her on the car ride home when he kept mentioning how he was going to savor every detail of the night. She wondered how much of her story he would disclose.

Pulling back the sheer white curtains and unlocking the window, Lucy raises the wooden frame until it's fully ajar and inhales the Miami air. The screen keeps the mosquitoes and other insects out; Lucy rests her nose up against the miniscule wires. George, who has been resting peacefully on the cool floor, lets out a loud snore that startles him awake. He stands on all fours and finds his master in the windowbox. Climbing into the space beside her, he rests his head in her lap and falls back asleep.

The mesh screen, on close inspection, resembles a cage. She is most positive that the Keller family is living in a private cell, each of them experiencing his or her lone punishment. Levon escaped from his cell tonight. She hopes he would find a way not to return to it. His grief and loss will be forever, though his personal pain is self-imposed.

The air feels funny in her nostrils, and she backs away from the panel. The light is on in Levon's room, and she thinks about proposing a Morse code or an old-fashioned wire telephone to communicate from her window to his. She is reminded of her childhood in Atlanta; she doesn't understand why so many things are stirring up memories of Atlanta. Perhaps because she let Levon in; she shared her story and moved it south. Before, it lived and died in Georgia.

George is happily snoring, and Lucy is restless. She feels a burst of energy that usually results in her getting in downward dog position or breaking out into dance, but there is a steadiness to George's loud grunts that keep her rooted in her seat.

The listlessness agitates Lucy as she eyes the golf bag resting in the corner of her room. Levon had asked her how she had recovered so quickly. He said, "How can you be so forgiving, so normal?"

"Normal," she laughed. "Nobody's normal. We're all messed up. Some of us more than others."

Everyone had been suspicious of her ability to bounce back from such a heinous violation. In an era when therapists are the norm, Lucy chose to speak of the assault only with the female officer who questioned her the hours following. Barbara was also a victim. Their shared experiences bound them in horrid, yet hopeful ways. Barbara still called from time to time. Ricky and her father had never asked for details, which would be much too disturbing for the men in her family to bear. Her mother begged and pleaded with her to talk to a professional, but Lucy would have nothing to do with any stranger who claimed they could "fix" her.

Now she is compelled to wake George from his slobbery stupor. She carefully lifts his head and hopes he will return to his Scooby Doo dreams. She glides across the room and finds the envelope in the top drawer of her desk. Holding it, she heads back toward the window and scoots herself adjacent to George's damp nose. She kisses him on the soft patch between his ears, and for a short while, this quiets him.

Levon's light turns off, and their street falls into a similar slumber.

The envelope is worn and crumpled, and she thinks about reading its contents again. She hasn't touched it since moving. Perhaps she needs to read the words tonight. Her head begins to feel light and drowsy. Her earlier energy has faded and has been replaced with a quiescent calm. Holding the envelope has that effect on her. Its nearness comforts in ways no mental health practitioner ever could. She finds the throw that's tucked in the corner of the seat and looks out at Levon's window one last time. It leaves her feeling close to him. Her lids are heavy, and she snuggles around George, the envelope near to her heart.

Hours later, Lucy awakens covered in sweat, the blanket on the floor and George licking the wet from her cheeks. The dampness drips down her back, like the boy's fingers once did, and she sits up and swats the imaginary touch. Light coming through the open window causes her to blink, and she catches her flustered reflection in the mirror across the room. She should have known it would make an appearance last night.

How was it that she could go to sleep at peace, and wake up in disarray, haunted and broken? It has been weeks since the dream snuck into her room, beneath her sheets and swathed her in its ugliness.

It always played out the same:

The May afternoon was warm and humid.

The golf course was recently tended to.

The smell of fresh cut grass permeated the air.

Her group was there: Jill, Ava, Natalie—the girls—and Nate, Brett, and Eli—the boys. Ricky and Lucy brought the number to eight. Indeed, Ricky's absence had been noted. Without him, the group felt lopsided. They were lounging across the rocks that bordered the tiny brook adjacent to the ninth hole. They had chosen the shaded area a year earlier for its location and privacy. The guys were kicking around balls; the girls engaged in end-of-the-year high school chatter. Someone, Lucy would never remember who, had brought a case of beer, and they were sipping from the cans, relaxing, minding their own business, and discussing the school year drawing to a close.

Lucy never liked the taste of beer, though she drank it sometimes. While the others finished off several cans, she would slowly nurse the one. Her friends were good people, good students from good families. Undeniably, they drank and experimented with drugs like most kids do in high schools across America. But, they never touched the heavy stuff. Weed was as far as they went. Until that afternoon. That it was the first time was irrelevant once police and parents got involved.

Nate was one of the most beautiful boys in their class. He had a combination of chiseled features, welcoming eyes, and delicate cheeks that blushed easily. Lucy and Nate were good friends. Both of their last names began with B, so they were relegated to the same homeroom year after year. And besides being someone nice to look at, he could always make her laugh.

Nate liked to get high. It was he who brought the packet of cocaine to the course. That, she remembered. Already gifted in comedy, Nate was at his best and funniest when he was doped up.

Lucy was not drunk, nor did she ask for the assault. What began as fun and games turned wickedly fast into senseless and mad.

All she had to do was walk through the trees to the spot the girls had called the *pissing point*. Lucy remembers her hair that afternoon. It was long and lustrous, falling down her shoulders. It smelled like apple and felt like silk across her back as she made the fifty or so steps to the secluded spot behind the bushes. She would remember later how the silk turned into sticks and the scratches left on her back appeared more animal than earth.

"Lucy," a voice called from behind her. She could hear the others laughing about something in the distance.

"Nate?"

He was there beside her, tall and fit; his brown hair left long in the front and brushed over to the side. "What are you doing?"

What happened next plays in Lucy's mind like an old movie that someone has edited. The movie jumps from the two of them talking, Lucy thinking how cute Nate is, standing there in the trees— she's giggling at something he says—to her on the ground, and he's on top of her. His lips are on her cheeks, her mouth, her neck. Kissing Nate feels good at first. He's all hands and tongue. He grabs fistfuls of hair and tugs on it as though he can't get enough of her. And he couldn't. The strong smell of beer on his breath creeps up into her nose. Soon, the power of his kisses become less of a thrill and more of a fright. His fingers reach under her shirt and claw at her breasts. There is nothing sweet about the way his hands clamp down on her and wrestle her when she says to stop.

"No, Nate," she begs, "get off me." It is a half-cry, half-wail.

The eyes that are staring back at her are no longer those of the boy she grew up with. The beautiful blue is flecked with red; they are glassy and unfamiliar. His hand covers her mouth when she begins to scream. The other pulls at her shorts and rips at her underwear. Nate is a strong boy; his weight bearing down on her makes it impossible for her to move. She squirms, she scratches, she pleads with her eyes, but Nate is crazed, unable to reach. When he tears inside of her, she screams beneath his sweaty palm, though no sound comes out. It's muffled in his grasp, stifled in the violation of her body and spirit.

This is the part when the film slows down and the sharp colors fade to a dusty gray. Lucy has left her body and like a patron in a theater, she is watching herself from above, unable to stop the animal from his attack. She is no longer fighting him. She is focused on the sky above and not the quake below. The trees are blocking the sun as it tries to peek through. She doesn't dare close her eyes. She counts the leaves on the trees. She silently prays. It is through someone else's eyes that she sees him whisper in her ear, a dull, grainy menagerie of words, "You feel so good, Lucy…," followed by a quickening, a shudder. Only then does he release her mouth, let out a gasp, and drop his head against her chest. He rolls over and pulls her along so that she is resting against his shoulder. His fingers tickle her back beneath the stained shirt.

Earlier, Lucy was dressed in a bright yellow tank top with denim shorts, but when she is forced to drag her body through the damp mulch, bordering the course where her best and closest friends sit, she is naked from the waist down. She has been taught that yellow and red make orange, though where her blood stains the cotton fabric, there is no mistaking the deep, pure crimson.

And that's when Lucy wakes up.

She tells herself it is the dream again, but she cannot dispute the accuracy of it. She had been excited by his touch. This realization shrouds her in shame. She is angry that she didn't fight harder. She is sad that the police and lawyers did. When the facts were sorted out and Lucy learned she was not pregnant, and that Nate was a virgin himself, other accusations came into play. Natalie blamed her for *flirting* with Nate. "How could you?" she asked. And while Lucy tried to wrap her mind around the sting of that biting remark, forensic experts concluded that Nate had no recollection of the incident and was suffering as badly as Lucy. Discerning who was the victim had become part of the tangled mess. In the middle of it, the anti-drug advocates made their message clear: Drugs were dangerous and play with your mind and your inhibitions. Use once and your life can change forever.

Lucy leans over and feels her tattoo. Smooth to the touch, it slows the frantic beats of her heart. The envelope is there too, but she can't bring herself to touch it.

chapter 19

Levon steps on the scale and can't believe what he sees. He is three pounds lighter. Had the stitches reduced his poundage when they were removed? Or, is it the result of his disclosure? Did the weight of his words—his burden—amount to that much?

Days have passed since his tryst with Lucy, and he has finally set the truths onto the page. Her secret has liberated him. The chronicling of that fateful night both invigorates and purifies. Now more than ever, he knows what he has unloaded onto the pages must be safeguarded.

The tattoo inscribed on his bottom has healed, and it's slowly reshaping Levon. He is not only writing in his journal with fierce abandon, but he has been piecing together an assortment of short stories of which he is relatively proud.

Things on the home front are unchanged and depressing, with the exception of his mother's jaunts to the synagogue. Her refusal to visit the cemetery has her at odds with his father. "David's not there," she says with a scowl. "He's in here," she adds, pointing to her heart. Solace is found in a language she can't read or write. They are now commanded to kindle the Sabbath lights on Friday evenings, eat challah, and sip from David's Bar Mitzvah Kiddush cup before she heads out the door. Sometimes, she invites Chloe along though never Levon or his father. Ironically, Friday nights were when the family used to worship David, while watching him during his weekly football games.

Levon's mother can be overheard saying to her half-listening husband, "David wasn't the one I was worried about."

A recent visit to Gainesville with Dr. Gerald was discouraging. Dollars were being pulled from his research. Gene therapy with dogs at the university had yielded positive results—dogs are now fasting three hours, up from one hour—and Dr. Gerald's team of associates believe they are close to a breakthrough. Sadly, without the proper financial backing, the veterinarians were laid off. What that means for children afflicted with GSD: Hope for a cure is within reach, though ultimately economics could be the difference between a child living a normal life and one living by the strokes of the clock.

In the past, fundraising events had raised substantial dollars for GSD research. Madeline Keller, once the organizer of such swanky evenings, wasn't planning on coordinating the winter gala, choosing to hibernate instead. Shuffling between two extremely bad scenarios—mourning loss and preventing loss—she had all but given up on life.

Levon had not.

Ellen DeGeneres, with uplifting and humorous contagion, has sparked a lightbulb in Levon's misty head. He steps off the bathroom scale, proud of his unexpected loss. He knows that it is ludicrous to think that he, a nobody from Miami Beach, can make a difference. Still, he had replayed the episode with the cornstarch multiple times and each time he is overwhelmed. After visiting Ellen's website, he drafts a letter and a children's story about kids with GSD, all with the intent of impressing her enough to lend an ear to the disease and other rare disorders.

"You are amazing," Lucy exclaims to Levon when he finally shows her the letter, the story, and the TiVo version of the episode that he has saved in his Now Playing list.

"Let me draw the illustrations for the story. We can go to Target and get one of those binders and send an actual book. She'll love the effort you put into it."

"You can draw?" he asks. With that, she snatches from her backpack a pile of drawings from art class.

"Wow," he says, "you're really good..."

"I know," she quips.

"And modest."

"This is good for you, Levon, very constructive."

His mother keeps walking in and out of the room. At least she isn't hiding in her darkened bedroom under the covers. Maybe she can sense Levon is on to something big.

Lucy is polite and happy when greeting Levon's mother. When a grunt escapes the tired woman before she flees back to her room, Lucy asks, "What is *up* with your mother? Has she always been like this?"

Levon shrugs.

"She acts like you're not in the room."

"I don't think she likes me very much. Bet you don't have a clever life lesson in response to that."

Chloe skips into the room and breaks up the grey cloud. Both Levon and Lucy stare at the star of their afterschool special. She has no idea what the two of them are up to, only that markers and paint are involved. "Can I help?" she asks.

"No," Levon says.

"Yes," Lucy insists.

"Which one is it?" the brown-eyed girl asks.

There is a lapse of prickly silence. Levon's thoughts fall back on David and Rebecca's baby. Was there a chance he or she could have been a carrier of GSD?

They are staring at the living, breathing catalyst for their pet project. She is speckled in freckles, and although she's not smiling or making a sound, her eyes are desperately pleading to participate. Levon is unsure of how she'll handle all the attention.

Lucy steps in front of Levon and says to Chloe, "We are going to do something bold to raise national awareness for GSD and get some funding to find a cure. You're going to be a part of it because it's your story. You are the star."

"You're scaring her," interrupts Levon.

Lucy turns to find a red-faced Levon. When she does, a strand of her yellow hair swats him in the face, and his hand reaches for his stinging eye.

"She's not a baby, Levon. She understands what I'm saying more than any of us."

"I don't want her to be involved more than she already is."

Lucy laughs one of her loud, obnoxious, grate-on-your-nerves chuckles. "She *needs* to be involved. Ask her. Ask her what it feels like to be different than the other kids at school. Ask her how it feels when she's at a birthday party, and the kids are all eating that sugary crap kids crave, and she's eating crackers and nuts? Look at her. Don't turn your head. She's the reason you're doing this." Then, as if Levon didn't get what Lucy was saying, she points at his beautiful, brave little sister and says it again.

"No," Levon demands, "I don't want her involved."

"What the heck is going on?" Chloe cries out. "You *are* starting to scare me."

Lucy says, "Your brother's starting to scare *me* a little bit."

Levon was starting to scare *himself* too. What had he gotten himself into and was it too late to pull the brakes on his plans?

"Why are you doing this, Levon?" Lucy asks.

She says this as though she knows the answer. It should make him grateful to have a friend who understood him so well after all the years he has suffered from ridicule and blatant disregard. Instead of feeling thankful, though, he feels uneasy, like she's standing too close.

Chloe sashays toward the pantry, considering her limited snack choices while Lucy leans in closer to Levon. "What's your problem? You know why this matters. Do you actually think *she'll* forgive you if you help your sister?"

Levon's silence is overshadowed by the loud pulsation of his heart. "Unbelievable," she says, rolling her eyes. "Haven't I taught you anything?"

Chloe returns to the table with a fist full of saltines. Levon checks his watch knowing that in his mother's physical and emotional absence, he is required to be Chloe's timekeeper. There is so much that goes into the maintenance of her illness: the clockwatching, the diet, the constant vigilance.

"Did I ever tell you about the first time Chloe went on an airplane?"

He doesn't wait for Lucy to answer; instead, he continues talking, more to himself then to her.

"We were held up at security for hours when they found a gram scale and a white powdery substance in my mom's carry-on. And do you know how many people of supposed superior intelligence don't realize that bread has sugar in it? Or how troubling it is to hear a six-year-old ask a grown-up at a birthday party about the level of sucrose in her popsicle?"

Other than the sound of Chloe munching on saltine crackers, the three are quiet. The crunching noise is followed by a clearing of her throat. Perhaps she is reminding Levon that he is talking about her while she is sitting right there.

"Did you know that Chloe had to learn how to swallow because she spent the beginning of her life unable to eat solids since she was fed through a feeding tube? And that those tasty flavored medicines for headaches and colds are so loaded with sugar they can send her into metabolic crisis? Try being in first grade and having to explain to others about the aide who shadows you around all day and your frequent visits to the nurse's office."

Chloe sidles up to him, but Levon doesn't pay attention until she is tugging on his shirt. Crumbs are caked across her shirt and hands, dotting her ruby lips. "Stop it," she says. "Stop it already."

"I'm sorry, Chloe."

"No," she continues. "Don't treat me like I'm some weirdo—"

"All I want is for people to understand…"

"*You* don't understand," she exclaims. "I'm okay. I never minded Mrs. Bethel being in the classroom with me, and I don't care if I can't eat all the stuff the other kids eat. I'm used to it."

"You shouldn't have to be used to it. You should be out having fun like other ten year olds who aren't afraid and aren't sick."

"I'm not the one who's afraid," she quietly adds.

"I'm trying to help you, Chloe," he says, and then turning to Lucy with a sneer adds, "and I think I found a brilliant way to help Dr. Gerald, so you can get better."

Chloe is silent. The younger, spirited child takes hold of her big brother's arm.

"It's not your job to fix me, Levon."

Lucy says, "Let her help, Levon. Do it for *you*, not for *her* approval."

Levon knows she's not referring to Chloe.

The letter took three days to perfect. Lucy critiqued it and edited it, while Levon added the finishing touches.

Dear Ellen DeGeneres,

Before I knew what was happening, I had fallen in love with you. It was subtle and strong, a mere flick of the remote, and there you were, parading across my television screen in fits of self-deprecating humor. You have inspired and touched millions of viewers nationwide. It is no wonder your name sounds less like "onerous" and more like "generous."

I have never written or contacted a television personality before—though you hardly personify the typical self-serving celebrity of talk show infamy. After I witnessed your recent episode with Wacky Steve, the Science Guy, I was compelled to put pen to paper. My aim is to bring to light the relevance of Steve's cornstarch experiment: the obvious, the obscure, and the ironic.

My ten-year-old sister, Chloe Keller, was diagnosed with

Glycogen Storage Disease when she was three months old. I have enclosed with this letter a detailed, clinical description of the disease, but in short, Chloe's body can't break down sugar. GSD, as it is abbreviated, lends itself to an expansive range of consequences, the majority of them life-threatening. Chloe must avoid all foods with sugar. She must eat every two to three hours in order to steer clear of hypoglycemia, liver damage, or the risks associated with stroke and death; Chloe will have this chronic disease for the rest of her life.

Cornstarch is what keeps Chloe and the other children with this menacing disease alive. That's correct, cornstarch. It's not a scientifically sound, unpronounceable brand name that has pharmaceutical companies clamoring for market share and distribution, nor does it come with an inflated price tag. Cornstarch, in the arena of groundbreaking medical breakthroughs, is as generic as it comes. No complex name can hamper its power. It is merely a white powder that, when mixed with cold water, saves lives.

Imagine my surprise when 2,000 gallons of this precious powder was used on your show for the purpose of Silly Science Experiments! Did the producers of the show have any idea that their wacky trick contained a dual meaning: light-hearted entertainment and a life-saving cure?

Like diabetes, patients with GSD can live with proper maintenance and management of the disease. Unlike diabetes, there is limited funding for a cure. Because GSD only afflicts 1 in 100,000 of our population, and diabetes 23.6 million, it gets left behind, an orphaned disease amid more publicly known life-snatchers. GSD is not cancer or heart disease. Funding does not come easy for rare illness nor does it generate extensive revenue for the drug companies. Diseases such as GSD are nameless and faceless until they attack someone you can't bear to lose.

Dr. Max Gerald, the research pioneer for GSD, has been working on gene therapy in dogs at University of Florida's Shands Hospital with great success. His efforts on behalf of many sick

children have been indefatigable. Sadly, in recent months, Dr.
Gerald's already limited funding has been cut short, and many of his
dedicated veterinarians and loyal staff have been let go. Dr. Gerald
has remained steadfast and undeterred by these cutbacks, caring for
the dogs himself and working tireless hours. When contacted by
GSD specialists worldwide, the largest distributor of cornstarch
nationwide was not interested in offering their support in the battle
against GSD.

Human-interest stories are your specialty. Though you speak to
us from our TVs, your voice is loud, warm, and vibrant, and your
compassion is visceral.

I write to you today, not for GSD alone, but for all the rare
diseases worldwide that are in dire need of exposure and support.
By using your influential voice, please help us shed some light on
them. An orphan disease may not afflict millions of people, but when
it affects someone you love, it's the most important disease in the
world.

Sincerely,
Levon Keller

"It's perfect," says Lucy, "and better that we took out the part
about David. You want her to do this because she cares, not because
she feels sorry for you."

Chloe is gluing the last of the children's book decorations to the
cover. Lucy draws a caricature of Chloe and uses brown yarn for her
hair and a button for her nose. When she finishes, she holds up her
masterpiece and smiles. "Do you think Ellen will invite us on the
show? I've never been to California."

The front door opens and closes and then opens and closes
again. It is Levon's mother, and she has charged in and out of the
house carrying with her a pile of mail. The box hadn't been emptied
in weeks, and sympathy cards and bills were stuck together, tightly

wound in rubber bands. Levon, Lucy, and Chloe are cleaning up their mess at the table, while Madeline is poring over the notes and bills. She is barefoot, clad in silky, black pajamas, and sips from a coffee mug.

"Where are my glasses?" she asks of no one in particular.

Chloe circles around the table and finds them resting next to the sink. She hands them to her mother, who snaps them on her head with a force that very well might knock the little girl over. Madeline is studying one of the letters very carefully. Her hands are grasping the pages, and her face is contorted. Levon thinks about asking her what's the matter, though, instead, lines up the rainbow assortment of markers, fitting them into their plastic case. Lucy is biting her lip and Chloe is singing some Disney song, blind to the tension filling the room. Levon makes out the AT&T insignia and can't imagine what's gotten his mother so shaken up. Has she forgotten to pay the bill?

Reaching across the table, Madeline Keller lifts the cordless phone from its charger and begins to dial. She's holding the invoice upright while her other hand is dialing numbers she is reading from the page. Levon immediately feels sorry for the poor soul at the other end of the phone line. Whoever it may be, the wrath of his mother is about to unravel and strike. His mother, though, abruptly hangs up and reaches for a pen in the kitchen drawer. She begins to mark up the bill, checking off numbers in manic obsession. Her eyes are darting back and forth, and her hands seem possessed as they travel compulsively down each page. Levon and Lucy busy themselves so as not to intrude on the private agitation that has Madeline's face knotted and flushed. When she drops the pen and hides her eyes behind her flattened palms, Levon knows whatever is there is going to prove disastrous. Madeline hastily stands up and heads toward the stairs. The cold air that follows her raises the hair on Levon's arms as if they are in a salute.

Lucy runs to see the piece of paper that now looks like something a kindergartener has used in a game of battleship.

"What are you doing?" Levon asks, jumping in her way, blocking her.

"Aren't you the least bit curious to see what's got her panties in a wad?"

Chloe is spinning around on one of the barstools that faces the island in the middle of the room. "What's a wad?" she asks.

"Stop it, Chloe," Levon barks at her, irritated by both girls in his kitchen. "You're going to throw up." At which point, Lucy has squirmed passed him and grabs the papers.

"Taking someone else's mail is a felony," he says.

She hands it to him and says, "I'm not taking it, you are."

The bill is for his father's personal cell phone. Levon recognizes the number across the top.

"Looks like Daddy's been letting his fingers do the walking…"

Levon studies the bright blue asterisks of his mother's pen. There are hundreds of them lining the pages like perilous scientific data. He doesn't recognize the number. There it was in scandalous repetition: all hours of the day, all hours of the night, calls from Key West when his father was there on a business trip, lots and lots of hours of talk time.

"Let's call it," Lucy says.

Levon shoots her a look that means *not in front of Chloe*.

"Give me the number," she says, picking up the electrically charged phone. Then she remembers something and winks at Levon. "Redial! Gotta love modern technology."

"No, no," Levon yells. "Hit *67 first. I don't want our number to show up."

"Good one, Sherlock," she smiles, hitting the keypad with a burst of pride and willfulness. Levon is scared to hear who's on the other end of the line. He prays silently that Lucy hangs up or says *wrong number*. Seconds tick and Lucy looks at Levon, not breathing a word. Then she presses *end* and drops the phone on the countertop.

"What happened?"

"It was voicemail."

"Did it say who it was? Was there a name?"

Lucy is unsure of what to say, and it's that hesitation that sends Levon into a mild panic. His heart jumpstarts at an alarming, unruly speed. His hands get sweaty and slam into his pockets.

She says, "Who's Olivia?"

chapter 20

For those who think reality television is entertaining, try spending Thanksgiving at the Keller house. Tonight's episode is commercial free—minus the scripted sensationalism provided by overzealous producers looking for a ratings boost. Lucy calls it a bad sitcom. Levon is sure her family won't ever accept an invitation to their house again. She assures him that "all families are dysfunctional." It sounds reasonable, though it doesn't do much to cheer him up. Replaying the night's events in his head, he is embarrassed and disgusted beyond words, and for him, that's saying a lot.

Levon was shocked when his mom invited the Bells over in the first place. Her distaste for Lucy is obvious, and they haven't been in entertaining mode lately. When there was no mention of the holiday, he assumed they were going to coast right through it, and then Sid and Lyd arrive at their doorstep from Westchester with a frozen Butterball turkey cradled in their arms. This sends Mom into a fit of nervous agitation. What better distraction than to invite innocent bystanders to a tense, family gathering?

The Bells can't resist, and in light of Lucy's most recent discovery, she can't wait to see the drama unfold. The afternoon has all the elements of great TV: mystery, murder, immoral behavior, and with the inclusion of the Bells, a captivated studio audience.

They are sitting around the table, talking and passing food around, when Dad asks Mom if she wants stuffing or mushroom orzo. Madeline, without skipping a beat, replies, "Neither, I want a divorce."

Diet coke comes shooting out of Lucy's nose. Her parents, who are seated at the other end of the table with her brother Ricky, have no clue what has happened and have been cheerily talking among themselves while the clicking of their forks becomes louder and louder. Sid plays with his food until he can't bear it any longer, and, rising from his seat, he heads for the bar in the living room. Lyd snorts, "Madeline, it's about time you got your sense of humor back. That's a good one." She cocks her head, lifting her wine glass to her pink lips, and gulps the red liquid. Chloe is busy feeding George turkey under the table. The comment flies way over her head, smacking Craig Keller square in the face, right above the deep, cranberry stain that covers his jaw. It's either real cranberry or the blemish left by the slap of Madeline's remark. Clearly, no one is more blown away than Levon's father. Lucy gives Levon one of her pitiful, gloating stares, although to her, this is better than any episode of *Gossip Girl*, and she is hooked. His father excuses himself from the table and asks Madeline to follow. No, actually, he demands she follows. When they get to the living room, all hell breaks loose.

The thought occurs to Levon that he might have been able to prevent this from happening. He knows who Olivia is; he knows what his mother found on his father's phone bill. He could've warned his dad or even balled him out for his betrayal. But Levon was tired of cleaning up everyone's messes.

Their voices carry though to the dining room; accusations are hurled.

"Are you sleeping with her?" Mom asks.

Expletives—words Levon didn't know his mother knew—bounce off the walls and echo across the table. The overhead chandelier shakes, crystals clacking a tune none of them had ever heard. Mr. Bell is hiding his face in his hands. Mrs. Bell shifted nervously in her seat, afraid to look up and make eye contact with anyone. They all sit around the table motionless and mute, and then Lucy persuades Chloe to join her on a dog walk.

Lyd goes to find Sid, though everyone at the table knows it's an excuse to pop a pill.

Mr. Bell asked, "Levon, is everything okay?"

Ricky, who obviously has his sister's witty sense of humor, replies, "We ain't in Kansas anymore."

Mr. Bell stands up, folds the linen napkin on the table and, by the look in his eyes, demands that his wife and son do the same.

"And miss all this?" Ricky jokes, before both of his parents shoot him a glaring look.

The door closes behind them, and there is Levon, sitting alone on Thanksgiving, at a table of half-empty glasses and half-eaten turkey and stuffing. The smell of sweet potatoes and his favorite gravy fill the air, though he is too focused on his lost family to realize that he had lost something else: his appetite.

Time stands still and Levon, foggy, can not say how long he sits there or how long his mother screams and curses at his father before he begins to defend himself. She finally quiets down, and he can hear his father, in between sobs, trying to explain how long it's been since she paid him any attention, how long it's been since they've talked to each other. "And God damn it," he shouts, "I lost David too, and I worry about Chloe every time I take a breath. You've turned your back on us, crawling into your hole to shrivel and die. I need you. I need my wife."

Levon has always thought cheaters are pricks of the lowest form. So how come what his dad is saying rings true? Is that why he turned a blind eye to what he saw in his office? It had been so long since he has seen his parents kiss, touch, or smile at each other. It had been well before the accident. How can he blame his father for needing what his mother doesn't give?

Levon plays with his food, a novelty. He can't recall a time when he hasn't shoveled the feast of Thanksgiving into his mouth.

Tonight's delicacies are too tough to swallow. His mother has a full glass of wine by her plate, and he takes a swig as Lucy and Chloe come scrambling through the front door. Lucy sends Chloe upstairs, instructing her to take a bath, and she finds Levon in the dining room polishing off the glass of wine. It is too sweet for his liking, though he can't lie and say it doesn't diffuse the nerves that have him wound up.

"Now we're talking," Lucy smiles, as she collects the partially full wine glasses and pours them into her own. She raises her goblet before asking, "What are we toasting to?" Levon draws a blank. There really isn't anything he is grateful or happy about that he can think of, so he shrugs his shoulders, and they clink glasses. Lucy finally says, "To not being on the other end of your mother's rant."

He says, "I'll drink to that."

"Do you believe him?" she asks.

His father is repeating over and over how nothing happened and he just needed somebody to talk to, while Mom is sniffling and saying stuff like, "Emotional affairs are far more destructive than physical ones." Levon can imagine Madeline reading from her library of self-help books, never imagining the day would finally arrive that she'd be quoting psycho-babble out loud. For what it's worth, he believes his father.

Levon began thinking about physical versus emotional, and how boundaries often blur—mostly because Lucy looks so drop-dead gorgeous. She leans up against him, and says, simply, "Are you all right?" His worlds are crashing down on him, and he shivers inside. Then, she asks—with this sweet, breathy voice that implies she's not judging him or his crazy, psychotic family—"Is there anything I can do to help?"

The idea of crossing over to the physical with her is more than tempting. She is inches from Levon's face. All he has to do is come up with some clever line and she will lean closer, find his lips, and they will be joined in a way that surpasses the metaphysical. It takes all his strength to stop his hands from brushing the wisps of her blonde hair off her face. They keep falling in front of her eyes, brushing her cheeks, and he yearns to touch them. The wine has made him giddy and daring.

Instead, they clear the table in silence, dropping scraps of food for George, who nuzzles his nose against the burgundy tablecloth, his eyes begging for more. Every time they come near each other, he feels himself being pulled toward her, and Levon is convinced she feels it too. On TV, the good guys always end up getting the girl— even if they are chubby and a little nerdy. Is it time to stop watching so much television?

Hours later, Levon and Lucy say goodbye, and Levon caps off the night with a final gulp of wine. His mother's pill case is on the island in the kitchen, and he wonders how many Klonopins she downed before climbing into bed, shuttering herself off from the world. The kitchen is a mess. Daphne would be there in the morning, and it's anyone's guess how she might peel the film of deceit from their floors and walls.

A light tapping at the door startles Levon. With Chloe asleep, his father out back clearing his head, and his grandparents' snores filtering the hallway, he hopes it is Lucy.

"Hi, Levon."

It's Rebecca.

Levon's hand finds his chest because he wants to make sure his heart is beating. For the first time, seeing her does not take his breath away.

"What's wrong?" she asks.

Levon simply smiles and invites her in.

Rebecca has her hair pulled back from her face and the golden color has returned to her cheeks.

"Remember Thanksgiving last year?"

Levon smiles and leads her into the family room where they sit on the same chairs as the occasion she plucks from memory. "Yeah," said Levon, "that was a fun night." They were all gathered together while Rebecca's nine-year-old brother, Aaron, performed magic tricks. It was a pretty boring performance until he made Grandpa Sid's toupee disappear. They laughed so hard Levon's belly ached for hours and, for once, it had nothing to do with desserts.

Levon began again, "How have you been?"

"I'm okay. I'm learning to live the new normal, whatever that means. Everyone says the first year is the toughest." Her eyes catch his in hers. "Every minute hurts."

"I'm sorry I didn't call you after the procedure."

"There was nothing for anyone to say. Unless you're Shelly Kalegeris."

"That's a name we don't need to talk about."

"No," she shakes her head, "We need to talk about her."

Levon's head tilts in a question mark.

"She showed up at my house. You were right. He wasn't cheating on me."

If only that night were so simple and the explanations able to bring David back.

Rebecca plays with the buttons on her shiny, black blouse; she swipes at her jeans as though there are feelings she needs to swat off. Levon covers her nervous fingers, impeding the motion. "Becks."

"She was actually pretty lady-like. It's interesting how people react to death. Truths come flooding out, and the high school bullshit loses its significance."

The word *truths* sends a rush through Levon's veins. "What exactly did she say?"

She grabs the coffee-colored throw from the couch and drapes it around her shoulders. Her shoes come off and her legs tuck underneath her. She was always so comfortable in their house.

"She was decent, Levon, really decent. It was like someone had taken over Shelly's bitchiness and replaced it with this weird empathy."

"I bet," Levon snorts.

"She said David was really torn up about the pregnancy. They talked, she offered him some advice. She said she's never seen him so distraught. They didn't hook up. Though she said she wouldn't have minded."

Levon takes this all in and remains silent.

"What else did she say? Was that all?"

"She said he was so upset he made himself sick. Thank God you drove him home."

The ridiculousness of that statement is punctuated by the evening's ironic outcome. They all knew about designated drivers and never getting in the car with someone drunk or high. Not even Levon's sober offer could help save David.

"I'm sorry," she says. "You know what I meant." She covers her face with her hands, resisting the truths. "I don't know what I meant."

"Not much makes sense anymore. Everything's changed. The world will never be the same again."

Her hands leave her face and they find Levon's. Together they squeeze as though all the unsaid words could spread through their fingers.

Rebecca speaks first. "I'm sorry he felt he couldn't talk to me. We could have worked through it."

Nausea seeps into Levon's belly. It happens quickly. One minute he is deducing how this could have happened, and the next he is sure he is about to get sick. Rebecca mistakes the look on his face to mean something else.

"I'm sorry. This must be difficult for you to talk about."

She had no idea.

"I'm glad she contacted you, Becks. There's got to be some consolation in that."

"I'm going to get going," she says, "I just wanted to wish you a good holiday and let you know I have been thinking of you and your family."

The two stand up and form a hug. Levon detects again how his heart is beating at a relaxed pace. This allows him to pull her tighter into his arms. She rests her head on his shoulder while the waves of nausea pass through Levon's insides.

There is so much to that night that would never be understood.

Returning to his bedroom, Levon lies down, pulling the covers over his head. The room begins to spin while his mind soaks in wine and stormy thoughts. Before he has time to understand what's happening to him, he is thrust upright, and the alcohol-laced heaving commences. The noise must be loud and foul sounding because his father bolts through his door.

"Dad, I don't feel well."

His father takes charge, heading for the bathroom. He returns with a cup of cold water and a damp washcloth. "How much did you drink?" he asks.

"I'm not sure. Just what was left on the table."

"Drink the water and go sit at your desk. I'll strip the bed."

Craig Keller returns with the blow-up bed used for sleepovers. The grimy sheets and blanket are rolled into a ball in the corner of the room.

"Don't blow it up," Levon begs. "The noise will wake everyone up. I'll take a blanket from downstairs and sleep on the floor."

"Levon," his father says, "you don't have to do that."

"It's not a big deal."

"You've always been an easy child. I'm not going to lecture you tonight on underage drinking."

Levon stops him. "Dad, I didn't even like the taste of it."

His father sits down beside him on the floor and laughs. "I'll remind you of that in a few years." Then he puts his arm around Levon's shoulder. "I'm sorry about tonight," he says.

"Me too, Dad. I'm sorry about everything."

"Levon, I love you. I'm going to do whatever it takes to keep our family together. Your mom is going through the toughest time of her life. I'll never excuse her behavior, or mine, but if I've learned anything the last few weeks, it's that no one has the blueprint for dealing with grief. We're all innocent bystanders on an unchartered terrain."

Leave it to his father to cull together one perfect, incisive sentence.

"I can't believe he's not here anymore. It doesn't seem real."

"I know," his father agrees, "I catch myself wanting to tell him something. He was my son. I was supposed to protect him."

"He'd be pissed knowing he's missing all of this."

His father's eyes swell with tears, though he doesn't cry. "Something tells me he's with us."

"I saw you hugging that Olivia lady."

"I know."

"I should have said something."

"No, you shouldn't have."

"I could have helped you."

"No one can help."

"How can you still love me?" Levon asks.

It takes him a full, palpable minute to answer. He finally says, "You're my son."

chapter 21

"How are we doing this week?" Dr. Lerner asks Madeline and Craig in her heavily accented voice.

Craig mumbles something, giving his wife an encouraging glance.

"Madeline?" she asks.

She shrugs, less confident than her spouse. Today she is exhausted, beaten down.

"The last few sessions have not been easy, I understand, for both of you. Nothing worth saving ever is. Lots of couples come in here with problems—some bigger, some smaller than yours—and if there's one thing that separates those that last from the ones who end up dissolving their unions, it is the *desire* to make it work."

Neither responds.

"I see you working very hard together. It's clear to me you want to preserve the marriage. I am correct, yes?"

Madeline nods her head in partial agreement. Normally, she would have scoffed at the doctor's no-nonsense approach to marriage preservation, but today she finds her booming personality and heavily accented brogue sedating. Dr. Lerner is their savior, the lifeboat for their sinking ship.

She continues. "Let's consider how we got here." Madeline looks accusatorially at her husband.

When David first died, the two sat huddled together discussing their crushing pain. They were on the same team, reliant on one another to heal. Now, their anguish has been sliced in two. The added ingredient of adultery, both bitter and addictive, has the two of them seated at opposite ends of the sprawling, brown couch.

"Madeline, I understand your frustration and anger toward Craig. I'm going to ask you, though, to do something that probably won't be easy. It's the only way I believe our work can be productive." She pauses for a response from Madeline, which is taking an uncomfortably long time. The silence is ominous and unpredictable.

"This may be hard for you to understand right now, Madeline, because you're angry and feeling betrayed. Instead of looking inward, it's a lot easier to cast blame on someone else. For us to work through this together, we have to cease talking about this other woman. She is not the problem. She is not the issue. She is insignificant to our success in here."

Craig is fumbling in his seat.

Before Madeline can argue, Dr. Lerner continues. "Your marriage has suffered some terrible blows—the loss of a child being the most significant. Even the healthiest of marriages oftentimes can't sustain that type of tragedy. Coupled with Chloe's illness and Rebecca's pregnancy, there are additional stressors." Dr. Lerner's dark eyes dart between the two solitary figures. "The affair is not what I would term a stressor, although, Madeline, I'm sure you'd disagree. The affair is the result of stress. It is not the problem, but the symptom of the problem."

Madeline takes a quick look at Craig. The relief that has sneaked across his face has her incensed.

Dr. Lerner continues. "The model for how you handle stress in the marriage is dictated by your personalities—whether learned or inherent. Craig," she says, stealing a glimpse in his direction, "your stressors made you desperate and needy. Madeline, you turned controlling and hardened. Much like the person who suffers and turns to drugs, Craig, you became addicted to the emotional validation you couldn't get from your wife. Madeline, your addiction was control—your children's diet, your own..."

"Are you saying what happened was my fault?" Madeline stands up, agitated.

"We don't point fingers and lay blame in here," Dr. Lerner says, motioning for her to sit down. After jotting something on a pad of paper, she places the pencil behind her ear where it peers out from the unruly bush. She purses big lips and says, "You both must be willing to admit to your mistakes and hold yourselves accountable for the problems in the marriage."

Madeline is pissed and it shows. Instead of ripping her husband's head off, she carefully pulls her hair back behind her ears.

"I'm sorry to have to tell you," Dr. Lerner says to her, "but this problem in your marriage has been here for a long time, a very long time. It preceded the affair. David's death certainly began a spiral effect, but the groundwork was laid years ago. Small problems became big problems. Your husband was calling out for help. Good thing that he did."

With that, Craig lets out a heavy sigh that sends Madeline into a frenzy. She is fuming. Her arms flail when she speaks; her face turns a dangerous shade of red. There is no way she is going to let Craig off that easily.

"How can you absolve him like that? Plenty of people have problems in their marriages, but he betrayed the marriage. He betrayed the trust!" She shouts like a petulant child who's not getting her way. "You make it sound like I should be thanking him."

"Is this how you typically handle conflict with your husband, Madeline?" There is no mistaking the giant mirror Dr. Lerner is holding up in front of her face.

"He disrespects me and my family, and I'm supposed to believe that I caused it, that I'm to blame?"

"You are *both* to blame," Dr. Lerner says, leaning forward in her chair. "We're in this room to explore how you got into your present predicament."

"It's unforgivable," Madeline says.

"There are two types of people who cheat," Dr. Lerner begins in response. "One is egocentric and doesn't believe in the sanctity of marriage and never will. The other is weak and confused, hungry for affection, for something to fill the void. The difference in these two types is simple: one feels tremendous regret and remorse, while the other has none."

Madeline turns to face Craig, and his eyes tell her at once which category he falls into. They are swollen, red and damp.

He has begged for her forgiveness for days. He has cried and appealed for her to allow him to stay. "We need to work through our grief together. We're stronger together than apart." He is ashamed: a failure to himself, a failure to his wife, and, most importantly, to his kids.

The image of nubile Olivia and the attention she paid her husband was eating away at Madeline and eroding her reason to exist. Madeline was adamant when she asked for the divorce on Thanksgiving night. And although they fought and cried and argued through the early morning hours, she remained resolute. There was no mincing of words. Madeline Keller had had enough. She was unequivocally prepared to leave the man who stomped on their vows and made a mockery of her in public. Craig was unwavering too. "I never touched her," he said, yet, equally repentant for the admitted emotional connection. "The day David died, it was over."

To Madeline, his emotional attachment eclipsed the physical transgression. She deemed it a blunt fracture to years of trust and intimacy. That night, and the nights that followed, were typified by finger-pointing and Madeline-esque threats.

With the course of their future hanging on a string as delicate as spider's silk, Madeline was in a hollow state of suffering. Her knee-jerk reaction was to bolt, start fresh, and although the thought provided momentary relief, its long-term prognosis was deeply unsettling. She knew the grim statistic: Half of marriages end in divorce when a couple loses a child—and she didn't want to be a statistic. She didn't want Levon and Chloe to suffer as a result of their issues. Two of them needed to manage Chloe's care. And although she trusted none of her friends with the details of the cavernous crack in the façade of her marriage, she ached for their support, but she also knew the shared consensus of modern suburban wives: If my husband cheats on me, we're through. And she didn't want her friends to judge her if she couldn't walk away.

She had to wonder if her soiled reality smacked them in the face—stinking of lust and abandoned dreams—would they be able to forage ahead on an unpredictable path without looking back, without regret? Madeline didn't know what to do. Leaving was easy in some ways, yet harder in others.

"Madeline, do you think you're able to refrain from talking to Craig about the other woman?"

Madeline shrugs.

"When you walked in here today, whether you were aware of it or not, you made a decision to commit yourself to the marriage and to the healing process. We can't do that without addressing the problem, not the symptom."

Madeline crossed her arms in defiance. Earlier this morning, when she was blowing her hair, the hair dryer knocked into one of the bottles on her perfume tray, sending the others crashing like a fleet of crystal dominos. It should have been simple to pick each up one at a time. Instead, the more she tried to align them on the silver tray in her bathroom, the more bottles fell over. Hearing Dr. Lerner's words reminded her of that frustration.

Madeline is still so angry and hurt she wants to lash out at Craig, not baby him. Then there's David. His absence exacerbates Craig's betrayal. The feelings are so tangled together; often, it's easier to hate Craig and be angry rather than exerience the emptiness of David's absence. That he betrayed her before David's abandoning her makes his infidelity all the worse.

Her eyes are furious when she says to Dr. Lerner, "I don't know if I can forgive him."

"I'm not asking you to forgive him. I'm asking you to take a look inward—both of you—and focus on finding the problems in your marriage. Ask yourselves, how did I contribute to this? How did my actions help get us here?"

Madeline makes one more vicious appeal. How the hell was it suddenly *her* fault that her husband attached himself to someone younger? "Ask *him* to look inward," she hisses, gesturing in the direction of Craig and his beleaguered frown. "This is bullshit, really, utter bullshit. I can't believe we're actually paying you for this."

Pretending not to hear Madeline's attack, Dr. Lerner turns to Craig who is focused sheepishly on the hands clasped together in his lap. "Did you say something, Craig?"

"This should be good," Madeline utters, sarcasm and contempt dripping from her tongue.

"Craig?" Dr. Lerner repeats.

Craig concentrates on a spot behind Dr. Lerner because meeting her eyes would leave him defenseless. Instead, he gazes at the walls lined with prestigious degrees and chooses one—the one from Tulane University—to study. He can make out the woman's name and the sturdy strokes of the Old English lettering. Soon the calligraphy blurs together, and he is looking at another wall—and a regret that is crystal clear.

A lone tear glides down his face, though no sound escapes his mouth. It is as if the tear burst from a grieving heart, a leak that had nowhere else to go but through the misty eyes of neglect. He doesn't wipe it off even though he is certain it is staining his cheek and poising him for further disapproval.

Words are lost to him, and he shakes his head in disbelief.

He is thinking of one of the first nights they agreed to go out after Chloe's diagnosis. They were at a dinner party for some friends. Madeline looked stunning, and Craig told her so over and over in the car. She had taken to knotting her hair up in a bun because it required little maintenance. Craig found it classic, elegant, and he loved that he could see more of her face. She didn't thank him, she couldn't. She had a plethora of reasons to disagree with his assessment. She was tired, though it didn't show. She was worried about leaving Chloe, but she radiated confidence.

The group was settled in a private room at the back of the restaurant. Madeline was to Craig's right, and while he made small talk with the man across the table, Madeline was engrossed in conversation with one of the mother's from the boys' school. The man was going on about some property in Cat Cay, and Craig was bored and obligingly nodding his head. The mirror behind the man's head gave Craig a perfect view of Madeline, chatting away with the buxom blonde by her side. She was animated and smiling. Craig studied her face in the reflection, believing she would feel his gaze and turn her head. In between cocktails and hor d'oeuvres, he willed her to catch his eye. When the main dishes arrived, he told himself if she looked his way, it was because she could feel his love tapping at her shoulders. She never looked at him. Not through a steak that was too well done or through a molten chocolate lava cake that he savored.

They said their goodbyes and their thank-yous to the group and headed out to the car. She was checking her cell phone to see if the children had called. When he asked her for singles to tip the valet, she still didn't look up, instead, handed him some singles while studying something in her bag. His stare was prolonged and determined.

Back in Dr. Lerner's office, the words trickle out without emotion. "She stopped looking at me."

"Can you speak up?" Dr. Lerner asks.

"My wife," he says, clearing his throat of the debris that had earlier inhibited him from speaking. "My wife, she doesn't look at me."

Dr. Lerner eyes Madeline who has grabbed her pocketbook and is staring at her hands.

215

"Madeline, could you please look at your husband; look at Craig."

Reluctantly, she turns an unwilling body.

"Craig, look at your wife and tell her what you need from her. Don't tell her what she doesn't do for you. Tell her what you want from her."

Even though Madeline's body is facing Craig's, she is unwilling to move her eyes from the meticulous embroidery of her expensive bag. Craig's eyes are fixed on her face. He is mistaken if he thinks the sheer force of his will can induce a reaction. She is stubborn and angry, and he thinks for the first time since they walked into Dr. Lerner's office, that this is a waste of time. Their problems are too deep to fix.

"Madeline," Dr. Lerner urges, "listen to what your husband is saying. Let him tell you what he needs, so you can tell him what you need."

Craig tries something daring as he reaches across the sofa for one of Madeline's folded hands. Dr. Lerner clasps and unclasps hers while the clock on her desk counts the intolerable beats of Madeline's cruelty.

Madeline considers what she's lost. David. David's unborn child. Chloe's health. Slowly, she turns toward Craig, her movements as ridged as the clock that drones on in the same paced measure that she has grown to detest. Her eyes find his face, first his chin, still damp, and then his eyes. When she is sure his eyes are locked into hers, and a whisper of hopefulness sweeps across his cheeks, she opens her mouth to tell him how much she hates him and why she can't look at him, but tears swipe away her words.

Instead, her hand finds his.

She doesn't hate Craig. No. But hatred of him is so much easier to grasp than to admit how much she hates herself.

chapter 22

Levon tugs on the stainless steel handle of the oversized refrigerator and finds a carton of reduced-fat milk, which is strategically placed in front of the whole milk. The expiration date reads January 1, 2008. The date scares him. New Year's should be a time of a fresh start, yet he is considering expiration, endings. He wishes he knows his own future with as much certainty as he does the day the milk will go bad.

Pouring the velvety liquid into a tall glass, Levon guzzles it in one breathless gulp. The sound of the front door opening and closing yanks him from a chocolate Mallomar daydream, and he rests the glass on the countertop to make his way to see who just entered his house.

"You are never going to believe this, Levon," says Lucy. She is carrying a suspiciously large envelope in her hands. "I can't believe it," she adds. "This is outrageous. You're a rock star."

She is dancing around him, waving the manila envelope in the air, and Levon can see immediately that the addressee's name is his own. Levon enjoys the manner in which Lucy waltzes through his doorway without having to knock, but he feels that her checking their mailbox is crossing the line.

"Wait till you see what it says. They love you!"

Levon grabs the mail from Lucy's hands, which stills her

billowy movements. "You steal my mail and open it too?"

He didn't have to ask who *they* were because the name emblazoned across the top of the fancy stationery gives him the information he needs. Ellen DeGeneres—or one of her staffers—has written him back, and Ellen was devoting an entire episode to orphaned diseases. The timing couldn't have been better. The very first National Rare Disease Day was taking place in Europe that March. They've even invited Levon's family and a guest to the taping in California! The last line of the letter reads: "It is people like you who bring to the forefront the impact of some of life's greatest travesties. Your voice will be heard as we 'silence the silence' on rare diseases."

Levon reads the letter again, carefully concentrating on the words and sentences that affirm his accomplishment. Someone has listened to him and has taken him seriously.

"Are you sure this isn't some joke, Lucy?"

"My tendency to pull outrageously funny stunts could never have made up something this good. You did this, Levon, you!"

He tries to reel in the words. The only time he has ever been this close to superstardom was when he was ten and on a Carnival Cruise with his parents and David and Chloe. For the costume contest, his mother dressed him and David as toilet seats with *1st Seating* and *2nd Seating* written across their backs. The reference to cruise lingo for the designated meal assignments earned them top marks, and they won first prize for creativity and a seat at the captain's table. This was something much bigger than the toilet seat. Back then he was *2nd Seating*. Clearly, he had elevated himself to a better position.

Levon fiddles with the envelope and its contents. There are forms to fill out, necessary signatures, and the required parental consent.

"Do I have to invite them?" he asks. "Guess there's no way I'm going to be able to fly cross country and go on national television without telling my parents."

To this, Lucy replies, "You're mother's so drugged up she won't know you're gone."

Though Levon hears Lucy's words, his brain buzzes a warning. He steals a sidelong glance at the girl who seems to have slipped from the sky. Despite her beauty, Levon sees something in her buttery skin and glittery eyes. For once, he doesn't turn away. Instead, he focuses on the whole of Lucy, this person who has crept into his life and found a way to be his compass. It is altogether strange for him to consider how for weeks, months even, looking into her eyes had made him flustered, and he was sure his flushed cheeks had betrayed his feelings for her. Now he feels assured. His cheeks remain dull white. He no longer needs to turn away.

"Why are you looking at me like that?" she asks.

Levon has a hundred things to say, though he doesn't say any of them. She would feel weird if he revealed how she has become a part of him.

"Levon?"

"It's nothing," he says, lying. Looking at her is like having an entire meal without taking a bite.

Levon's mom screams from upstairs that she wants Levon to empty out the washing machine and put the clothes in the dryer.

Levon rolls his eyes. Daphne, their housekeeper, comes tomorrow, and he doesn't know why his mother is insistent on doing the laundry on her days off.

"This week, it's all about washing clothes."

He tells Lucy how the whirring of the washing machine can be heard at all hours of the day and night. The laundry room is teeming with cases of Tide, Clorox, and Shout.

"Maybe it soothes her."

They are walking down the hallway leading toward the laundry room. Lucy is a few steps behind Levon, and he can hear the humming of the machine as he approaches. "My mother has never cleaned anything in her life," says Levon, turning the knob of the espresso-colored door. "What can she possibly find soothing about doing laundry?"

"Quiet," Lucy says, raising her finger to her pursed lips. "Listen to the sound."

The digital display signaling the end of the spin cycle reads three minutes. Lucy hops up onto the adjacent dryer, leaning over the washer to watch the clothes spin through the clear, circular door. Her nose presses against the glass, and a cloud of her breath fills the window. "Look into the great abyss," she says.

Levon moves closer and sees his face gawking back at him.

"Stare down the center," she says, "it's like riding on a roller coaster. Maybe your mom comes down here and trips."

"I doubt Mom needs any more thrill rides in her life."

Levon is getting dizzy peering down into the machine. His brain has been tricked into thinking there are miles swirling in front of him. A part of him wants to tear up Ellen's envelope and the proof of his existence, lift the lid, and slip inside for a free fall through the Maytag experience.

Lucy asks pointedly, "Are those his clothes she's washing?" And when Levon doesn't answer, she continues cautiously. "Maybe she's trying to preserve them."

Levon almost laughs aloud. "David's clothes are untouched. No one is allowed to go near them, let alone wash away his smell."

This sad fact registers across Lucy's face.

He says, "Your attempt at turning dirty laundry into some symbolic ritual is appreciated, but you have it all wrong. Nothing makes any sense when someone dies. There aren't hidden meanings behind how people react. I think she's suddenly into washing clothes because she doesn't have to think about it. It's methodical. Wash. Dry. Fold. Repeat the cycle. I think she does it because it's safe."

"How do you mean?" she asks.

"She can't screw it up. There's a start and a finish. No surprises."

"You've obviously never done laundry," she says. "Guess what happens when you accidentally wash your black T-shirt with your white clothes? I think it's more than that. I think your mom's in a lot of pain."

"No shit," quips Levon.

"I'm serious. It's hard not to joke about her being Joan Crawford, but really, I think the washing and the cleaning are about her pain."

"I'm not seeing the correlation."

"She's trying to get rid of the ugliness, the dirt, the stains."

"Then why stop at clothes?" Levon bursts out. "You've seen her swoop in on her broom, and she's not sweeping floors or cleaning bathrooms."

"That's funny, Levon, even for you."

"A comedian and a shrink," he laughs.

"You don't have to be a shrink to figure your mother out. She's textbook."

The loud buzzer signals the end of their foray into his mother's psyche. "Saved by the bell," she says.

Levon begins to unload the damp clothes, while Lucy remains seated atop the dryer. Her feet are dangling in front of the machine's door. "Move," he says, and with the disobedience of a schoolgirl, she ignores him and positions her legs so that they are framing the door Levon wants to open.

"It would be a lot easier if you got down," he says.

"It would, wouldn't it?" she teases.

Ignoring her taunting eyes, he slowly fills the machine while she watches him in amusement.

What should have taken him minutes ends up taking him close to ten. Instead of filling his hands with fistfuls of shirts and shorts and jeans, he takes out each piece one by one, cradling them in his hands. He's not even sure which items are meant for the dryer. His mother is obsessive about things shrinking. He's having too much fun being close to Lucy to consider what clothes should hang on the rack against the wall.

"If Ellen could see you now," she laughs.

"Don't joke about that. Ellen has been known to show up unannounced at viewers' doorsteps with a microphone and a camera. Next thing you know, the whole school knows I'm doing laundry."

"The world," she says, correcting him, which reminds him of the girl from last week's show. Ellen and her crew showed up at the woman's house with a truckful of cash. The woman was then locked in a clear, Lucite chamber while a leaf blower blew around the money. She had two minutes to fill her pockets and clothes with as much as she could. Levon was eating a bag of Cheetos at the time. If there was food in the chamber, he'd know exactly where to put it.

The dryer door slams shut, and Lucy wriggles her body to the side, leaving room for Levon to manage the controls. She is fixed on him, a stare that is filled with a multitude of emotions. His fingers brush against the knob. Lucy's fingers are already there. They make room for his, where they remain.

"Delicate or heavy?" he asks.

"Delicate," she whispers.

Levon feels his palms sweating, and he knows it's not from the heat of the dryer.

"Any new theories about laundry you want to share with me?" she asks, her words taking on an echo of vibration as Levon powers up the machine with his other hand. She is so near to him that her breath touches his cheek.

He thinks back to his face in the reflection of the washer and the envelope that is folded and creased in his pants. Wash. Dry. Fold. Repeat the cycle. *No, no, no,* Levon thinks to himself. Time to break the cycle. Time to find the guy who wrote that letter to Ellen, the one whose backside boasts of courage.

"Levon?" she asks. "You have that face on again."

Well, duh, he wants to say to her. *There is this gorgeous person draped across my dryer, and I'm about to make my move, leap into oblivion.*

Without hesitation, he looks her squarely in the eyes and says, "I love you, Lucy."

"What?" she shrieks, simultaneously jerking her hand away from his.

"I think I love you," he stammers again.

"Oh, Jesus, Levon, you don't love me. Get a grip."

He steps back from the machine as she lets herself down.

"You can't say things like that."

"What am I supposed to say with you sitting like that?"

She's wiping the lint off her pants and bouncing around him. "Not that, Levon. Say something, anything, but not that. You don't love me. You hardly know me."

He thought they had grown to know each other pretty well.

"Slow down and think about what you're saying. There's no need to jump to conclusions. You think you feel something, but you don't. Trust me. You might love me, but not in the way you think."

The box of Bounce drops to the floor, and the fragrant towels scatter across their feet. Levon hides his humiliation by taking his time to re-stack the individual sheets in the box.

"Levon, don't be upset," she says.

"Easy for you to say. I'm like the dark that ruins your whites."

"It's okay. Boys tell me they love me all the time."

Of course they do. "Have you ever loved any of them back?"

"I'm not sure I'm capable of love."

"Do you think that will ever change?"

She is quiet, which is altogether foreign to both of them. She takes a white rubber band from off her wrist and pulls her hair from her face. He concentrates on her white sweatpants.

"Why white?" he persists.

Lucy grabs hold of the sides of the dryer. "You better sit, or better yet, document this in your journal. It's extremely personal. I don't share it with anyone." She's thinking about the letter that she slept with the other night and says, "I'm allergic to the dye in most clothing."

"Bullshit," Levon says.

"I never lie," she says, "except when I'm lying."

"Really," he says, "tell me about it."

"One day, Levon. Soon, I hope. I'll show you mine, and you'll show me yours. What do you think?" she adds, tossing her head to the side. "What do you say we spill all our secrets?"

Levon wrestles with this.

"But not here in the laundry room," she continues. "Not when we're puppets in Mom's little play. There are things neither of us will ever understand. That's okay too."

Levon's words are thick and clumsy like the Play-Doh he once shaped in his pudgy fingers. When they finally emerge, he stammers, "I'm not really sure why my mother insists on doing laundry everyday, and I don't think I'll ever make any sense of any of it—not my mother, not David, not the spin cycle, not even you. I do know that if you were to sit here like that with me, I'd never say no to laundry. I'd never say no to the great abyss."

"That's better," she says, "much better."

chapter 23

The holidays have arrived, and with them, a blast of exquisite weather and joyful tourists. Miami Beach is cramped and crowded; visitors from all over the world are bursting onto its pristine beaches. Restaurants and nightclubs are decorated with families and vacationing college kids, and Lincoln Road is vibrant and bustling with scantily clad bodies from around the globe escaping the frost.

Levon and Lucy are at the Miami Beach Botanical Gardens, and Chloe is finishing up a sticky collage with the help of a woman dressed as a clown. Levon is bored and losing interest.

"What's up your ass today?" Lucy asks. "I'm the one who's supposed to be upset." Levon knows she received a call from Ricky, and he wasn't coming home for another week. He's been invited to go skiing in Colorado with a bunch of what Lucy deemed, "smelly frat boys."

His parents had pulled out of the driveway that morning and within thirty seconds Lucy was at his door beckoning him to come outside. "Grab Chloe and whatever she needs for the next couple of hours because I'm getting the two of you out of this house." Her mother dropped them off at the museum. Levon noticed how Lucy's mom didn't ask how he was doing after the Thanksgiving fiasco. There were some questions that people generally knew the answers to. Carol Bell was too polite to interfere.

A little girl approaches Chloe with a cone topped with pink and blue cotton candy, and Levon hurls himself in front of her. The startled girl trips backward and reaches for her mother. The woman snaps Levon a nasty look before shielding her youngster with an outstretched arm and leading her away from the creepy boy. He hadn't meant to scare the poor child—his response was a reflex, the natural instinct to protect his sister from deadly sweets.

Chloe holds up her completed artwork for them to see, which helps Levon forget the hypersensitive mother and her sugary daughter. Lucy says, "It's awesome, Chloe. Nice job." Levon is staring. The disjointed myriad of textures and colors make Levon want to cry. Resting across the buttons and strips of yarn and lace are three cutout newspaper people. The two boys are taller than the girl in the middle. They are all holding hands, face-down on the construction paper. He knows they are boys and a girl because of their yarn hair. Levon doesn't have to ask why they are glued to the page backwards. Nor does he need to guess which one of the boys is him. Chloe has made that perfectly obvious by the hefty size of the one on the left.

Chloe's freckled face turns to Levon for his critique. Her brown, beautiful eyes would be enough to melt his resistance, but Lucy's are watching him as well. Seeing her flanked in a white sweatsuit, he wonders if her open closet looks like a giant cloud, if her drawers are layers and layers of deep snow.

Lucy throws her arm around Chloe and pulls her close. The picture rests between the two of them. If Levon had his cell phone, he would snap a photo of Chloe's masterpiece held by his two brilliant girls. He longs to be the center of their touch, the center of something.

"I love it," he says. "Almost as much as I love you, noodle."

"Noodle?" she giggles. "You haven't called me that since I was six and a quarter."

Somehow it felt right. Today more than ever.

"Where are we going now?" She asks Lucy, tucking the project under her arm, diminishing it to the crook of her elbow.

"Follow me," Lucy says, leading them out of the gardens.

Levon trails behind the two angelic creatures. They frolic and wave in the crisp breeze, spinning around each other, smiling and laughing. He is happy to see his sister relaxing and being a kid. Despite being denied a normal, carefree childhood, she is alongside Lucy, dancing in the breeze. That the two of them instantly bonded is not a surprise. Finding each other is just another string of coincidences.

The Holocaust Memorial stands proud and somber. Lucy and Chloe enter first. Levon takes his time. He thought today was going to be another thrilling adventure like Haulover Beach. "Maybe she's too young for this," he says.

"I know about the Holocaust, Levvy. They're teaching us about it in school."

Chloe spots a friend of hers from the neighborhood and runs toward her at full speed.

"Who knew this was such a hot spot?" he laughs, only because he's nervous as hell and unsure of what to expect.

"Levon, this is serious stuff," says Lucy.

He agrees in silence.

They walk through the arbor of history, garden of meditation, dome of contemplations, the lonely path, and finally stop to stare at the large arm jutting out from the tranquil waters, the sculpture of love and anguish. They reflect on what they have witnessed in the many galleries: children torn from their parents, the mass destruction of generations, the contrasting evil, black granite against the tender, unforgiving Jerusalem stone. Neither of them speaks. Lucy wears her glasses today. They darken in the sun and hide her thoughts.

Chloe returns with her friend and asks if she can go to her house. The mother appears cordial and capable so Levon pulls from his back pocket the folded list of instructions he keeps with him at all times. It outlines Chloe's illness, what she can eat, what she can't, her dosing schedule, and a list of their emergency numbers. Then he searches his backpack for Chloe's GSD bag, which contains suitable snacks and her next measure of cornstarch. He hands it over to the woman as though he's handing over his heart. "I know your mother," she says, "and we've had Chloe to the house a few times. I can call her if you'd like."

Levon imagines her interrupting them at Dr. Lerner's office.

"It's fine," he says. "I'll let her know."

The threesome hurry off and Levon is left with Lucy.

"Alone at last," he says.

She is surveying the surroundings and the breeze ruffles her pants and hair. The wisdom brought forth in the sacred spot incites her. "Let's sit," she says.

He follows her to a spot on the floor, close to the edge of the water lily garden. Levon longs for his journal. The world is becoming a much larger place. The symbols of the lost souls in the garden, the lily pads— he begins to see them anew. "The water sustains the pads," Lucy says. "Among the sadness and ruin there are signs of life and purity."

The two sit there for a while, awash in their thoughts and prayers. Levon stares up at the giant hand as it touches the bright blue sky. Its shadow falls on the dark waters below. *Lightness and dark. The forces of evil and good.*

"Do you see that?" Lucy hollers.

Levon turns to his friend who is pointing toward the water. "There's another one!" He follows the direction of her short fingernails and spots the white flower resting upon the green pad.

Lucy reaches into her bag and draws out an envelope. Handing it over to Levon, she takes off her glasses and dabs at her eyes and cheeks.

Levon wants to ask her about the ominous envelope, what it

means. Instead, he heeds its call and begins to read:

Dear Lucy,

Mrs. Bara and I will never be able to make sense of our loss and your pain, though we can offer you something that we hadn't offered our son when he was still with us, something he was not able give to himself: the lesson of forgiveness.

We have been angry, and we have mourned. We have repeatedly asked God why? No answers come. We find ourselves clutching to the belief that from darkness comes light. From the depths of misery comes hope. From black soil grow supple flowers.

I'm asking you to find it within yourself to trust the world again. I am asking you, a young girl, to find peace in your heart. I am asking you to understand that innocence is not lost unless you allow it to be.

Upon Nathan's death, we came across this book in his room.
The pages were earmarked, and we left them untouched.
Your name was scribbled throughout.
We are certain he wanted you to have it.

With my deepest respect,
Mr. William Bara

Levon folds the letter and places it carefully back in the envelope. Lucy grabs him by the hand and leads him to the sculpture of the mother who is hovering over her two frightened children.

"It was her book they gave me. Her diary."

Levon recites Anne Frank's words aloud. Lucy's eyes are pressed shut, and she mouths them as he speaks. She remains clutching his hand, and its hold implies she doesn't want to let go. She leads him away from the statue and back to the pond. They take their respective seats and watch the lily pads float along the water.

Lucy begins. "My mom got the call about Nate. He had been depressed, holed up in the house. Despite what everyone thinks, there was nothing gratifying about it. Even though I didn't provoke him, even though I didn't ask for it, I felt responsible in some roundabout way.

"He came to see me once, after the media circus died down. He wanted me to know he was sorry."

"What did you say?"

"I knew in my heart he was going to carry around a regret that would never go away. He needed to let it go. I wish that were enough for him. When his parents showed up with the book, I understood what Nate wanted from me. I chose the color white that afternoon. The same white as those lilies. Look at them, Levon. Proof that life goes on. Evil will never prevail."

chapter 24

"Namaste."

This word forces Madeline to halt as she steps out the back door of her home and through the short distance onto her patio.

It's a glorious day in Miami and, with status updates on Facebook, the locals are reminding their friends in the snowy North why they live in South Florida. It's cool enough for pants and warm enough for short sleeves. A mild breeze rattles the leaves on trees, and air, once dense, is clean and dry. Madeline has come outside to escape the tomb that was at one time her home. At the center of it is her son David's room.

Her legs cannot carry her fast enough to the door that leads outside. She promised herself and the rabbi and Dr. Lerner that she wouldn't visit the shrine this week, but she was never good at self-control. She has forbidden the others to enter. As his mother, though, she has the right to wipe the growing dust off the bookshelves and touch the clothes hanging in the closet. It is *her* right because he was *her* son.

Today, she opened the dresser drawers and was greeted by the smell of David. It was everywhere at once, the cologne he had recently begun to wear, the wholesome scent of a boy on the verge of becoming a man. The T-shirt on top was one of his favorites. She brought it to her face and buried her cheeks in it. She took a deep breath. Then she began to weep.

"Namaste," she hears again.

The lingering scent of David escapes her. She peers over her right shoulder—past the fence, and beyond the hedges and foliage that she often calls the spiky, death plant—and spots the neighbor, Lucy Bell, sitting cross-legged on the grass, eyes closed, palms pressed together beneath her chin. As a teacher, Madeline is accustomed to being around teens, she understands what makes them tick. Lucy Bell, though, is unfamiliar territory. Madeline has always prided herself on her objectivity when it comes to kids. Madeline has a feeling that Lucy is different from other girls her age. Something about her peaceful aura sets her apart. No longer privy to the gossip at school, since she hasn't been there since David's accident, Madeline hasn't heard what the other teachers make of the young girl.

Madeline's distorted picture of Lucy is fragmented. The unique position that Levon once held in the household—irresponsible and blameworthy—he now shares with his partner in crime. She was there when Levon siphoned the leftover wine and threw up all over himself. She was the reason Chloe's feeding tube got ripped from her belly by her unruly dog. She is the diversion responsible for Levon's defiance and sudden secrecy. Madeline can't help but ask herself why the gregarious, charming Lucy Bell chose Levon when she could have had her pick from the hundreds of boys at Beach High?

Madeline gazes at the girl and wonders if she stares hard enough, will Lucy's eyes open.

And yet, as Madeline peers over the fence and beyond the trees, her admonishing hands pressed on her hips, she is overcome with a gnawing emotion. The disgraceful feeling ricochets around her bony frame. A mild dizziness overcomes her, and she tries to find her footing.

Madeline is thinner than ever, though that isn't the reason for her fragility.

Lucy's flowing blonde hair is blowing in the breeze, and Madeline is sure she doesn't notice the wisps brushing against her cheeks. She is intent on her yoga pose, free and light. Watching Lucy Bell is painful. They are the antithesis of one another. Her youthfulness makes Madeline want to cry. Her serenity leaves the older woman feeling inadequate and alone.

chapter 25

Lucy doesn't feel the threat of Madeline Keller's disapproval while she's humming *namaste* and freeing her mind of recent clutter. Breathing in through her nose and out through her mouth, the cleansing both tickles and relaxes. Today is January 27, her sixteenth birthday, and she and her mother are going to drive to Lincoln Road with George and bask in all that Miami has to offer. Lucy notices she is humming. She does that when she is really happy.

Ricky eventually came home after his ski trip, and he, Lucy, and their parents spent a few days in the Everglades, hiking and camping. It was a nice reprieve from the congestion and crowds of South Beach. When they returned, they celebrated Carol and Andy's anniversary at Il Migliore in northern Miami, which has become the Bell's favorite place to dine. The managers know them by name, and to commemorate their special night, they etched their signature into the restaurant's walls, a treat reserved for the regulars.

It was a wonderful week—carefree and harmonious. Lucy, Ricky, Levon, and Chloe spent a fair amount of time together. Having her brother join their threesome made her aware of how much she has missed hanging out with a group of friends. Ricky was amazing with Chloe, just as he had been when she was the little girl's age. He would hoist her on his shoulders, and they would chase George up and down the sidewalk. By week's end, he could recite all of Chloe's safe snacks: popcorn, pretzels, and plain Cheerios. "That means plain, not honey-nut and not cinnamon-apple flavored," she shouted in his ears. "Dangerous, very dangerous." He would wink at her, and then they would high five each other in a playful manner. The fun wasn't limited to just Chloe. Ricky and Levon snuck off to play a long-awaited game of golf. "He's not very good," Ricky laughed, when they returned from the acclaimed Doral course. "Actually, he's terrible." Lucy chuckled. "Poof. My Tiger Woods fantasy evaporates."

The group, along with the elder Bells, spent New Year's Eve huddled on the couch in Lucy's playroom watching Dick Clark and Ryan Seacrest count down the seconds to 2008. They brought in Joe's Stone Crabs, and as tradition dictated, they completed a 1,000-piece puzzle while the Jonas Brothers and Miley Cyrus took to the stage. None of them were saddened by the passing of 2007. Moving forward was on everyone's mind. Which is probably why Madeline Keller had declined an invitation to her neighbor's home. The woman, understandably, was stuck in the past.

Saying goodbye to Ricky at the traffic-infested Miami International Airport was tough. Her parents had agreed to let her drive him; the melancholy deepened as they got closer to the airport. "I wish you didn't have to go back," she said. He took the hand that wasn't on the wheel of their Volvo and squeezed it. "You're in good hands," he whispered.

Now, reciting the final salutation, *namaste*, Lucy is reconciled and at peace.

And that is when an image of Levon pops into her brain.

Lately, it has been hard to ignore him pushing his way into her thoughts. Attempts to get him to participate in her Saturday morning yoga ritual were thwarted by Cruella de Ville who always has some type of *task* for Levon to do. Last week, it was accompanying her to their storage facility to sift through pictures. The week before, it was organizing the garage. "Yoga's good for you," she told him. "It'll clear the muck from your head."

"I'm not sure it's for me," he said, at once thankful for the tedious tasks that excused him from bending over and allowing Lucy to see his butt crack. Today he was working diligently on birthday preparations. There was no time for stretching and holding in the occasional fart.

Levon would sometimes have Lucy in stitches, laughing harder than Nate ever made her laugh. When Levon told her he loved her, it took all her strength to hold in a loud, hysterical chuckle. And not because the idea of love and Levon in the same sentence were not possible. She cared about Levon, deeply, and she was well aware that he cared about her, too. But love? Neither of them were capable of giving away their heart.

Lucy is smiling at the thought of that first afternoon she sat on the dryer and the many that preceded it. Theirs was a friendship that defied high school logic. Lucy was immune to the way in which she and Levon broke from tradition. Levon restored her faith in humanity. With him, innocence was not yet lost. People, as Anne Frank suggested, were quite possibly innately good.

Did it matter that he did not sport a six-pack or have the presence of Josh Duhamel? She remembers the way her fingers tingled when his hands found hers on the dryer. It was not the rumbling of the machine that sent the signal to her brain. She had thought her body was numb to touch. Suddenly it was awake.

Ricky picked up on the chemistry between the two. "Are you sure there's nothing you want to tell me?"

"Yes, I'm sure," she replied, even though the subtle coloring of her flesh was telling her brother all that she hoped to disguise.

Levon was changing, and it was thrilling for Lucy to witness while at the same time weird. Timid and shy were being replaced with bold and gallant. Tonight, he had planned an adventure. "Be ready at five," he said. When she told him that was early, he smiled his big, Levon grin. "I like being with you."

Could the gradual shedding of pounds have been the catalyst for change? Lucy was positive he hadn't even noticed their long walks from the bus stop and the afternoon strolls with George were turning his extra cushions into solid rails. Lucy was sure her grin had sprouted from deep within and caused her lips to turn upward and her cheeks to blush.

When her eyes open, the first thing she sees is Madeline Keller. Adjusting to the bright sunshine, she blinks. It is not an apparition. Levon's Mom is hard-core staring her down. Lucy rises from her cross-legged sit, planning on rolling up her mat and heading into the house, though the ogling pulls her into an unexpected direction.

"How you doing, Mrs. Keller?"

Lucy strolls the short distance to the fence that separates the two houses. Her yoga mat is nestled under her arm. The hour and a half on the patio renewed her energy, and she is open enough to feel plain empathy, compassion, for Levon's mom. But her sheer proximity has Lucy quaking inside. There is enough sorrow in Madeline Keller to drain anyone's good feelings. Had Lucy known Levon's mom prior to the accident, she might have remarked on how youthful the woman looked. Now, the whispers around town were about how the disconsolate mother had aged twenty years.

Madeline ignores the lingering question and proceeds to wish Lucy a happy birthday. That it has registered in her tortured mind astounds Lucy, though she accepts the wishes with a raised eyebrow.

"Levon told me," she continues. "I really don't keep track of the calendar that much anymore." She reaches into her pocket and pulls out a cigarette, lighting it in one swift flick of a lighter. "Want one?" she offers Lucy.

Lucy shakes her head. "I don't smoke."

"Good, kids today are too reckless."

She's puffing away on the cigarette, and Lucy's unease is beginning to replace her peace and tranquility. She shifts her weight from one foot to the other; the yoga mat falls to the ground.

As she leans down to pick it up, she says, "Levon's taking me out tonight. He won't tell me where we're going."

Mrs. Keller tosses the cigarette butt on the grass and steps on it.

Lucy continues, "He's a good friend, Levon."

Madeline Keller tightens the knot on the bathrobe around her waist. She says, "There's a lot about Levon you don't know."

Lucy finds her center again, "Forgive me for saying this, Mrs. Keller, but I think you have it wrong. There's a lot about Levon *you* don't know."

The possibility that this girl is right disturbs Mrs. Keller, who says, "Are you always so disrespectful to adults?"

Lucy says, "No, never, unless I'm forced to be. You really don't know Levon at all."

"David will never have another birthday," she says. "Soon, all of you will pass him in age. Even Chloe."

"I'm sorry for that," Lucy says. "If Levon could change that night, he would."

"What makes you so sure?"

"Levon loved David. He worshipped him. Still does."

"David was the perfect son," she laments.

Lucy ponders this. Since the day she sat next to Levon on the bus, Lucy knew something was not right about that night. Nothing in life is perfect, especially not people. She already knew that David had gotten Rebecca pregnant. Maybe there were other mistakes or errors in judgment. Lucy wants to scream at her. Lucy wants to tell her she has a wonderful son with talent and compassion who is starving for affection.

Instead, the sorrow in the older woman's eye engulfs her, wrapping around her like chilly air, sending goose bumps up and down her arms. She thinks about parents losing their kids—she thinks of Nate—and says, "Levon needs you, Mrs. Keller."

The older woman is on the verge of tears, and the sight of this spins Lucy into a spiral of worry. She moves closer toward her house and is thankful for the wall that separates them. She wonders if she should walk over and offer a hug. She's not sure she can touch her. Yet, sitting there staring at her is driving her nuts, and it would be even ruder to turn and walk away. Mrs. Keller's shoulders are shaking. She is about to say something when Levon sticks his head out the back door. He doesn't see Lucy standing there, and she can tell he's worried about something. His mouth opens, though his words fall on themselves in a jumble of regret. "Dr. Gerald called."

To which his mother turns her head and says, "Are you kidding me?"

"I'm sorry. I was listening to my iPod and didn't hear the phone."

"I've been waiting for that call for *two days*."

Lucy is following the exchange. *Don't look away, Levon. Look at her and fight. Stand up for yourself.*

Levon stammers and a flurry of buts, ifs, and apologies litter the air. He is no match against his mother's sharp punches.

"Stop screaming at him," Lucy yells.

The interruption causes the two faces to turn in her direction. One is angry, the other interested.

"You're wrong about him," Lucy continues, raising her voice with each word. "Levon's a good kid. Give him a chance."

All heads turn to face Levon who appears as though he wishes the ground would swallow him up.

"Lucy," he stammers, "go away. This is none of your business…"

"It is my business. Stand up to her. Show her who you really are so she can take those blinders off."

"Why is she getting involved in our family business?" asks his mother.

"I don't know," he answers. "She doesn't know what she's talking about."

The look he shoots Lucy is insistent, part plea, part *I'm gonna kill you.*

"Levon," his mother repeats.

Lucy's face is one of disgust. There is no hiding her disdain for the way in which Levon handles his domineering mother.

"Levon," she says, in a tone that is sad and wishful at the same time. "The only person you're fooling is yourself."

"Happy Frickin Birthday," he says to her before turning around and stomping off into the house.

sunday, january 27, 2008. 2:08 p.m.

I'm writing because I hate Lucy Bell right now. I hate her. I hate her. I hate her.

She is not invited to the taping of Ellen. No fucking way.

sunday, january 27, 2008. 2:27 p.m.

I'm so angry at her I could scream.

sunday, january 27, 2008. 3:08 p.m.

There's only one thing left to do.

chapter 26

"Why did you do that? Why would you set her off?"

"I did you a favor," Lucy replies. "One day you'll be thanking me."

Levon lets her do the talking, knowing what's coming. The jitters take over his arms and legs.

"You're mom doesn't get it. If you're not going to stand up for yourself, I will," she says.

They are in the Volvo pulling out of the driveway. Chloe is standing outside waving frantically and wishing Lucy a happy birthday. You'd think they were leaving for the prom.

Levon almost canceled the evening, but when he caught a glimpse of Lucy stepping out the front door, he was glad he had changed his mind. She is dressed from head to toe in some shimmery, white, unpronounceable fabric. When she walks, it falls around her like waves.

Lucy is driving with the precautionary grace of a girl who has never driven a car. She is watchful, heeding all the signs on the road and careful to keep both hands on the wheel. Whenever Levon has been in the car with her before, she has always been an alert and confident driver. "It's much more serious once you have a license," she turns to him and says, "But you know that already, don't you?"

"I can't believe she let me out tonight," Levon says.

Without taking her eyes off the road, Lucy replies, "That would be punishment for her, not you."

"Don't try to sugarcoat it," he says.

Stealing a glance at the golden locks that punctuate her cheekbones, he thinks she looks different, already sixteen. He looks down at his black polo and jeans and hopes he made the right choice. Cool and understated were what he had in mind.

"Which way am I going?"

"Take La Gorce to Forty-first, and we'll go up Alton."

Levon checks by his feet to see that the present he had Chloe wrap is there on the floor. It is a system of checking and re-checking that tames his jumpy legs. He doesn't answer.

Lucy drives with the windows and sunroof open. She says it's her favorite thing so far about Florida, letting the cool air in, feeling the breeze against her hair and face. The fresh air steals the day as the warm sunshine fades, and they make their way along the traffic-infested streets of South Beach. Wyclef Jean is filling the car with "The Sweetest Girl." His famous voice mingles with the breeze while Lucy sways her arms and hips against the torn upholstered seat, mouthing the words.

She stops swaying and says, "My dad thinks the Internet's ruined music."

When she realizes that Levon has no witty comeback, she continues. "When he was growing up, they listened to songs on the radio and waited for the DJ to tell them the name of the song and who sang it. Then he'd wait for an eternity for his parents to drive him to the record store to buy it. Sometimes, when he had to have a song, he'd sit there with his tape recorder against the radio speaker, and press record when it came on, which was always a crapshoot. He'd sit there for hours waiting and waiting."

Levon agrees that music is certainly more accessible these days. He couldn't imagine having to actually wait to hear a song on the radio.

Lucy goes on talking. "He says that songs today don't have a shelf life. We hear a song on Monday, hold up our iTouch to the speakers, and Shazam tells us the name and the artist. Then we download it to our phones or our computers and listen to it over and over again for days, and we're sick of it by Friday. We're killing my father's business."

"We didn't," he objects, "the Internet did. You said it yourself."

"It's kinda sad," she says, "how the evolution of technology, however efficient, diminishes the humanness of things. We'll never know what it feels like to really yearn for something, life without instant gratification." She turns away from the road to sneak a glance at him. "You know, the excitement of things to come?"

Levon reminds himself that Lucy is a girl who has been violated in the most inhumane way. Her experience of the most intimate, loving act has been spoiled by a boy who was out of his mind and out of control.

But Lucy wasn't talking about love and romance. She was talking about cassette tapes and a new technology named after a Marvel superhero.

"Sure I do," he says.

They reach the end of Alton Road where the dilapidated South Shore Hospital sits in sharp contrast to the sparkling green bay behind it.

"Get on the MacArthur and head west toward downtown," Levon says. Wyclef has ended and he notices the familiar call letters of Y-100 on the radio dial and asks, "Do you only listen to his stations?"

"I cheat sometimes," she says. "Clear Channel owns 105.9 and Zeta and Love 94, but I've been known to crack open a little Power 96. Don't tell my father that though. It's all about the ratings."

"Does he get to meet a lot of the musicians?" Levon asks, wondering why they have never discussed this before.

"The artists?" she asks. "All of them, though he leaves most of the courting to his radio promotion people. He would much rather be home with my mom than out at clubs and restaurants with musicians."

"That's nice," Levon comments.

"My parents are weirdly cute together," she smiles, which leaves Levon speechless.

"How's that situation been going?" she asks, her smile dissolving into sympathy.

"She wants him to move out."

He says it like it means nothing when it's everything.

"Are you serious?"

"Would I lie about something like that?"

"My mother always told us to pick a spouse carefully. Rule #501. A huge percentage of our joy and pain will come from this single decision. Where would he go?"

"He has a bunch of properties. He can stay at any one of them."

"Do you think he wants to go?"

"Wouldn't you?" he asks, a question that really does not require an answer, though speaks volumes. "That's why she ripped my head off this morning."

"She's always ripping your head off," Lucy adds.

"Last week we all went to family counseling together. They were talking like I wasn't in the room. I tried to put myself in her shoes, and you know what I came up with? I'd hate me too."

"Don't say that, Levon."

They are back on the MacArthur, and the last of the cruise ships is sneaking out of the harbor. Darkness continues to creep through the car windows, and Levon watches Lucy hug her white scarf closer to her shoulders. The afternoon in Dr. Lerner's office with the three of them together was intended to heal the family, and all it did was leave Levon feeling crappier about himself than ever. Their family had many obstacles to overcome, the shrink told them. The death of their son and his brother would change them forever. In addition, there were deep-seated issues that had to be dealt with if they were ever going to manage their grief together as a unit, which was ironic because his father was on the cusp of moving out.

"You have a lot of decency, Levon. If you didn't, I wouldn't be caught dead with you," she teases. But the joke is lost on Levon who is staring at the Miami skyline and missing his brother with an ache so profound he gasps for air. It sneaks up on him, paralyzing him with sadness. He wants many things, none of them possible: to talk to his brother, to watch him carry Chloe around on his shoulders. He is starting to forget the sound of David's voice and that scares him. And what if he loses Chloe too? His little sister's disease has always been at the forefront and has taken a backseat since the accident.

Levon begins to hyperventilate. Why did he have to pick now, Lucy's big day, to fall apart? Clutching at his neck, he says, "Something's wrong."

She either doesn't hear him or she can't discern the worry in his tone.

"Lucy," he tries again, "I can't breathe."

"I hear you panting. You're breathing fine."

"I think I'm dying," he says between exhales.

"You're not dying, Levon."

"It's happened before."

"What's happened? Your dying?"

Levon fights the urge to jump out of the car. He's dizzy and can't seem to swallow. "Lucy, stop the car. I've gotta get out of here."

He must be dying because Lucy has never so willingly adhered to his orders. She pulls the car into the parking lot of Jungle Island.

"It'll pass. Just breathe," she says, "in through your nose, out through your mouth."

Levon pants, "This is just great, spending your birthday breathing in and out like a rhinoceros."

"Don't worry about my birthday," she says. "Just relax and concentrate on your breaths. I told you yoga would be good for you."

Levon is wheezing, every breath a gasp for more air. He tries to swallow and thinks he can't, that something has taken hold of his esophagus and obstructs the otherwise natural reflex to gulp. His head feels light and dizzy. He is ninety-nine percent certain he is going to pass out. The heightened state of panic sends a tremor through his body. "Give me a minute," he whispers, finding mild relief in resting his head in his hands along the dashboard.

"How long do they usually last?" she asks.

His eyes are clamped shut, though he hears her words knocking loudly at his ears. Her voice is loud and muffled. He is annoyed by the question. *What the hell does it matter how long the terror lasts when he is on the cusp of death? How can she be asking such stupid questions?*

"You're having a panic attack, Levon. Focus on something pleasant."

Levon ignores her.

"Go to your favorite place in your mind."

That was once easy for Levon: Carvel. Now his favorite place is sitting beside him in the car. "You're not helping."

"All right, then let's get out of here and take a walk. The fresh air will help."

"No, no," he shakes his head, changing his mind. "I can't get out. Something is really wrong." He is thinking about something and unable to say it out loud. It is gnawing at him. Lucy is right about that night. The truth is surfacing in the form of a chokehold. He thinks she had better call 911.

"Let's make out, that'll distract you."

Even the image of her lips against his can't prevent the spiral of dizziness in his head. "Talk to me," he says, "tell me about your day today." The detailing of concrete facts is certain to help him suppress the urge to jump out of his skin or shout out words that will alter many lives.

She begins to highlight her day spent with her family on Lincoln Road, replete with crowds of beautiful people, when George's tail swats across a table of four and the glasses of wine in its path shatter on the sidewalk. Levon doesn't hear a word. The lively timber of her sentences and the pandemonium emphasize the commotion ripping through his body and leads him to obsess about other things, other thoughts. He is thinking about the fancy restaurant at the top floor of the Wachovia building—the tallest in Miami—that is waiting for the two of them to arrive. He is thinking about David's face and how when he smiles, his lips are sometimes crooked. He is thinking about Chloe and what her future will be like.

"Are you hearing a word I'm saying, Levon? Get a hold of yourself. You need to get out of your head and into your life."

Her words are harsh, but they are true. They snap Levon from the spell that has him spinning and bouncing like a pinball. His breath flows smoother now; his heart rate drops to a steady pace. He can feel his fingers. The tingle and numbness have dissipated.

He gets out of the car and takes a walk around the deserted Jungle Island parking lot. When he returns, she's waiting for him.

He says, "That wasn't so bad."

"Ha!" she laughs. "You looked like you saw a ghost."

"I'm pretty sure I did," he says, letting his fingers run through his hair.

Reaching across the seat, Lucy touches him, sending a new wave of terror through his veins. She says, "I know you've put a lot of effort into tonight, and it means a lot...*you* mean a lot...but Levon, I'm not as complicated as you. Here's a tip: Don't overthink. Keep it simple. Rule #126. Take me to Bayside. I heard it's fun. Or," she says, eyeing the jumbo green letters adorning the café au lait walls beside them, "we can be really naughty and sneak into the parrot cages."

"I've had enough animals for one night."

"You're cute. Even for a rhinoceros."

Levon stares ahead. "Hilarious."

Bayside is filled with vacationers when they arrive at the outdoor marketplace in downtown Miami. Levon hasn't been to the tourist spot in years, though today he is more tolerant of the noise and the Mexican man who is enticing him to pay a few bucks to hold an obscenely large python. They pass through the square and reach the often-photographed Banyan tree. Lucy grabs her cell phone from her purse and throws it at Levon. "Take a picture of me," she demands.

Lucy is dwarfed by the breathtaking trunks and limbs, which measure over seventy-five feet tall. "The tree is over one hundred years old," she proclaims, reading from the sign beside her. Levon snaps Lucy in a pose that has her arms and legs tangled amongst thick, descending roots. She is staring up at the lush branches that form a canopy overhead and shade the main entrance to the shops. He likes to photograph her when she isn't looking; she is beautiful against the tree.

"Let's get a picture of you in Forrest Gump's shoes," Levon suggests, referring to the restaurant across the cobblestone path where a bench sits with a box of chocolates and a waiting pair of sneakers.

"Forrest had some pretty good quotes," she says, taking a seat on the chair, resting her glasses on top of her head, and quoting how life is like a box of chocolates. Her sedate outfit is a contrast to the oversized and scuffed sneakers. "Should we eat here?" she asks.

Levon's mind runs wild. Forrest was no Casanova, though he got the ethereal Jenny to love him. How could he say no to that kind of fate?

The hostess guides them through the gift shop and beyond the pastel, floral walls before deciding on a table. Lucy takes her time reading all the quoted wall plaques that are sure to grow her inspiration repertoire to alarming numbers. She punches him on the arm as she recites, "If Mom ain't happy, ain't nobody happy."

Levon takes a seat at a bright red booth. Lucy sits across from him under the sign that reads, "A balanced diet is chocolate in both hands."

"This wasn't what I had in mind when I planned your special

night," Levon says.

"I didn't expect to have to resuscitate you," Lucy shoots back.

Over hamburgers and strawberry lemonade, they touch on every subject except Levon's panic attack. Lucy continues to amaze him. He has no idea there's a clinical name for his recent bouts of suffocation. Instead, they discuss the latest scandal at their school that's centered on one of its administrators and a student. Numerous repetitions of *I heard that* and *Do you believe?* fill the conversation. From there, they move on to Lucy's lively descriptions of previous birthdays dating back to age four (her earliest memory) through to the present. And finally, Harper Collins.

"Why would anyone with the last name *Collins* put their child through a lifetime of publishing house jokes?" Levon asks.

"I heard that her father died when she was a baby and her mother remarried Mr. Collins. Hence, Harper Collins."

"How do you find out about this stuff?" he asks.

"I heard she has a crush on you."

"Right, and so do Simon and Schuster."

That gets a smile out of her. "It's true."

Levon reaches for his glass; the unfamiliar attention leaves him feeling self-conscious. Lucy is the last person he wants to hear from about a different girl having a crush on him. Music is blaring—a song Levon has never heard before—and Lucy is mouthing every word while she tortures him with her smirk. She is swaying her body against the red vinyl and her hair—half pulled up and the other half down—is dragging across the table. She is amused with *being in the know*. She throws her head back in delight when it smacks the wall behind her and the dark wood sign with its painted words comes crashing down on her.

A snicker escapes Levon's mouth. It bursts out of him and sends a bubbly vibration through the air.

Lucy is fighting with the wooden board, trying to pin it back onto the wall. Levon's laugh is unstoppable; tears of happiness drip from his eyes. His belly allows the laugh in—a deep, bellowing, wonderful sensation he hasn't felt in weeks. For a minute, he forgets that someone has a crush on him, and it's not Lucy.

When she finishes the assault on the sign and secures the piece back in its place on the wall behind her, the torment begins again.

"Don't change the subject," she says, falling back against the cushion, careful about ardent displays of excitement. "We're not through discussing your latest crush."

"Random House or Little, Brown?" he asks, spent from the bout of hysteria.

Lucy rolls her eyes.

"HarperCollins published James Grippando's new novel."

"So you've noticed her, too?" Lucy says.

"No, I'm reading the book."

"So you've been thinking about her?"

"Jesus, Lucy, you're such a pain."

"Aha," she says, "you like her."

Levon shakes his head and motions for the waitress. He had cornered her by the bathroom and asked her to bring out a dessert for Lucy's birthday when he waved to her. Lucy is eyeing him while she uses a straw to clean the cracks between her front teeth.

"Does this mean you're finally done pining over Rebecca? I bet her pregnancy thing wasn't much of a turn-on." And before he can respond to such a wildly outrageous statement, she continues with, "Harper's pretty, Levon. Don't say you haven't thought about it."

"She's a midget."

"But a charming midget," Lucy says.

Levon sighs.

"Can't you just be happy?" she asks, plainly.

The young waitress with the bouncy blonde hair arrives at their table flanked by her fellow wait staff. She is shy, holding a plate in one hand and a lighter in the other. No one had told her that her job description included mild forms of humiliation. Slipping the chocolate chip cookie sundae in front of Lucy, the enthusiastic group sings in unison while Maggie, according to the friendly name-tag, lights the candle. She reminds Levon of a book he read as a child, *Muggie Maggie*. Maybe *Muggie Maggie* was also published by HarperCollins.

Lucy's green eyes are closed, and the revelers have parted. Levon longs to reach across the table and touch her warm cheek—with his lips or his hand.

Lucy is thinking hard about her wish; her lips are mouthing private prayer.

Levon is savoring the time that has allowed him to gawk. He thinks to himself:

I am in love with you, and then, *can you feel how much I love you?*

She opens her eyes and stares at him, long and hard, before blowing out the candle.

Levon's heart races, and his reckless thoughts litter the space between them. They are words without sound; she does not hear the loud timbre of his thoughts. Instead, she is busy devouring the vanilla ice cream with its gooey cookie. Her lips are glazed in thick syrup, her tongue swirling around buttery crumbs. Ordinarily, he'd be dying to join her in the food frenzy, but watching her is enough. She looks more beautiful than ever, and Levon is aching inside.

He would never tell Lucy that he knows about Harper's crush. Unlike Lucy, Harper censors her speech and is soft-spoken. The signs she sends his way that let him know how she feels about him are subtle yet noticeable—the way she blushed when he caught her looking his way, how she always manages to turn up by his locker when they've finished lunch. Levon isn't blind. Harper's cute, albeit in a teeny human sort of way. She has pretty blue eyes and stick-straight black hair.

"She's got a huge rack," Lucy says, while Levon is thinking she's disproportionate. Some things are hard to miss. Harper Collins is known to have the largest breasts in the tenth grade. "Do you like big-breasted girls or are you an ass man?"

"I don't know. Are you an ab girl or an ass girl?"

"Ass for sure. And don't think I haven't noticed yours shrinking in those Levi's. You've lost a lot of weight, Levon. How come you're hiding it under loose fitting clothes? Do we need to take you shopping?"

The numbers on the scale had dwindled into digits he had not seen for some time. Folds have been replaced with lean lines, and muscles he never knew existed have made themselves known. He thought he was the only one to notice, but Chloe asked him the other day if he was wearing high heels. *High Heels?* Had what he lost in weight been made up for in height? He locked himself in the bathroom and studied his face. The Vitamin E was working and the battered skin was fading into a nice macho battle scar. Pulling at his cheeks, there was a noticeable difference in the elasticity. What had once been pliant, rubbery flesh has transformed into a term once used to describe David's profile: smooth and noticeable. He supposed most boys his age emerge from being unbearably awkward into a man.

"You look good," she says, before adding, "not that I had a problem with you before, and don't get carried away. You can still afford to lose a couple more pounds. I'd hardly call you *skinny*."

"How do you do that?' he asks. "How do you manage a compliment and an insult all in the same sentence?"

"Think of it as me saving you from a lifetime of vanity and self-importance."

"How noble of you."

Levon contemplates her words. "I haven't told them yet."

"What are you waiting for? They'll be so proud of you!" He didn't have the answer. Perhaps he was merely accustomed to not sharing.

"If it makes any difference, I'm really proud of you." Her eyes sparkle, and she seems genuinely impressed with his recent accomplishments. The timing couldn't be better.

"Here," he says, reaching under the table and handing her his gift, which Chloe wrapped in white.

"You didn't have to get me anything."

"I know."

She takes it in her thin fingers and shakes it. "Doesn't sound like much."

"It's a lot," he says, feeling his heart jump-starting, the thump thump thump growing hideous and loud as she tears at the paper.

Lifting the lid, Lucy peers inside.

"There's only paper in here."

He knows that. He was the one who placed the neatly stacked sheets along the bottom of the Bloomingdale's box he found in his mother's closet. Strategically placed upside down, she reaches in for the first lined sheet. Turning it over, she sees Levon's scrawly handwriting.

It's not easy watching someone read your most private thoughts. And what's on the six pages changes everything. Lucy is the kind of girl who would jump to the ending of a book because she lacks the patience to plod through. Levon notices how she carefully reads each word, every sentence, eventually holding the stack in her hands like valuable treasure she often teased him about. She is reading his words, and her face reacts in this order: her cheeks turn pink, her eyes enlarge, the eyebrows rise and fall in harmony, and her lips, processing what she's reading, release the final *Oh*. Her chin is resting on her left palm as if unable to hold the exclamation in.

"Oh my God, Levon, you have to tell them about this."

"I can't," he says.

"You have to."

"David's gone."

She says, "There's no way you could have predicted…"

"How's that for a birthday present?"

"This craziness? You think this is a gift?"

"No, that you get to be right about me."

"Right about what?"

Levon shakes his head back and forth. "My secret. You were

right all along. I have a big one."

"Levon, you have to tell them. You owe it to everyone, especially yourself."

"How can I do that to my brother?"

"Jesus, Levon, what about *you*? How could your brother do this to you?"

Levon doesn't have an answer. David is gone. He's the real victim.

This isn't the response Levon predicted. Her birthday is ruined. All he wishes for is to disappear, like he has done for most of his life. Lucy is irritated, or angry, he can't tell. He thought he was giving her a gift by sharing this piece of him. He sees he was wrong.

She gets up from her side of the table and, instead of walking out of the restaurant, she scoots him over and takes the seat beside him in the booth. Her hands are clasped in her lap and she nudges him with her shoulder. No sooner has the chaos inside him diffused, when she says, "You're so brave, Levon. David was lucky to have you."

"How come I don't feel brave?"

"You need to tell them. This changes everything."

"I know," he says. "That's what scares me the most."

sunday, january 27, 2008 10:55 p.m.

I take it back. I don't hate Lucy at all.

chapter 27

There is a stranger waiting at the door when Levon pushes through. She looks a lot like his mother, but there is a sparkle to her that has her lit up like a Christmas tree. There is a pep in her step he hasn't seen in months; this was not the woman who had persecuted him hours before.

"Is there something you want to say to me?" she asks, lingering around the doorway.

Levon is taking off his shoes and setting them alongside the collection along the floor of their foyer. His mom's latest obsession is maintaining clean floors. The dirt and grime on sneakered shoes are no longer permitted throughout her house. She has gone so far as to purchase guest slippers, so anyone could walk around her spotless floors with germ-free feet.

There is something amiss about her, though Levon can't put his finger on it. He appraises her again, searching for the piece that has her resembling someone softer and serene. That is when his father walks in the room.

"How could you keep this from us?" he asks.

There is no physical way Lucy could have gotten to them this fast. Coincidence? Or was someone playing with his head?

"Don't you think you should have said *something?*" his mother adds.

"I'm sorry," he says, while air fills his hungry lungs.

"Come on, Levon, something more than that. Had we known…"

Levon finally says, "I'm sorry I lied." *There.*

"This isn't a lie, son. It's a sin of omission."

"I did what I had to do," he says, liberated, free, joyously at peace.

"And that's some story you concocted," interrupts his father with a smile.

A smile? How could he be smiling at a time like this?

"Dr. Gerald faxed it to us."

Levon stiffens while his dad continues the interwoven tale.

"Ellen DeGeneres! Who knew I'd be praising you for the countless hours you've sat on that couch watching her show?

"It's wonderful what you did, Levon," says his mother. "Dr. Gerald got a call from Ellen's producers, and they've invited him to participate on the panel of experts for rare diseases, *and* they've donated money toward his research, so the dogs can be taken care of…"

His dad says, "What a beautiful thing you've done for your sister…"

Levon hears what they're saying, though he misses the feeling that washed over him a moment earlier—one that came from him believing they knew the truth. The idea was freeing, fleeting, and he wants to get it back. He wants to take it all back, what he did to rewrite the story, the preservation of dignity, the life-changing sentence. He wishes for a different kind of truth.

Madeline Keller moves closer to her son and extends her arms around him. The facts are so near he wonders if they can spread through osmosis. He allows himself to feel the warmth of her skin and the safety of her grasp. She doesn't smell so bad anymore. It's not Shalimar but something citrusy that warms his nose. His father comes close and pats him on the back. He should be happy and soaring with pride, sandwiched between these two strangers who fill him with such emotion. Instead, tears roll down his brand new face.

When they pull away from him, his father asks, "Why didn't you tell us?"

Levon didn't have an answer.

"Honey, I'm proud of you," she says. "What you did was really special."

Levon can see that this is hard for her. She is smiling and her hair actually seems washed. She made an effort to style it. She is less ugly to him, though there are fragments of the damage that will never go away.

That night he writes:

I should be focused on the good that came from today; the look in their eyes. They are softening and it shows. But I can't escape the feeling, the way they held me in their arms together, like a Levon sandwich. Ha, I always find a way to analogize with food. When I closed my eyes, the feeling was....well, for someone who overflows with words, it was indescribable. I closed my eyes to let the feeling seep in.

I saw this TV show once. I don't remember the name. But the mom and dad were in their bed, their son lying between them. The kid had to be around ten, the time when it begins to get embarrassing when your parents garner you with so much attention and affection. They were kissing and hugging the kid, and he was giggling and laughing and absorbing the attention like the vanilla cream between the Oreo cookies. The mom whispered in the boy's ear, "How does it feel to be so loved?" and the boy replied, "You know, Mommy." But she didn't. She turned her head so he couldn't see. She tried to hold back the tears, but they just surged down her cheeks like waterfalls. I wasn't sure at the time why his response provoked such a reaction; now I think I may have the answer. If she was like me and hadn't felt her parents' arms around her, like I did today, then, no, she wouldn't know what it feels like to be loved.

Anyway, here I go off. Tangents. Tangents. They were proud of me, and it felt nice, although the reasons were not what I originally thought. I thought I was finally free from this mess that's been caged inside my gut, and even though having my parents' arms around me was the best feeling I'd felt in years, the regret was worse. The secret I have had to bury is fighting to come out. I don't think I can hold it in much longer.

chapter 28

"The other night changed a lot of things for us," Craig says.

They are seated in Dr. Lerner's office, and instead of sitting across the couch from him, Madeline is close, their fingers intertwined.

"I want to make this work," she says.

"It's going to be hard work," Dr. Lerner answers.

"This is nothing compared to what we've been through."

Unmistakable was the look that crossed both of their faces. They were pleased with their decision though inhibited about showing their devotion to one other. It would take much to rebuild and restore the home they had once built together

"I don't know," she continues. "Holding Levon and having Craig there with me felt right. My tendency has been to resist; I couldn't this time. I couldn't extract myself from the feeling we are meant to be together."

Madeline has never before studied Dr. Lerner. Today, she takes in her curls and the moles that Levon had noticed before. She finds the office—its pale beige and orange tasteful—less off-putting. She notices that the doctor is on the skinny side. Madeline can't imagine how that's possible when she spends all day on her tush.

Dr. Lerner pretends not to notice Madeline's stare and says, "I'm happy to see you've come to this decision, Madeline. It's much easier to walk away from a marriage. It takes far more will to make one work."

"I've lost too many things. I don't want to lose any more." She looks at Craig when she says, "We need to take it slowly. We need to get to know each other again."

"And yourselves," Dr. Lerner adds.

"I suppose that too. I've thought a lot about what you said, and I see how it's not all Craig's fault. I contributed to his emotional detachment. I haven't been the most attentive wife."

"That's a difficult admission, Madeline. It must have taken a lot of reflection for you to come to that conclusion. This is particularly good for Levon," the doctor adds. "I have been worried about him."

Craig is usually the one to respond to the mention of Levon. This time, Madeline perks up.

"I think something else is going on with him, something we're all missing. He holds back in our private sessions in a way that worries me."

His father says, "Levon expresses himself more effectively on the page. Talking hasn't always been easy for him."

"This is more than a shy teenager withholding."

"During our last few sessions, he has been very upset. Most recently, we barely talked before he became inconsolable."

"Can you tell us specifics?" Craig asks.

"I can give you a summation of his issues, though I cannot repeat to you what Levon and I discuss. In order for me to help Levon, he has to know that he can trust me completely."

"And his issues are…," Craig beckons.

"Number one, he has lost his brother, and he is blaming himself. That's tough on anyone. For a teenager who doesn't have a sense of self within his family unit, it exacerbates the problem." She pauses before putting her pencil behind her ear and says, "You're probably wondering what that means."

They both nod.

"Levon is stuck. There's grief and guilt about his role in the accident, and it's compounded by his belief that he's invisible within your family."

Last week, Madeline would have shouted out one of her derisive remarks, questioning the validity of Lerner's accusations and telling her to just get to the point. Today she is humbled and anxious. She is patient to hear about the son who is becoming more of a stranger with each passing day.

"Much of your time, energy, and attention has been spent traversing between Chloe and David."

"Are we talking about middle-child syndrome?" Craig asks.

"Levon doesn't strike me as the classic middle child. I don't like to use the MCS label, though for the sake of this conversation I will. He is not rebellious. He is good-natured, and I know from our visits that he has deep love for his siblings. There doesn't, or didn't, appear to be jealousy or competitiveness between his brother and him. He loved David. I think it's tearing him up inside to live with what he's done."

"Is he angry at me?" Craig asks. "Do you think what I've done has affected him?"

"It has scarred all of you," she says. "But Levon is a wise boy. I think he understands better than the two of you why your marriage had been in disarray. As you neglected each other and failed to nurture your family center, you also neglected to take care of your son."

Madeline is the first to reply. "It's been hard for us. You know that."

"I'm not talking about the current situation, Madeline. I'm talking about many, many years of Levon going unnoticed."

It was the first sentence Dr. Lerner said that made sense in a nonsensical world. The pair evaluated this slowly. Nobody moved. Nobody talked. Madeline squeezed her husband's hand. He whispered, "Maddy," and his breath caressed her cheek, and she closed her eyes and welcomed the tears. Madeline cannot defend their actions, but having it explained to her helps her understand what they've done.

"What do you think he's hiding? What are we missing?"

Dr. Lerner tells them. "Levon's keeping a secret."

chapter 29

It is mid-February, and Florida is chilled with temperatures in the forties and fifties. Jackets and scarves are yanked out of hiding, and although it has been weeks since the night when Levon's mom held him close, the temperatures have plummeted in opposition with her temperament. It is four months since the accident, and her icy exterior has begun to dissolve. Levon might have accepted full responsibility for the shift in her personality, though he knows that Ellen DeGeneres shares the credit. First, there was the bun. It came back. And Levon noted that his mother was wearing clothing in the morning and had rid herself of the bathrobe that had her wrapped up like an enchilada. When Sid and Lyd called from New Yawk (that's how they pronounce it), Levon answered their question in a new way. He said, "She seems to be doing better."

A colossal shift is that his father is no longer sleeping in the guest bedroom. He is the first to comment on the changes in Levon.

"There's something different about you."

His mother turns to look at him, unconvinced, and looks away again.

Could it be that I've lost like ten pounds? he thinks to himself.

"I can't put my finger on it, but there's something."

Had their hours of counseling really distracted them that much? All the time they spent repairing themselves and each other, they failed to notice one of the largest changes of all. He stared at Levon, up and down, for a full minute before the lightbulb went on.

"Oh my God, look at you! Look at how thin you are!"

This gets Madeline's attention, and she whips around in great delight. Levon pretends the bulk of his winter jacket has hidden his weight loss. When she reaches for his hands and raises them high so she can get a good look, he feels for the first time that he is no longer invisible, even though there was less of him to see. Madeline is bursting with pride at having a thinner son. She cradles him in her arms. Her skin is less white, and it is returning to its usual caramel color. "This is wonderful, Levon," she says. "You look fantastic."

All Levon has ever wanted was to be noticed for some accomplishment. Ellen was only the beginning. He thinks that shedding pounds has shed his mother's distaste for him. How he oozes with pride inside his newfound physique. It doesn't even bother him that her bun is pressing hard into his cheek.

Their family has begun to repair itself in the only way it knows how, and for the moment, it has Levon singing inside, although, a short, erratic jingle.

The letter from Brown could not have come at a worse time. It had been David's first choice when choices were his to make, and the thick, bulging envelope, with its promising contents filled the entire mailbox.

Levon retrieved the mail that afternoon. The Brown logo emblazoned across the top left corner of the packet jumped out at him and sent pieces of junk mail and an important bill or two onto the ground. Seeing David's name bold and unconcealed brought forth the truth that Levon had spent months suppressing. He reached for the metal mailbox to steady himself.

His mother's car is in the driveway. He does not have the heart to share the bittersweet news with her. He's sure its contents will set her back months. He wishes he can walk over to Lucy's house, but he knows she is at a yoga class.

Mano is the spiritual guru she has been talking about for weeks, a yoga instructor who also has the ability to heal the inner spirit with his Korean massage table, crystals, and magical touch. Lucy has been visiting him once a week on the north side of town for private lessons, and what she calls "spiritual cleansings." She would talk about Mano for hours—the chakras and moving the negative energy around so it isn't stuck inside fighting to come out.

"His hands can't cure this body," Levon once said, only he was not referring to his physical being. In truth, Levon was terrified of someone like Mano. The way Lucy explained him, he sounded like a clairvoyant, someone who could look into her eyes, read her thoughts, and see inside her soul. He was afraid of what Mano would find in his own eyes and that kind of vulnerability scared him.

Pushing through the doorway of his house, he holds the envelope from Brown close to his chest and wills his mother away. Chloe is watching TV. He can hear the sounds of her favorite television show, *The Suite Life of Zack & Cody,* filtering through the air. The envelope is burning his skin, searing right through his shirt. He puts it in his backpack where he fears it might explode and take the house down with it.

His mother calls from upstairs and asks him to feed his sister. Levon checks his watch, and it is time for her cornstarch. Carrying his knapsack into the kitchen, he drops it onto the floor by the island and begins opening and closing cabinets in preparation for Chloe's feeding. His nerves are on high alert, and he is afraid his mother will march in, trip over the pack, and she, herself, will explode. He places the box of Argo cornstarch on the counter and measures the powder. He looks back at the floor to make sure the bag is still there and that the zipper is still closed. He searches another cabinet for the boxes of sugar-free Kool-Aid, and he realizes they are out. He measures the water, knowing that for Chloe it will taste like chalk. His bookbag is still there. His mother is still upstairs. Turning to Chloe's mixture, he fuses the water and cornstarch in a purple sports bottle.

275

"Chloe," he calls out, "it's time."

His sister comes bouncing into the kitchen, the TiVo remote in one hand. Ordinary day. Ordinary treatment. Levon imagines the drink that Chloe grabs rather hastily will taste like crap, yet she never winces. She finishes it and heads to the family room to zap the twin boys on the screen back to life.

The backpack beckons him again. He sits at the glass table and rubs his temples. He hears the sharp voices coming from the TV. The beating of his heart is pronounced as he fantasizes about destroying the letter. Finally, he reaches down toward his black bag and finds his journal. He writes:

I can't do this anymore.

Then, he writes it again and again and again and again—pages of denial and forgiveness as he succumbs to defeat, begs for mercy.

The clock says four o'clock. He has been sitting at the table, staring at the same sentence for almost an hour. Homework. He takes out his math assignment and the numbers jumble his brain, so he tosses the book aside and returns to the journal.

Miguel Lopez has a secret. (His characters are often Spanish because he feels in Miami his potential for commercial success improves with multicultural appeal.) *Miguel is in love.* He crosses that out and begins again. *Miguel Lopez is hiding the truth.*

Miguel is an asshole.

The story needs some work. He knows that. Though words have always come easily to him, right now he is stuck.

Dr. Lerner told him the healing process would take time. She said that he might never get over losing his brother, only the good minutes would occur more frequently than the bad. What was most important, she said, was that he was kind to himself, allowing himself to grieve. He flips back the pages to when he last saw Dr. Lerner and reads over his entry.

It was about doctor-patient confidentiality. She said he could tell her anything, *anything* (she repeated it twice), and his face reddened, knowing she was reading the pages inside of his thoughts.

It was implausible that she knew, though when a trained psychologist had her hypersensitive antenna fixed on him, he suspected she was like a mindreader. He told her about the "panic attacks" thinking Lucy made up the diagnoses, but she was right. Dr. Lerner had this checklist of symptoms, and Levon had every single one of them. She said, "For some people, anxiety presents when our unconscious pushes through. The repression of sad or angry feelings emerge and the anxiety symptoms, similar to the fight or flight response, protect you from those intense emotions." Levon didn't understand at first. It was too clinical. Then she explained it to him in terms that appealed to the psychologically-challenged: when true feelings that are too hard to cope with want to come out—ones that are deeply rooted in our unconscious—they often present in the form of anxiety. Then she added, "Is there something you want to tell me?

Two hours pass before Levon looks up from his homework and hears his mother's wail coming from the other room; she's shrieking that he should call 911. He is almost sure the backpack has exploded, and she is choking on its sharp, bitter pieces.

"Levon," she screams again wildly.

Levon jumps from his seat at the table, grabs the cordless phone from off its cradle and dials the foreboding number. He follows his mother's cries to the frenzied spot on the dark, wooden floor where Chloe lays unconscious in the throes of a seizure.

"What happened? Did you give her the feeding?" she asks.

Levon does not answer because he is frantically giving their address to the placid, yet commanding voice on the other end of the line. Chloe's body is violently shaking; a river of wet stains the front of her jeans. Madeline turns her onto her side so she will not clamp down on her tongue. She is leaning over Chloe, holding her head in place, while her daughter's eyes fall back into her forehead.

Levon races into the kitchen and trips over the backpack, the source of his distraction.

The measuring cup he left on the marble countertop remains where he left it, along with the box of cornstarch.

He gave her the wrong amount.

Acting on adrenaline and impulse, he finds Chloe's nighttime feeding apparatus and fills it with glucose. Levon is focused and in charge. He knows exactly what to do with the concentrated sugar water that his parents have marked in a cabinet for emergencies. The lack of cornstarch caused Chloe's blood sugar to drop. He knows he cannot give her more cornstarch because it would take too long to digest. He has to get some glucose in her. Fast. The feeding tube is the only way.

With the life-saving device in his hand, Levon heads toward his baby sister and his panic-stricken mother. She is patting Chloe on the head, kissing her, stroking her forehead. Her hair is damp and clumped, matted to the sides of her freckled face. He waits for his mother to accuse and point fingers, but she does not.

The device connects to Chloe's feeding tube, and within five minutes, Chloe stops flapping against the floor. Her eyes become focused and clear. The sirens are heard outside, and a moment later, EMT paramedics race through the door, Lucy by their side.

Chloe is awake, alert, and asking why everybody is staring at her.

The paramedics are brought up to speed on her condition, while they are poking and prodding her tiny body. She has awoken from an extraordinary slumber and finds herself in the starring role of a medical drama. Levon's mother is quiet, still.

"How is she?" Madeline asks the blonde-haired young man working on her daughter.

"She'll be fine. You saved her life."

The other paramedic, a man with a long, gray ponytail and a fair amount of facial hair adds, "Her vitals are good. She's stabilizing."

Madeline looks at Levon.

He says, "That's never happened before. Never."

She doesn't yell. Actually, she doesn't even speak.

The paramedics pack up their things and head for the door. As they walk out, Craig Keller walks in. He is shaky, but they assure him that everything is fine. Chloe is resting comfortably on the couch. She is thirsty. Levon heads for the kitchen and a bottle of water. He eyes the backpack and believes it is a curse. When he returns, Chloe is already sound asleep. His mother is on the phone consulting with Dr. Gerald.

They gather around the kitchen in silence.

Lucy is dressed in her yoga outfit, white flowing pants with a matching white tank top. Her hair is pulled back in a ponytail. She is flushed from Mano's supernatural hands, and the thought leaves Levon seething a little inside.

Madeline cannot acknowledge to herself that her son has just saved her daughter's life. She is in a knot of confusion.

Craig Keller asks, "How did this happen?"

Levon is looking down at the floor and at the bag that contains one of the secrets that has him tangled up inside. "I don't know. I used the measuring cup, the one that's always on the shelf with the cornstarch. I didn't notice it wasn't the right one."

His father speaks up, "It's possible someone accidentally switched the cups. Thank God you knew exactly what to do."

Thoughts and words and compulsions are filling Levon's head. Lucy is there beside him. The daggers in his mother's eyes have returned. He feels the heaviness in his chest, the air that is trying to escape. He is leaving his body. He is close to panic. He tries to identify the source, the "repressed feelings that are fighting to get through," but they are moving too quickly for him to decipher.

Lucy breaks the silence. "It's time, Levon," she says, pressing her hand on his shoulder.

Levon listens to her words and considers the many interpretations of time. Is it time for another panic attack? Is it time for Chloe's feeding? Is it time to face the truth?

Levon cannot breathe. He is gasping for air, convinced again that he is about to die even though Dr. Lerner reassured him that no one has ever died from a panic attack. Lucy is the only one who notices the physical changes in him.

"Tell her, Levon," she demands.

"Tell me what?"

"The truth."

"Levon, what is she talking about?"

"Enough, Lucy." He is sure he is going to faint. The paramedics are probably still near the neighborhood. It won't take them long to carry him out of the kitchen and into the safety of their ambulance.

"I love you, Levon; I can't watch you do this anymore."

Her eyes are glazed over with a compassion that halts the symptoms of panic. "You love me?" he asks.

"Oh geez," she says, "don't lose focus here. Tell them the truth about that night."

Madeline looks to her husband and asks, "What is she talking about?"

Lucy reaches into her bag and pulls out the stack of papers.

sunday, october 14, 2007
12:18 a.m.

"Levon," David repeats, his words are faint, interspersed with gasps, "there's something you need to know."

Levon turns toward his brother who is trying unsuccessfully to unfasten his seatbelt. "I gotta get out of here."

Levon says, "Don't move. We have to wait for someone to come."

"I can't," he says, raising his voice in agitation. "Listen, bro, I'm fucked. If they find me here, I could go to jail."

A sharp pain pierces Levon's right side. He hopes he is not about to die from internal bleeding. "What do you mean?" he asks, each word searing his stomach.

"Oh man," David, cries out. This time his voice is riddled in panic, and Levon cannot tell if he is wincing because of pain or fear.

"I have drugs in me. Jesus Christ, I snorted fucking coke with that bitch Shelly." Now he is crying. "There's been so much shit with Becks, and Shel said it would take the edge off." He is trembling. His body is shaking wildly. "Fuck, it made me feel like crap. That's why I needed you to come get me. No one at the party wanted to leave, and Becks was pissed at me. Bro, I've never taken a drug before. Never. And now they're going to test my blood since I was driving. I'm going to get busted by the cops. Shit, what have I done?"

Levon listens as his brother's sentences run into each other. Fear is flooding out of his every pore. When he saw David walking toward the car from the party, he had thought he looked like shit. When he insisted on driving them home, David refused. "You've already done enough tonight. I'll drive so you don't get in any more trouble."

The pain in Levon's side is mounting. What feels like water dripping down the front of his face is something else. He touches the liquid, and the red stains his fingertips.

Levon thinks of only one thing for them to do.

"Switch places with me."

"What?"

"Switch places with me," he says again with more insistence. "I'll take the rap."

"Levon, no way," he grunts. "Mom'll ground you for life. You could go to jail."

Levon is pulling himself up and out of the seat. It is dark, and he cannot see what's around him. He feels sharp metal, pieces of the cushion, the airbag thrusting into him, against his cheek. His entire body aches. He is certain something inside of him is broken.

The ground swallows him up as Levon realizes the car has been cut into two pieces. He reaches for his brother and feels for him in the dark. That is when he sees the blood. It is everywhere. "David?"

No answer.

"David, we're gonna take care of this. I promise."

A moan escapes David, a whisper. "No." The hysteria has been replaced with a quiet stillness.

Levon tugs at his brother and says, "Come on, help me move you to the other side." For an instant, David pulls himself up and allows his brother to help him. Together, they reposition the older boy to the passenger side. David falls into the seat that has been carved out by his brother's body and rests against the window. For Levon, it is extremely difficult to fit behind the wheel and the airbag left by David's narrow frame. He throws himself into the seat; it is cramped and he can barely breathe. He has been so caught up in his head that he hardly notices the music drifting from the radio.

"Listen to the music," he tells his brother. "Help will be here soon."

Levon's breathing steadies. He rests his head on the seat and closes his eyes. He is going to be the hero. He is going to save David. Who would care if his future is compromised along the way? It would be worth it to see the gratitude in his brother's eyes. David will be thanking him tomorrow.

As they switched places, it never occurred to either boy that David would die.

a cold day in february, 2008

I'm not mad at Lucy for what she did. I gave her the pages from my journal so she would do exactly what she did, even though I didn't realize it at the time.

When she handed my mother what I wrote, I took the backpack with the letter from Brown, grabbed my wallet, and ran out the door. It was freezing, and I didn't have a jacket. I ran up La Gorce for what felt like eighty frigid miles and when I hit Forty-First Street, I flagged down a cab. A cab. Sid and Lyd would say how Manhattan I'd become. I knew exactly where I was headed. I needed to see him. I needed to talk with him. The whole ride in the smelly cab I was thinking of him and whether he knew I'd ratted him out. I thought when I got there I could explain what it's been like for me, and he would understand.

The cemetery had changed since we were last there, or maybe it was me who changed. It was getting dark, but I wasn't afraid. There was something peaceful about the trees and the flowers. I found his plaque and rested my hand across his name. I gave him the acceptance letter by placing it across the dates under his name. It was so cold, though I hardly noticed. He was close by, and I could feel him warming me up, not just on the outside, on the inside too. That I wasn't shivering when the cold wind whipped through my hair and ears was the sign I needed, the signal that he was okay with it all.

I didn't hear the car or her footsteps. She just seemed to appear there, kneeling beside me, my mom. She was bundled in a bulky coat. It was hard to find her face, though there was no mistaking her eyes. They had been crying. With her eyes wet, she was the beautiful, strong woman I once knew. We didn't talk much. We didn't have to. We just sort of huddled close together and felt the fierce ache of missing David together.

Sometimes in life, it's easier to see what we don't want to see. My mother isn't a horrible person. Her scope is just limited at times. That's what Dr. Lerner said. Here was a woman who lost her son, her firstborn, and there was Chloe, the one she worried about the most. I am no longer her middle child. With her arms around me, I knew we would find a way back to each other.

Lucy would later say to me:

Rule #20 –Be forgiving of yourself and others.

Rule #55 – Stop blaming others. Take responsibility for every area of your life.

Rule #60 – Admit your mistakes.

Rule #222 – Think twice before burdening a friend with a secret.

Rule #314 – Never underestimate the power of forgiveness.

And Rules #448-451 she lumped together:

Don't be afraid to say I don't know, I made a mistake, I need help, I'm sorry.

author's note

Though *The Mourning After* is a work of fiction, glycogen storage disease is not. This perilous disease, a rare genetic disorder that afflicts 1 in 100,000 babies worldwide, is lifelong and incurable. My brother-in-law, Dr. David Weinstein, is the world's leading expert on GSD. Since 1998, he has completely dedicated himself to researching and treating the disease in the hope of finding a cure. Children with GSD are missing an enzyme that enables the body to release stored sugar from the liver. Without proper treatment, massive liver enlargement occurs, and the inability to release sugar during periods of fasting causes hypoglycemia, seizures, and even death. As stated in the novel, cornstarch is the medical treatment for patients to maintain a healthy lifestyle.

The Mourning After was written in 2007 when GSD was in the beginning stages of animal trials. Dogs (maltese) naturally have GSD, and it is a fatal condition for the animals. In 2005, David moved to the University of Florida to pursue treating the dogs and humans, and the treatment has allowed the dogs to thrive. The goal is to translate this success to humans in the near future.

In August 2013, our family will be joining David and his family in Warsaw, Poland, when David is awarded the Order of the Smile Humanitarian Award for his efforts to help children with this disease. Prior winners of this award include Pope John Paul II,

Mother Teresa, Nelson Mandela, and Oprah Winfrey. David lives in Gainesville, Florida with his wife, Geraldine, their son, Justin, and their adorable dog, aptly named, Argo.

Proceeds from this novel will benefit research on GSD through the Dr. Weinstein Dream Fund created at the University of Florida. For more information about Dr. Weinstein, GSD, and how you can help, please visit www.glycogenstoragedisease.com.

acknowledgements

Thank you to all the readers who have welcomed me into their hearts and homes. I have been humbled by your support and enthusiasm.

Thank you to H. Jackson Brown, Jr. for allowing me to use his Life's Little Instruction Book (1991) for the following rules: #20, #55, #60, #222, #314, and #448-451, as noted in the novel. All other "*Rules*" came from my mother.

The lyrics to Everclear's "Wonderful" were made possible by Doug Cohn and Brian Lambert in conjunction with Marilyn Alkire and Paul Brooks at Universal. "WONDERFUL" Written by Alexakis Greg Eklund and Craig Montoya. Irving Music, Inc. on behalf of itself and Commongreen Music, Evergleam Music and Montalupis. Music © Publisher, Courtesy of (BMI).

Warm appreciation to Rabbi Harold Schulweis of Valley Beth Shalom in Encino, California, for permission to use the poem, *It's Never Too Late*, In God's Mirror: Reflections and Essays. Thank you to Jane Jacobs.

Martine Bellen, Jan Blanck, Amy Berger, and Merle Saferstein, for editing, cutting, streamlining, and deleting my favorite lines.

Jim Grippando, for supporting an indie author with enthusiasm and kindness.

Rabbi Alan Litwak, for providing spiritual and religious

insights.

Odalys Medina, for teaching me about texture, architecture, and design.

Jessica Jonap, Lisa Palley, and Stephanie Norman, for their creativity, wisdom, and guidance.

Allen at www.ebformat.com, the master of book formatting and ebook conversions.

Creating the book cover was a collaborative effort. Thank you to Edwin Pineda (www.bluemonkeydesign.com), Larissa Meek at BGT Partners, and my most talented friend, Hester Esquenazi.

Blake Feder, for being a gifted thesaurus.

Thank you to the many wonderful friends and loving family who fortify my life on a daily basis.

My siblings, Randi Berger, Robert Berger, and Ron Berger, for the love, laughter, and friendship, as well as the tears and sadness. Mom blessed us when she gave us to one another.

Dr. David Weinstein, my brother-in-law and friend, your tireless efforts on behalf of GSD patients worldwide is remarkable. Thank you for allowing me a glimpse inside of your world. I am honored and proud to be your sister-in-law.

Jordan Weinstein, for your smile and laughter, your voice in the shower, and for understanding why I can't write your seventh-grade book reports.

Brandon Weinstein, for our conversations about writing and professional sports. Here's the good news: you can do anything you want when you grow up. You are that good.

Steven Weinstein, thank you for being the first person I see in the morning and the last before I go to bed at night. You are my staunchest supporter, marketing extraordinaire, and the one who dreams up the perfect twists. Your kindness, big heart, and selflessness keep me grounded in a lopsided world. I love you, Bear.

To my mother, Ruth Berger, I didn't know when I wrote *The Mourning After* that I would be mourning you during the editing phase. Words can't encapsulate the loss we felt when you left us. We miss you every day, with every breath. I know in my heart you are smiling down on us in your UM baseball hat, Heat jersey, and Dolphins sweatshirt. The world is not the same without you.

questions & topics for discussion

1. How far would you be willing to go to protect someone you love? Did Levon go too far?

2. Why was it so difficult for Levon to open up to his parents? What holds any of us back from complete honesty and disclosure?

3. Do you believe Middle Child Syndrome really exists? Do you have any personal experience with it?

4. How much of Lucy's resiliency is inherent vs. learned?

5. The dangers of drugs are evident throughout the novel. What is our best action for keeping our children away from drugs?

6. The Holocaust and Anne Frank are used in the novel to illustrate the horrors of genocide and resiliency of the human spirit. What can we learn from this analogy? Share a personal experience with the group.

7. What would be easier for you to forgive in your marriage, a physical transgression or an emotional one?

8. Why was it so difficult for Levon's parents to see him clearly?

9. Weight is an issue for the Keller family. How does it influence and change Levon's personality throughout the course of the

novel? How does Madeline's weight and Chloe's diet factor into Levon's eating habits?

10. How does Lucy change Levon's life? How does unconventional friendship work for the two?

11. Ethereal Lucy appears in Levon's life on the day the family buries David. What does Lucy symbolize for Levon?

12. How does anger work throughout the novel in displacing sadness?

13. How does Craig Keller's indiscretion influence his wife, Madeline? Was that the turning point for change?

about the author

Rochelle B. Weinstein is a former entertainment industry executive living in South Florida with her husband, twin boys, two dogs, and two cats. Her highly acclaimed debut novel, *What We Leave Behind*, is for any woman who has loved and lost and wondered what could have been. She is currently writing her third novel—a love story based in Beech Mountain, North Carolina, her family's second home.

Ms. Weinstein enjoys connecting with her readers. She is available for book clubs and other speaking engagements. To inquire about an appearance, or to share your thoughts on her novel and read her blog, please visit her at: www.rochelleweinstein.com.